A CAR BACKFIRED LOUDLY. EMMA'S HEAD snapped up, her gaze locking on a brown Buick idling in the parking lot. The woman at the wheel had a wrecked look to her, her hair a wild black tangle, her cheeks sunken and pale. "Oh my God," Emma whispered.

And just like that, I knew: It was Becky, our birth mother. I recognized her from Emma's memories. And yet she seemed familiar to *me*, too. My father had met Becky in secret the night I'd died—what if I had, too? I willed myself to remember. But my mind was a blank and I was left with a feeling of dread and doom.

My father had said Becky was troubled, possibly even dangerous. I couldn't help but wonder: Was she disturbed enough to kill her own daughter?

BOOKS BY SARA SHEPARD

CROSS MY HEART, HOPE TO DIE

A LYING GAME NOVEL

BY

SARA SHEPARD

HARPER TEEN

An Imprint of HarperCollinsPublishers

alloyentertainment
Produced by Alloy Entertainment
1700 Broadway, New York, NY 10019

Library of Congress catalog card number: 2012953621

ISBN 978-0-06-212820-1 (pbk.)

Design by Liz Dresner

13 14 15 16 17 LP/RRDH   10 9 8 7 6 5 4 3 2 1
❖
First paperback edition, 2014

Betrayal is the only truth that sticks.

—ARTHUR MILLER

∽ PROLOGUE ∽
A FAMILIAR FACE

I watched the two teenagers sitting together outside the
Coffee Cat Café on a sunny Saturday morning. They
leaned toward each other, their voices low and almost
intimate, their bodies close but not touching. Most people
probably thought they were a couple—a really attractive
couple. The boy had high cheekbones and a lean, athletic
build. His blue-and-green striped polo shirt brought out
the green flecks in his hazel eyes. He was movie-star hot.
But maybe I was just biased: Thayer Vega *was* my boyfriend, after all.

Or at least he was before I died.

The girl next to him looked exactly like I did, back

when I had a body. Her bright blue eyes were lined with my velvety chocolate liner, and her light brown hair spilled down her back in thick waves just like mine used to. She was wearing a gray cashmere sweater and dark-wash skinny jeans from my closet. She answered to my name, and when a tear streaked down her cheek, my boyfriend leaned over to hug her. Instantly, I felt the ghost of my heart constrict.

I should have been used to this by now: living a bodiless existence as a dead girl, floating around like a plastic bag behind my long-lost twin, Emma, watching her inhabit my life, sleep in my bedroom, and talk to the boyfriend I'd never get to kiss again. The night Emma and I were supposed to meet for the first time, I never showed up—because I'd been murdered. My killer threatened Emma into taking my place, or else. She'd been living my life for months now, trying to solve the mystery of my death. But knowing all of that didn't make it any easier to watch moments like the one I was seeing now.

When Thayer had first returned to Tucson from rehab a few weeks ago, Emma had thought *he* might be my killer. But even though he was with me that night in Sabino Canyon, her investigation proved—to my great relief—that he definitely hadn't killed me. She had cleared my adoptive parents, too, even though they had been hiding a huge secret from me—that they were actually my *grandparents.* Our birth mother, Becky, was their troubled daughter. She had us when she was a teenager, leaving me with her parents and taking Emma with her when she left town, only to abandon her in foster care five years later.

I watched Thayer and Emma talk until a car backfired loudly. Emma's head snapped up, her gaze locking on a brown Buick idling in the parking lot in front of the café. The woman at the wheel had a wrecked look to her, her hair a wild black tangle, her cheeks sunken and pale. And yet I could sense that she'd once been pretty.

When I looked back at Emma, her hands were trembling. Her coffee cup tumbled to the patio tile, and the lid flew off, spilling lukewarm coffee all over her black flats. But she didn't even flinch.

"Oh my God," Emma whispered.

And just like that, I knew: It was Becky, our birth mother. I recognized her from Emma's memories, although she looked even more ragged than the last time my sister saw her, thirteen years ago. And yet she seemed familiar to *me*, too. I wondered if we'd ever met. So far, I had only been able to remember my life in disjointed flashes, usually preceded by a disconcerting tingling sensation. I felt tingly right then, but when I closed my eyes, I saw nothing. I had found out about Becky the night that I died. My father had met Becky in secret that same night—what if I had, too? I concentrated on the tingling feeling, willing myself to remember more of that night. But my mind was a blank and I was left with a feeling of dread and doom.

Just last night, my father had told Emma that Becky was troubled, possibly even dangerous. As I watched the car take off in a cloud of exhaust, I couldn't help but wonder: Was she disturbed enough to kill her own daughter?

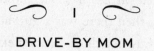

1

DRIVE-BY MOM

Emma Paxton stared hard at the woman in the Buick. At first, all she saw was a haggard woman with a lined face, sunken cheeks, and cracked, thin lips. But then she realized that beneath her dull, spotted skin the woman had a familiar heart-shaped face. And if Emma squinted, she could picture the woman's brittle, frizzy hair a shiny, raven black again. And her eyes—those *eyes*. An electric jolt ran through her. *Our eyes are our best features, Emmy,* her mother always used to say, as they stood in front of the mirror in whatever run-down apartment they happened to be living in that month. *They're like two sapphires, worth more than any amount of money.*

She gasped. It was . . .

"Oh my God," she whispered.

"What did you say, Sutton?" Thayer Vega asked.

But Emma barely heard him. She hadn't seen her birth mother in thirteen years, ever since Becky abandoned her at a friend's house when she was five.

The woman looked up and her eyes—two blue sapphires—locked on Emma's. Her nostrils flared like a spooked horse's, then there was a gunshot-like bang and the car peeled away in a thick cloud of exhaust.

"No!" Emma cried out, leaping up. She clambered over the wrought-iron railing that surrounded the café's patio, scraping her shin in the process. Pain rocketed through her leg, but she didn't stop.

"Sutton! What's going on?" Thayer asked, hurrying after her.

She raced toward the Buick as it accelerated out of the parking lot and turned left into the Mercers' subdivision. Emma followed it across the street, barely noticing the traffic whizzing past her. Horns honked at her in anger, and someone even stuck his head out the window to yell, "What the *hell* are you doing?" Behind her, Emma heard Thayer's labored breathing and uneven footsteps as he did his best to keep up with her despite his injured leg.

The Buick turned down the Mercers' street and picked up speed. Emma forced herself forward at a faster clip, her lungs heaving in her chest. But the car pulled farther and farther away from her. Her eyes blurred with tears. She was about to lose Becky *again*.

Maybe that's a good thing, I thought, still shaken by my almost-memory—or, at least, my hunch. Whatever was going on, I had a feeling Becky didn't come to town for a happy family reunion.

Suddenly, the brakes squealed and the Buick screeched to a stop so quickly that the smell of burnt rubber permeated the air. A bunch of kids playing kickball in the street screamed, and a boy stood inches in front of the car, frozen in fear, a bright red ball in his arms.

"Hey!" Emma called out, sprinting for the car. She cut across the Donaldsons' lawn, hurdling their Kokopelli lawn ornament and narrowly dodging a staghorn cactus. "Hey!" she yelled again, plowing into the back of the car, bracing herself against the trunk to stop. She slapped her hand on the rear window. The exhaust steamed out hot against her knees.

"Wait!" she yelled. Her eyes met Becky's in the rear-view mirror. Her mother stared back at her. Her lips parted.

For a split second, it felt as if time stood still as Emma and her mother looked at each other in the mirror, cut off from the rest of the world. The boy ran off toward the sidewalk, clutching his kickball. Birds splashed in the Stotlers' rock fountain. The grumble of a lawn mower vibrated through the air. Was Becky hesitating because she thought Emma was Sutton? Or was she thinking of Emma, remembering all the good moments they'd shared? Sitting in bed, reading chapters from Harry Potter. Playing dress-up with the clothes Becky brought home from the dollar bin at the thrift store. Making a tent out of blankets during a thunderstorm. For five years, it had been just the two of them, mother and daughter against the world.

But then Becky broke her gaze. The engine snarled once more, and the Buick shot off in a billowing cloud of dust. Emma choked back a sob. She turned away—and stopped in her tracks. A police car had driven silently up behind her.

The driver rolled down the window, and Emma sucked in a breath. It was Officer Quinlan.

"Miss Mercer," Quinlan said acidly, his eyes hidden behind aviator sunglasses. "What's going on here?"

Emma turned as the Buick sputtered around the corner. For a fleeting second, she hoped that Becky had taken off because the cops had pulled up, not because she wanted to get away from her daughter. "Was that a friend of yours?" Quinlan asked, looking at the car, too.

"Um, no. I thought I recognized her, but I . . . didn't," Emma finished lamely, wishing it had been any other cop patrolling the street. Quinlan knew enough about her as it was—at least he thought he did. He had a file five inches thick on her twin, mostly about dangerous pranks she'd played with her clique called the Lying Game. Like the time Sutton had called the police to tell them she'd seen a lion prowling around the golf course, or the time she'd claimed to hear a baby crying in a Dumpster, or the time her car had "stalled" on the train tracks, only to miraculously spring back to life just in time to escape an oncoming train.

My friends had been particularly pissed at me for that one. They'd put together a revenge prank that was so dark, I hated to think about it even now. A video of it, which showed a faceless assailant strangling me, had been leaked on the Internet. And it was that video that had led Emma to me.

Quinlan squinted suspiciously. "Well, if you do know her, make sure she drives a little more carefully. She might hurt someone." He looked pointedly at the swarm of kids watching with interest from the sidewalk.

Irritation seized Emma. She crossed her arms over her chest. "Don't you have anything better to do?" she asked brazenly. Pushing the envelope was Sutton's M.O., and it felt liberating to channel her sister's attitude sometimes.

Thayer finally caught up to her, panting. "Afternoon, officer," he said carefully.

"Mr. Vega." Quinlan looked weary at the sight of

Thayer—he didn't trust him much more than he trusted Sutton. Thayer placed a hand protectively on Emma's arm.

I twitched. I knew Thayer was trying to be supportive, but I felt jealous all the same. I wasn't the kind of girl who shared, even with my own sister. Especially not my boyfriend.

Finally, Quinlan shook his head slowly. "I'll see you both around," he said, and drove away.

Thayer ran his hands through his hair. "Déjà vu. At least no one ran me down this time."

Emma laughed weakly. The night of her sister's murder, Sutton and Thayer had been together at Sabino Canyon. He'd snuck home from his rehab center in Seattle to visit Sutton, but what had started as a romantic moonlit walk had quickly gone sour. First, they'd seen Mr. Mercer talking to a woman who they'd assumed was his mistress. Then someone had stolen Sutton's car and rammed it right into them, shattering Thayer's leg. Sutton's sister, Laurel, had picked Thayer up and taken him to the hospital, leaving Sutton behind in the canyon. She had then met with Mr. Mercer, her adoptive father, who'd told her the truth about the woman he was with: Her name was Becky and she was Mr. Mercer's daughter—and Sutton's biological mother.

But as for what happened next, Emma wasn't sure. All she knew was that Sutton hadn't survived it. Emma had been piecing together that night in the canyon ever since she arrived in Tucson. Every clue brought her a little closer to the truth, and yet she still felt so far from solving the puzzle. She had figured out that Sutton, furious at Mr. Mercer's betrayal, had run back into the Canyon—but where did she go next? How did she die?

Emma looked down to see a ribbon of blood trickling into her sandal from the scrape on her leg.

"Here," Thayer said, following her gaze. He took a blue bandana from his pocket and knelt by her feet, carefully dabbing at the wound. "Don't worry, it's clean. I keep it on hand just so I can offer it to hot girls in distress," he added with a grin.

As the faded piece of cloth turned dark with my twin's blood, a memory flashed before me. I saw Thayer, his eyebrows furrowed, handing me that same bandana to wipe the tears from my eyes. I couldn't remember what I'd been crying about, but I remembered hiding my face in the fabric's soft folds, breathing in the warm sweet scent of Thayer's body that lingered on it.

"Who did you say that was?" Thayer asked, tying the bandana snugly around Emma's ankle to cover the wound.

Emma scrambled for an explanation, for yet another lie. But then she looked at the boy who'd loved her sister, his hazel eyes soft and concerned, and all that came out was the truth: "My birth mom."

Thayer blinked hard. "Seriously?"

"Seriously."

"How did you know it was her? I thought you'd never met."

"She left me a picture," Emma said, thinking of the note Becky had left in the Horseshoe Diner.

For a few horrible days, Emma had thought that Mr. Mercer killed Sutton, in order to keep her from revealing his affair. Knowing that Sutton had seen Mr. Mercer with a woman in the canyon, Emma had searched his office and discovered he was secretly paying a woman named Raven. She'd arranged to meet with Raven at her hotel, but the mysterious woman had sent her on a scavenger hunt that ended with a note at a diner. Raven had left behind a letter and a photo of herself—only, it had been Becky's face staring back. Raven/Becky had vanished, but Mr. Mercer had explained everything.

It was actually why Emma had asked Thayer to meet her for coffee. She'd wanted to tell him that Mr. Mercer hadn't been the one who'd run Thayer down in Sabino Canyon the night I'd died—and that the woman Thayer had seen Mr. Mercer with was actually her biological mother.

"It was her, Thayer. I know it was," Emma protested.

"I believe you," he said in a low voice.

Behind them a garage door rattled open, and they

stepped aside so that a freshly waxed Lexus could back out past them onto the street. They stood in silence for a moment, saying nothing.

"Are you going to be okay?" Thayer asked finally.

Emma felt her jaw tremble. "She looked . . . sick, didn't she?"

"She'd have to be sick not to want to talk to you." Thayer reached out and squeezed her arm, then pulled away cautiously, as though afraid he'd been too intimate. He nodded awkwardly back in the direction of the café. "I should probably get home. But Sutton—" He hesitated again. "If you want to talk about any of this, I'm here for you. You know that, right?"

Emma nodded, still lost in her thoughts. He was three blocks away before she realized that she still had his bandana knotted around her ankle.

I watched him go. Maybe he and Emma were right. Maybe the reason that Becky was acting strange was that she was ill. But I couldn't shake the feeling that I'd encountered her face before—while I was alive, before I became Emma's silent shadow.

I wondered if it had been the last face I'd ever seen.

2

THE GOOD, THE BAD, AND THE SEXY

Later that day, Emma parked Sutton's vintage Volvo outside the Old Tucson Movie Studios. A rickety, old-style western saloon stood in front of her, complete with swinging wooden doors and an overpowering stench of booze. Next to that was a bank building with bullet holes in the wall, a hitching post, and even a house that must have been a brothel, judging by the overly made-up women fanning themselves on the porch. In the fifties and sixties the studio had been a real movie set for westerns, but now it was an amusement park, a Wild West Disneyland full of tourists. Ethan Landry—Emma's boyfriend and the only person who knew her true identity—had suggested they come here instead of the municipal tennis courts, their usual meeting spot.

"Howdy, ma'am." A man in cow-print chaps and spurs nodded his Stetson to her. Emma waved halfheartedly, not really feeling in the Wild West spirit. She wished she *could*—it would be reassuring to swagger confidently down the street, a gun at her hip, finally in charge of her destiny after feeling helpless for so long.

The studio sparked something in me, too. I was pretty sure I'd been here on a class trip and had laughed at the fakey-fakeness of it all with Char and Mads. We'd ditched the tour to sneak into the saloon through the outhouse in the back. Even half remembering how much fun I used to have with them filled me with longing.

After wandering for a few minutes without seeing Ethan, Emma plopped down on one of the benches facing Tucson Mountain Park and pulled out her copy of *Jane Eyre*, which they were reading for English. She had opened to the middle of the book when suddenly she heard gravel crunching behind her.

Ethan was passing by the general store, squinting into the afternoon sun. Her knees weakened slightly as she took in his broad shoulders, muscular legs, and dark, piercing blue eyes. He wore a pair of camouflage cargo shorts and a black sweatshirt, and his dark hair had a cute tousled look that made her want to run her fingers through it.

His shadow stretched out toward her in the sunset as he approached.

"Reach for the sky, partner!" she said, jumping up and aiming her fingers at him like twin pistols.

Eyes round with mock terror, Ethan lifted his hands, then quick-drew an imaginary gun from inside an imaginary coat. "Bang!" he said.

She clutched her chest and staggered backward, sinking to her knees. Then, despite all of the drama that had unfurled that day, she started giggling. That was one of the things she liked most about Ethan—she could be herself with him, goofy Emma Paxton of Las Vegas, Nevada. The girl who wrote a secret newspaper about her life, who kept detailed lists of snarky comebacks she should have said to people who'd been rude to her, the girl who hadn't known Marc Jacobs from Michael Kors before she stepped into Sutton's shoes. Ethan didn't judge her for any of that—he liked her just the way she was. No one had ever accepted her at face value before. Even back when she'd been herself, everyone had immediately made assumptions about her because she was a foster child.

Ethan strode over to her bowlegged, like a cowboy, and drew her close. Their lips met in a brief kiss. Emma felt as though her body might melt.

When they parted, she glanced around them. "I've never been on a movie set before."

Ethan turned around. "I keep forgetting you didn't grow up here. We used to come to the studio on school trips all the time." Ethan took her hand in his, and together they strolled down the dusty street. He pointed at the saloon, where a red-faced man with a beard was wiping down a bar covered in bottles of whiskey. "They built that for *Rio Bravo*. And they shot a bunch of *Gunsmoke* and *Bonanza* episodes out here in the sixties."

"On one of the signs out front it says *Little House on the Prairie* was filmed here," Emma said. "I used to love that show."

Ethan looked surprised. "I didn't take you for the *Little House* type."

Emma shrugged. "I watched reruns of it after school. I think I liked it because even though they were poor, the family was so loving and happy. Ma and Pa would do anything for their children."

Ethan glanced at her sideways. "And what do you think about the Mercers? Are *they* a good family like that?"

Emma nodded slowly, knowing that Ethan was referring to her recent discovery that the Mercers were her family, for real. It was still unbelievable that Mr. and Mrs. Mercer were her grandparents—and Laurel her aunt. She felt grateful to have finally found them, but in some ways, it had made things even more complicated. The Mercers didn't know they had *two* grandchildren. Nor did they know the granddaughter they'd raised as their own child was dead. What would they do if they found out? What would they say if they discovered Emma had been impersonating Sutton, that she had known Sutton was dead all this time?

It was something I thought about a lot, too. I wanted my parents to embrace Emma, I really did. I wished that I could help explain everything to them. But lies can hurt, especially a lie this huge.

"So." Ethan took Emma's hand, leading her to a bench across from a church. This part of the lot looked completely abandoned. "Why did you want to meet?"

Emma took a deep breath. "I saw my mom earlier," she admitted, biting the corner of her lip. "My *real* mom. Becky."

His eyebrows shot up. "Where?"

"She drove past me. I tried to run after her, but she gunned it. I guess she didn't want to talk."

Ethan turned Emma so that she was facing him. "Are you okay?"

She shrugged, forcing a smile. "It's not *me* she's avoiding, right? It's Sutton she doesn't want to talk to."

Ethan scratched his chin. He opened his mouth like he was about to say something, and then closed it.

"What?" Emma asked.

He shook his head. "Nothing."

Emma cocked her head to one side. "Say it."

He took a deep breath. "Well, you said Becky was kind of . . . *crazy*, right?"

Emma nodded slowly. She had told Ethan about how erratic her mother had seemed when Emma was just a little girl. Some days Becky would take Emma to the park, or let her have ice cream for breakfast, lunch, and dinner. Other days she stayed in bed with the blinds drawn, crying into her pillow. The summer before she'd abandoned Emma, Becky had taped cardboard from cereal boxes all over the windows, certain that someone was watching them at night. Emma still cringed when she saw the Captain Crunch logo.

Ethan scuffed the edge of one Chuck Taylor against the other. "Do you have the letter she left you at the diner?"

Without speaking, Emma pulled Sutton's wallet from the Madewell messenger bag over her shoulder and unfolded the note, wincing once more at Becky's handwriting, which was familiar even after all these years. It didn't say much; just *I wish things had gone differently that night in the canyon*, and some vague advice for Sutton not to make the same mistakes she had. Emma wished it had said more.

I did, too. It was the first note my mother ever wrote to me. I wished it said how much she loved me, how much she regretted the decision to give me up.

Emma held it out to Ethan, who studied it intensely. Finally, he looked up and handed the note back to her. "Have you noticed that this isn't addressed to Sutton?" He turned it over. "Not on the front. Not in the greeting. Not *anywhere*."

"So?" Emma asked.

"What if that letter was written to *you*? What if she knows you're not Sutton?"

Emma's body went rigid. "The only person who knows that is the murderer."

Ethan's expression didn't change. Emma shook her head. "Becky's unstable, but she's no murderer. She sent me on treasure hunts all over our apartment complex. She helped me paint big colorful murals on the walls of one of my bedrooms. She's my *mom*."

But even as the words spilled from Emma's mouth, a different type of woman came to mind. Manic Becky. Mad Becky. She pulled out *Jane Eyre* and looked at the cover. It was the same edition she'd had when she'd first read the book, back in Nevada when she was twelve. On the cover was the twisted face of the madwoman Mr. Rochester hid in his attic: her eyes scrunched shut, her face pale, her mouth open in a scream. The image was an archetype of mental illness. Emma remembered how she used to look at that face and shiver with fear—but also something else, something she couldn't quite put her finger on. Now she understood what it was: recognition. Bertha Mason's face reminded her of her mother.

She shut her eyes, pushing away the memories. Her mom had been under a lot of stress. It didn't make her a murderer. What motive would she have for killing Sutton?

I hoped Emma was right. I'd dreamed of meeting my birth mom since I was a little girl. The idea that she could have wanted me dead left me with a deep, hollow ache. I fumbled again at the elusive memory—*had* I met Becky? Had something happened between us? But it remained maddeningly out of reach.

"Forget I mentioned it," Ethan said quickly. He pulled Emma tight to his chest. She just stood there, shell-shocked. "Emma, I'm sorry. I didn't mean to freak you out. I don't know anything about your mom. It's a stupid idea."

She buried her face in his sweatshirt, listening to the thud of his heart as the sunset blazed bright pink over the mountains. She hadn't wanted to admit it to herself before, but Becky *had* looked deranged as she drove past the café. She was suddenly glad it had been Thayer with her and not Ethan. If Ethan had seen her, she couldn't have denied the possibility that Becky could be dangerous.

"Can I ask you something?" he asked, his fingers playing lightly with her hair.

"Anything."

"Do you think you'll get to stay here? You know, after Sutton's case is solved?"

Emma paused. It was something she'd fantasized about since the first moment she'd discovered that she had a twin. She had never fit in anywhere before—even her best and most well-intentioned foster parents had never made her feel like part of a family. Now she had the loving family she'd always dreamed of . . . but would all that change when they found out how many lies she'd told?

"I hope they'll understand why I did this, when it's all said and done," she said quietly. "I'd hate to leave them."

"I've been thinking." Ethan sounded almost shy. "We're both eighteen. Other than finishing up school, we're free to do whatever we want. So if for some reason your living situation with the Mercers doesn't work out, we could . . . I mean, maybe we could get a place."

She blinked. His cheeks burned scarlet even in the dark. For a moment she wasn't sure she'd understood him.

"Together," he added. "As a backup plan, I mean. I don't want to rush you into anything. But it's not like my mom would really miss me." A sad look came over his face, then he met her eyes again. "And Emma, I couldn't stand it if you left. If I lost you."

Emma smiled bashfully. She wasn't sure she was ready to move in with anyone, but the fact that he'd been thinking about their future together brought a warm glow to her heart. She traced the contour of his cheek with one finger, then leaned up and pressed her lips to his.

The world glittered behind her closed eyelids. She wound her fingers into his thick hair and pulled him closer. His breath made her skin hum with excitement. She had never realized how much she longed to be touched by someone who truly cared about her. She had never realized how little she had been touched at all. Now that Ethan was in her life, she sometimes felt as if the only thing keeping her grounded was the promise of another kiss.

I knew the feeling. Thayer used to have that effect on me.

A rustling came from the weeds behind the church steps. Emma looked up. "What was that?"

Ethan tilted his head. "What was what?"

Emma stared at the church's facade, and then strode across the dry street to look around it. Nothing. The desert stretched out beyond, empty except for a few scattered cacti. If someone had been spying, he'd slipped away.

Ethan put an arm around her shoulder and squinted into the sunset. But it no longer seemed beautiful to Emma. Somewhere out there, a killer was watching her every move. Somewhere her sister's body lay undiscovered, unmourned.

She turned to Ethan. "I'm pretty wiped out. We'd better get home and rest up for the big flag football game

tomorrow." She reached for his hand. "You're still coming, right?"

"I wouldn't miss it," Ethan promised. The sand
crunched beneath their feet as they walked past the busy
part of the town, where tourists were buying hand-
kerchiefs and Stetsons.

Sutton's Volvo was at the far end of the parking lot, but
Emma spied the note folded under her windshield wiper
immediately. Her heart seized in her chest. She ran for the
note and snatched it off the glass. The muscles in Ethan's
face were taut as she unfolded the note.

"Oh my God." Emma gasped, looking around the
empty desert. The message was in the same familiar
handwriting that had greeted her on her first morning in
Tucson, the same scrawl that had announced her sister was
dead, and she had to play along or she'd be next.

*You should thank me. Before you came here you had noth-
ing. Now you have everything you want. Just don't slip up.
Sutton thought she could have everything she wanted, too.*

For once, Emma and I were thinking the exact same
thing: Those footsteps by the church had been real. My
killer was still watching Emma's every move.

3

THE FACE THAT LAUNCHED
A THOUSAND FISTS

"These shirts are *so* lame," Laurel whined, pulling at the collar of her blue cotton tee. "Why couldn't they have gotten American Apparel instead of Hanes Beefy-Ts?"

It was a beautiful Sunday afternoon, and Emma, Sutton's friends, and the Mercer family were gathered in Saguaro National Park for the annual Hollier High Parent-Student Football Fun Fest—that was what the banner arching over their heads called it, anyway. An artificially green swath of grass splayed out before them, and a bunch of families flipped burgers on the public barbecues and loaded plates with potato salad and watermelon slices. Little kids tumbled across the freshly chalked lines of the football field, playing freeze tag. Mr. Mercer tossed a U-of-A-branded football in the air, seeming pumped for the flag football game that was about to begin.

Emma laughed, tucking her own red shirt into Sutton's mesh Adidas shorts. "It's a fund-raiser. I'm sure the shirts were donated."

Charlotte Chamberlain rolled her eyes. "My mom does plenty of fund-raisers. Everyone knows if you want to get big money, you have to spend big money. Last year she held a raffle for a vintage Chanel coat and got three times what it was worth."

"What was the charity?" asked Madeline Vega, another one of Sutton's friends, who was tall and lithe next to Charlotte's short and curvy frame.

Charlotte shrugged, pulling her reddish curls into a ponytail. "Does it matter?"

There was shuffling and giggling behind them, and the girls turned. The Twitter Twins, Gabriella and Lilianna Fiorello, twirled over. They'd come dressed in short cheerleader outfits—Lili in black and red, with giant safety pins pierced through the skirt, and Gabby in sky blue and white, her blond hair in a high ponytail. Both of them carried sparkly pompoms and made a lot of noise when they shook them.

"Oh my God, *what* are you guys wearing?" Madeline snickered.

"It's *ironic*, duh," Gabby trilled, lifting a pompom high in the air.

Emma smiled at all of them. These were Sutton's friends, but she'd begun to think of them as her friends, too. Aside from Alex, her best friend from Henderson, she'd never been close to any girls, let alone a whole group of them. It was a nice feeling, even if she couldn't talk to them about her actual problems.

I wasn't sure I had talked to my friends about my serious problems either. We loved each other with a fierce loyalty, but we weren't the best at saying it. I think we were all so focused on maintaining our fabulous images that we forgot they weren't always real.

Emma pulled her hair into a knot and did some deep knee bends to stretch. Her legs still ached from chasing Becky's car, but she'd gotten a lot stronger while pretending to be Sutton—she'd had tennis practice almost every day.

"Oh my God, Sutton, are you actually *playing* this year?" Madeline asked, incredulous.

"I thought I'd try something new," Emma said lightly. Though football clearly hadn't been Sutton's thing, she was actually looking forward to this game. The closest thing to a family outing she'd ever had in foster care was a trip to the recycling center to turn in soda cans. She loved that the Mercers had annual traditions like this. Plus, it was just the kind of distraction she needed after the panic of receiving another note from Sutton's murderer.

"But you always complain about how much you hate grass stains and that Dad's end-zone shuffle makes you want to die of embarrassment," Laurel said cautiously.

Emma elbowed Laurel, grinning. "Scared I'll beat you, little sis?"

"You wish." Laurel laughed. "Bring it on!"

Emma surveyed the field. Besides Sutton's friends, plenty of other kids from Hollier were gathered to play. Emma waved at Nisha Banerjee, who sipped an iced tea under the awning, and Nisha gave her a friendly wave back. Nisha and Sutton had been rivals, both on the tennis court and off, but Emma had recently forged a tentative friendship with her. Sutton's ex-boyfriend Garrett Austin was here, too, sharing a hot dog with his younger sister, a sophomore with Buddy Holly glasses and purple hair. Emma avoided catching his eye—she'd broken his heart after he'd offered his willing body to her on her birthday.

Charlotte grabbed her by the elbow. "Don't look now, but you have an admirer."

Emma glanced around, looking for Ethan, but it was Thayer whose eyes she met. He stood in a group of guys across the field. The other boys were punching each other on the arm and horsing around, but Thayer just stared at Emma. When she caught his eye, he grinned bashfully and looked down.

He meant that look for me, I repeated to myself, but knowing it didn't make it any easier to watch.

"Here we go again," Madeline groaned.

"What?" Emma turned to her friends. They were all watching her with varying degrees of skepticism on their faces. She swallowed nervously. It wasn't that hard to guess what they were thinking—that something was going on between her and Thayer. Ever since he'd returned to Tucson, things between Emma and Sutton's friends had been a bit tense. Charlotte hated the fact that Sutton always seemed to get all the guys—which Sutton hadn't exactly helped when she'd stolen Garrett from Charlotte several months ago. Madeline didn't think Sutton was good for Thayer, who was recovering from his alcohol addiction. And as for Laurel, she and Thayer had been best friends for a long time. She'd always had a crush on him, which had made it especially humiliating when Sutton decided to go for him. Emma could only imagine how upset Laurel had been when she found out Thayer was meeting her sister in secret the whole time he was supposedly missing.

"You guys, it's not like that!" Emma said, hoping to avoid what was clearly a touchy subject. "Thayer and I are just friends."

"Oh yeah?" Charlotte looked across the field at Thayer, whose eyes were still locked on Emma. "That's a friendly look he's sending you."

Emma felt her face getting warm. Fending off boys was a new experience for her. She'd never stayed in one school long enough to connect with any would-be boyfriends. She leaned over to retie her shoelaces, trying to ignore Charlotte's accusing glance.

When she straightened, she noticed another familiar figure on the other side of the field, and her heart lifted. She waved at Ethan, but he didn't seem to see her. Then she caught his expression. He was watching Thayer with fire in his eyes. Emma recoiled. She knew he was jealous of Thayer, but she had never seen him look so venomous before.

"Ethan!" she yelled, but the crowd shifted and he disappeared from her line of sight.

"So which one of them are you bringing to my party in two Saturdays?" Charlotte asked with a smirk.

"You're having a party? Since when?" Madeline interrupted, fingering the collar of her T-shirt, which she'd cut into a boat neck.

"Since about an hour ago," Charlotte said coyly. "I just found out my parents are going to Vegas that weekend. We can't let an opportunity like that pass us by, can we?"

"Nice," Gabby whispered, reaching for her iPhone and starting to type. Lili followed suit. In twenty seconds, the whole school would know about it, thanks to their Twitter feeds.

"Well, I'm taking Ethan, obviously," Emma said. She looked for him across the field again, hoping she'd just imagined the terrifying look he'd given Thayer. A headline popped into her mind, an old habit from the days of imagining herself an investigative journalist: *Rumored Love Triangle Drives Teen Couple Apart; Details on Page 11.*

The referee blew his whistle, signaling the players to assemble in the middle of the field. Emma, Madeline, and Charlotte were with Mr. Mercer on the red team. Ethan joined them, giving Emma a kiss on her cheek. Laurel and Mrs. Mercer stood on the other side in blue, along with Nisha and Thayer.

"You're going down!" Laurel screamed at Emma from across the field. Emma rolled her eyes good-naturedly. Not long ago, a threat like that from Laurel would have scared her, but she and Laurel were now on good terms. And Laurel *definitely* wasn't Sutton's murderer.

"Okay, everyone," Mr. Mercer said, tucking a yellow flag into his waistband and gesturing for the group to huddle. "Madeline, Charlotte, you girls flank us and keep those blues off our backs. After the snap, Sutton, you run downfield as fast as you can. I'll pass it to you when it looks clear." Then he squeezed her arm. "I'm glad you're playing this year."

Emma couldn't keep the smile off her face. Since she'd discovered Mr. Mercer was her grandfather, she'd felt close to him, not just as Sutton but as herself. But then the usual guilt flooded back. He didn't know her secret. And as much as she wanted to tell him, she couldn't. She thought about the locket tightening around her throat at Charlotte's house, the stage light that had crashed danger-ously close to her head, all the times the murderer had warned her never to tell anyone. She couldn't bear the thought of her grandfather being hurt—and if he knew the truth, his life would be in danger, too.

The referee blew the whistle again. Emma saw the ball snap back and bolted, weaving quickly in and out of blue cotton shirts. The Twitter Twins' high voices chanted from the sidelines: "We've got beauty, we've got class, the other team can kiss our . . ."

"Sutton!" Mr. Mercer cried, drowning out the rest of the cheer. Nisha was in front of him, trying to grab the flag from his belt, but he danced backward a few steps and threw.

Emma's body tensed as the ball hung in the air. It fell neatly into her arms, and she took off toward the goalpost.

"Where do you think you're going?" From the corner of her eye she saw Mrs. Mercer come her way. Her grand-mother was surprisingly dexterous, limber from the hot yoga she did three times a week. Emma zigzagged around her and put on a burst of speed. Laurel joined the chase, and she and Mrs. Mercer flanked Emma as she pelted up the field.

Emma's hair came loose from its knot and billowed behind her. I was pulled along by her speed, but I couldn't feel the wind in my hair or the earth pushing away under my feet. I wondered how many times I'd gone to this tournament only to stand on the sidelines with my friends, complaining about the heat. Maybe I should have actually played once, just to experience it for myself.

The goalpost loomed in the distance, so close Emma could taste it. Suddenly, a pair of arms encircled her waist. She tumbled to the ground, the football rolling away from her. When she flipped to her back, Thayer's face hovered over hers. "Gotcha," he said softly, in the same feathery tone of voice he might use to say *I love you.*

Time stood still for a moment. Emma smelled the sweet grass, saw the light freckles on his cheeks. His face was so close to hers, she thought they might kiss.

I would have given anything in that moment to be able to feel what Emma did.

Then Thayer cried out as someone lifted him from behind. Emma looked around, confused, and saw Ethan shoving Thayer to his feet.

"This is *flag* football," Ethan said angrily. "You're going to hurt someone."

Thayer pushed Ethan away. "Touch me again, man, and I'll hurt *you.*"

"Oh yeah, you going to knock me down like you did

my girlfriend?" Ethan shoved him again, this time a little harder.

Thayer took a few steps back. A dangerous grin broke over his face. "I'm going to enjoy kicking your ass," he snarled. Then he lunged. Soon the two were a tangle of limbs and dirt thrashing around on the ground.

"Stop it!" Emma cried, struggling to her feet. There was blood on Ethan's cheek. Thayer's shirt was torn at the collar. The referee's whistle blasts kept breaking through the air uselessly. Spectators stood with their hands clapped over their mouths. People ran toward them, including Mr. Mercer.

"Break it up, boys!" he yelled. But only a few feet from the fight, a divot of grass snagged his foot. He went flying face-first into the turf, rolling a few feet before coming to a stop. A low groan of pain escaped his mouth. Ethan and Thayer stopped fighting and stared at him.

"Dad!" Laurel screamed, dropping to his side. Emma and Mrs. Mercer were just behind her.

Mr. Mercer let out another groan. Both of his shins were skinned, and blood trickled into the grass. He clutched his left knee, which had already swollen to twice its usual size.

"Oh, man," whispered Thayer, wiping his own blood from his purpling nose.

Mrs. Mercer looked into the impotent crowd, her face

pale. "Can someone help me get him to the car?" she asked firmly.

Thayer and Ethan scrambled to either side of Mr. Mercer. Between the two of them, they managed to get him unsteadily to his feet, guide him across the field, and angle him into the family SUV. Mr. Mercer groaned the whole way. Emma followed, her heart pounding loudly in her chest. She barely felt Madeline's hand on her shoulder or heard Charlotte's promises that he was going to be okay. She and Laurel climbed into the backseat, and Mrs. Mercer turned the ignition. No one spoke as they pulled out of the space.

Emma turned and stared back at the parking lot. Ethan and Thayer stood several feet away from each other, looking sheepish. Ethan's arms were crossed over his chest. Thayer rubbed the back of his neck awkwardly.

"Still think they're not fighting over you?" Laurel mumbled.

Emma didn't answer. She didn't want to be squabbled over like some medieval damsel. Maybe they'd learned their lesson since Mr. Mercer had been hurt.

Don't count on it, I thought, remembering Thayer's almost-kiss when he'd tackled my twin. The only way he'd stop fighting for me was to find out the truth—that I was dead and Emma was simply standing in.

4

KARMA'S A BITCH, AND SO AM I

News of the fight between Sutton's two boyfriends was all over the school by Monday. Emma had to deflect constant questions about the quarrel, the details getting more exaggerated as the day wore on. Ethan had almost strangled Thayer to death. Thayer's leg had miraculously healed, and he'd given Ethan a deadly kick to the groin. Thayer was going to hire a hit man from his shadowy past to finish Ethan off. Ethan now carried a gun to school.

Emma tried to shrug off the stories, but they dogged her even when she got to tennis practice that afternoon. As she joined the rest of the team on the courts, girls kept asking her about it as though she'd literally been caught in the middle of the fight. "I heard that Ethan and Thayer are going to have a rematch on Friday," Clara Hewlitt, a sophomore, said wistfully.

"How very Clint Eastwood of them," Emma joked. But she felt uneasy. She hadn't said much to Ethan after the fight except to send him a few texts, yelling at him for being so rash. Ethan had apologized, as had Thayer. But Emma didn't exactly like having the two of them fighting over her.

The late fall air was dry and hot, the sky a robin's-egg blue beyond the mountains. The moon hung visible even in the afternoon, a pale disc in the cloudless sky. The courts were busy with girls warming up, adjusting ponytails and gossiping—probably about the fight.

Laurel nudged Emma. "Check out the new girl," she giggled, thankfully changing the subject.

Emma glanced up at the thin, elfin-looking girl standing a few feet away. Her long blond hair was swept back in lots of little braids, and she had about a dozen earrings in her earlobes, and silver rings shaped like ankhs and Wiccan spirals and Celtic crosses on every finger. While the other girls on the team were doing deep, athletic-looking stretches and exercises, this girl stood on one leg in some kind of yoga pose, her hands at her chest in prayer position. She hummed distractedly to herself as she lifted her arms in the air, balancing perfectly. Emma recognized

Joni Mitchell's "Free Man in Paris," which Ursula, one of her old foster mothers, used to play nonstop.

Charlotte snorted. "What's she doing, balancing her chakras?"

Laurel laughed, and the girl's eyes snapped open. She gazed at them as if she was seeing them through a deep mist and could just barely make them out.

"Be quiet, Charlotte, you're disturbing the cosmic forces," Laurel teased, slapping her friend lightly on the arm.

Emma shifted her weight, a twinge of guilt gnawing at her. She'd been the new girl often enough in her life to know how hard it could be. She straightened her spine and strode across the court toward the strange girl.

Practically everyone on the team stopped what they were doing. Nisha paused mid-push-up to follow Emma with her eyes. Clara, who'd been demonstrating a backhand grip to some low-ranked players, dropped her racket and openly stared.

It wasn't the first time Emma had been struck by the power of popularity. When Sutton Mercer talked, people listened. Sometimes that influence made Emma uncomfortable—she'd never had that kind of sway in her own life, and she'd been on the receiving end of the popular kids' cruelty a few times herself. But now she had the opportunity to use her role as Sutton Mercer to do some good.

"Hi," she said, holding her hand out to the new girl. "My name's Sutton."

The girl didn't budge from her yoga pose. After a moment Emma was forced to lower her hand awkwardly. It was only then that the girl gracefully dropped back to a standing position, opened her eyes, and gave Emma a big smile.

"Sorry about that—I like to see how long I can balance in *vrksasana*. My record is twelve minutes thirteen seconds." She blinked placidly. "My name's Celeste. Do you practice yoga?"

Emma pursed her lips. "Uh, no . . ."

"You totally should," Celeste said, a languid smile on her face. "Not only does it improve your focus, but it can really put you in touch with the flow of the universe. My tennis game has improved so much since I started. Once you learn to move with the racket, it's like it just finds its way to the ball."

"That's . . . cool," Emma said.

Celeste grabbed a SmartWater from the bench and took a long swig. "We moved here from Taos. Daddy got a new position in the art department at the U. He's a painter. He just finished a big exhibition in Berlin."

Emma perked up. This at least sounded more interesting—she was a huge fan of art, especially photography. Ethan had taken her to an opening a month ago, and she'd loved it. "What kind of work does he do?"

"You like art?" A hint of skepticism had entered the girl's voice. "I wouldn't have guessed that. Daddy's work is very conceptual. People don't get it most of the time, at least not in *Arizona*." She wrinkled her nose.

Emma frowned. "Arizona's not so bad."

"Oh, it's fine, I suppose," Celeste said. "I'm just used to Taos. It's so beautiful there, and the people are all *brilliant*. They all live in such harmony with the earth. Tucson is, well . . . different."

"The university has a great art department. I'm sure your dad will be really happy there." Emma glanced around her, looking for a way to escape the conversation. Celeste was kind of snooty. She took a step backward. "Anyway, it's nice to . . ."

But then Celeste cocked her head curiously. "You know, Coach Maggie told me all about you, Sutton. But I thought you'd look . . . *stronger*." Her eyes went up and down Emma's frame, clearly giving her the once-over, and she smiled dismissively.

Emma gritted her teeth. "Good things come in small packages," she mumbled.

Thankfully, Coach Maggie chose that exact moment to blow her whistle. "Gather round, girls!"

The team trotted over to Maggie, a short, muscular woman who wore a baseball cap over her strawberry-blond hair. When Maggie put a hand on Celeste's shoulder, Celeste bowed her head like a Buddhist monk. "All right, everyone, this is our newest Lady Chaparelle, Celeste Echols," Maggie said. "She just moved here from New Mexico."

Laurel nudged Emma. "What did she say to you?"

"You know who she is, right?" Clara whispered beside them in a reverent tone. "Her grandma is Jeanette Echols."

"Who's that?" Laurel crinkled her nose.

"The novelist?" Emma asked, before she could stop herself.

Charlotte, Laurel, and Nisha turned to stare at her. "When was the last time *you* opened a book?" Charlotte asked, a hand on one hip.

Emma feigned a cough to hide her misstep. One of her foster moms used to be into Jeanette Echols, who wrote fat paperbacks about vampires and witches and bloodthirsty fairies. When she was bored one day and couldn't catch a ride to the library, Emma had finally caved and started to read the whole series. But they definitely weren't the kind of thing Sutton would have read.

"Please make her feel welcome," Maggie continued. She looked at Emma. "Sutton, are you ready to scrimmage?"

"Born ready," Emma said, marching toward the court. For once she actually believed her own Sutton bravado. How big of a threat could Celeste be?

Celeste pulled her mass of braids up into one large

ponytail and gave Emma a placid smile. "I should warn you, Mercury's in retrograde and I'm really sensitive to that. I'm a Virgo."

"Got it," Emma said. She exchanged glances with Nisha, the only girl close enough to overhear. Nisha made a tiny index-finger-circling-the-ear gesture. *Crazy*, she mouthed. Emma giggled.

Maggie blew her whistle as a signal to play. Emma bounced the ball twice on the ground, stepped up to the baseline, and hit a hard serve over the net. Celeste returned it effortlessly, dropping the shot in the far left corner of the court. The ball sailed easily past Emma's outstretched racket.

"Love-fifteen," Maggie called out, pointing to Celeste's side.

Emma gritted her teeth, twirling her racket. She crouched low and tried to refocus, but the same thing happened on the next serve. Celeste sent the ball back to Emma with a graceful swing, somehow finding a pocket of the court Emma couldn't reach in time.

"Emma!" I groaned, wishing I could cover my eyes. She was destroying my badass tennis image.

"Love-thirty," Maggie called.

Even the girls who were supposed to be involved in their own scrimmages stopped to watch. All Emma could do was shrug and serve again. This time she was able to return

Celeste's backhanded volley, but it arced straight up in the air as a lob. Celeste smashed it back down onto Emma's side of the net, as easily as if she were swatting a fly.

"Nice try," she said, her voice oozing sweetness. "I'm sure you'll get the next one."

But Emma didn't hit the next one, or the next. Forty-five minutes later, Celeste had trounced her in five straight matches. Emma braced her hands against her thighs, panting, as the team stared in confusion, no one daring to clap *against* Sutton. Only when Maggie encouraged everyone did a few of the girls muster up halfhearted applause. Laurel and Charlotte crossed their arms over their chests, looking disgruntled. Nisha had done the same. Emma shuffled to the sidelines in humiliation.

"That was something else, Celeste!" Maggie cried, clapping loudly to make up for everyone else.

Celeste smiled, a thin sheen of perspiration glowing on her skin. She bowed her head to Emma. "*Namaste.*" Then she drifted off to one of the far courts. A few girls trotted behind her, and Emma could hear them talking about astrological signs and yoga poses.

Charlotte shook her head in wonderment. "Who does she think she is?"

Emma tried to look disdainful as she wiped the sweat off her face and shoulders, but a flutter of anxiety twisted her stomach. Her twin would have decimated that girl, she was sure of it.

"We're done for the day!" Maggie called a few minutes later, guiding the girls to the locker room. Emma had never been more relieved for practice to be over. Steam billowed through the green-tiled room, the sound of the showers hissing in the background. Colorful shower poufs hung outside some of the lockers, laced through the combination locks to dry between uses.

Emma hooked Sutton's basket of toiletries over her arm, threw a towel over her shoulder, and slid out of the aisle of lockers. On the end wall was an oversized display case that said HOLLIER HIGH CHAPARELLES MVP across the top. It featured the MVPs through the years, from girls with big eighties hair and massive earrings all the way to Sutton's photo from last year, her dark hair sleek and straight, her eyes bright. Emma paused to look at it for a moment, suddenly sad. Someone stopped beside her and gasped.

"Who is this?" Celeste asked, her voice low and tremulous. She pointed at Sutton's photo.

Emma stared at her. Was she joking? Was this some kind of game, an extension of the you-don't-look-very-strong comment from earlier, her way of saying, *There's no way you're going to be MVP this year.* But Celeste's eyes were round and ingenuous. She seemed to be looking right into Emma and struggling to understand what she saw there.

"Obviously that's Sutton. Who else could it be?" Nisha

had come up behind them to peer over Emma's shoulder. She curled her lip.

Celeste shook her head, a pained crease between her eyes. "No, it's not. The energy in this picture is nothing like yours, Sutton. You seem much . . . sweeter. Like you've lived a hard life and know what it's like to suffer."

Oh, great—since I'd died I'd had to hear time and time again what a bitch I'd been, and now I had to listen to the fact that my *energy* was mean, too?

Emma recoiled from the other girl's gaze. It had been months since she'd been seen for herself by anyone except Ethan, and for better or worse she'd gotten used to being able to hide behind Sutton's persona. Now she felt uncomfortably like someone was peeking behind her disguise, seeing how she really felt and what she really thought.

She gave Celeste a cold sneer. "Whatever you say," she said, tossing her hair over her shoulder. "Excuse me, I need to shower." She sauntered past the other girl, forcing herself not to look at her again.

Careful, sis, I thought. I didn't believe in premonitions or astrology or auras either, back when I was alive. But then again, I didn't believe in ghosts. Sometimes there are things in the world beyond what you can see with the naked eye.

5

DADDY-DAUGHTER DINE-AND-DASH

Tuesday evening, the maître d' of the La Paloma Country Club dining room hurried to the podium to meet Emma and her grandfather. Mrs. Mercer and Laurel had a mother–daughter community service meeting, so it was just Emma and Mr. Mercer for dinner that night.

"Oh, Mr. Mercer, your knee!" the maître d' cried.

Mr. Mercer was propped up between two crutches, his knee buried in the straps and padding of a brace. He smiled ruefully. "You should see the other guy," he said, wincing.

The maître d' laughed mirthfully and waved for him to follow her to the dining room. Luckily, the room wasn't crowded, so Mr. Mercer was able to maneuver easily around the tables. A piano tinkled in the corner, blending in with the low conversations and scrape of silverware. A few men in suits sat at the bar, talking golf, while women in designer dresses and pearls nibbled on colorful salads, the dressing in cups to the sides of their plates. The big floor-to-ceiling windows on the far wall offered a panoramic view of the Catalina Mountains. As they passed a large gilded mirror, Emma studied their side-by-side reflections. She'd inherited Mr. Mercer's straight nose and jawline. She smiled at her own reflection and saw the matching smile on his face. It seemed so obvious that they were related, now that she knew to look for it.

"What happened?" a woman called out from a nearby table, glancing in concern at Mr. Mercer's crutches. Mr. Mercer just smiled at her and passed on, but not before Emma noticed that *a lot* of the women in the dining room were eyeing Mr. Mercer appreciatively.

Ew, were they ogling my dad? Sure, he was good-looking in that salt-and-pepper way, dignified and handsome in his tan sports coat and Italian leather shoes. But he was here with his daughter, for crying out loud—well, really his *grand*daughter. *And* he was on crutches.

Emma helped Mr. Mercer into a chair at a large round table in the corner. "I'm so sorry again about your knee," she mumbled.

He shrugged. "It's not your fault."

"It kind of is. If it wasn't for me . . ." Emma trailed off, still annoyed at Thayer and Ethan.

But Mr. Mercer waved her protestations away. "Let's not talk about it anymore, okay?"

A waitress handed them leather-bound menus, and Emma's mouth started watering just reading her choices: portobello ragout in truffle oil, butter-poached lobster, rosemary-rubbed pork tenderloin, pecan-crusted snapper. Eating in nice restaurants instead of Jack in the Box was definitely on the list of *Things That Do Not Suck About Being Sutton Mercer*.

But then Emma thought of the killer's most recent note—YOU SHOULD THANK ME—and suddenly didn't feel as hungry. The cost of her new life made it hard to enjoy the perks.

When the waitress returned, they put in their orders: fettuccine alfredo for Emma, a filet mignon, rare, for Mr. Mercer. Then Mr. Mercer reached into his coat and pulled out a folded manila envelope. He looked down at it in his hands for a moment. "I found these for you," he said, setting it on the table between them.

Emma opened it to find a thick pile of photographs. On the top was a glossy picture of Becky around age twelve or thirteen. She was sitting on a horse and grinning broadly, braces glinting on her teeth. The next was of Becky in a

Girl Scout uniform, pointing proudly at a merit badge on her sash. Becky in a cat costume for Halloween. Becky on a beach building an elaborate sand castle. There were a few of an older Becky, sixteen or seventeen years old. She'd lost all her baby fat and had a pale, waifish beauty. She no longer smiled for the camera. Emma paused at a picture of her mother in an oversized plaid flannel shirt, standing on a canyon trail in California. The expression on her face was hard to read. Sad, maybe, or just distant.

A wave of sorrow washed over Emma, too. What had happened to that smiling girl on horseback? How had she become the haggard woman she'd seen in the Buick?

It was hard for me to look at them, too. All my life, I'd wondered who my birth mother was. Admittedly, I'd pictured someone amazing: an international reporter called away to cover a dangerous war zone that was no place for a child, or a fashion model working the runways in Paris. But Becky was so ordinary, plain. Damaged.

"There are more in the attic, if you'd like to see them," Mr. Mercer offered.

"I would," Emma said, flipping through the photographs again. She paused on a picture of a junior-high-age Becky scowling playfully from a tent, perhaps on a camping trip. "She's really pretty."

The Becky she'd known had been beautiful, with her big blue eyes and milky white skin. But there was a brittleness to her, an unease that kept most people at a distance, as though some tangible sadness clung to her. Emma remembered being at a playground once when a man in a basketball jersey had tried to flirt with her mother. Becky had stared silently at him from within the depths of her long, loose hair until he'd moved nervously away.

Mr. Mercer nodded as the waitress set down their appetizers. "She is. She looks a lot like her mother. So do you, for that matter."

Emma could see it: All three generations of Mercer women had the same eyes, the same cheekbones. In one of the pictures, Becky sat side by side with her mother at the end of a dock. Mrs. Mercer's smile looked forced, while Becky just stared blankly at the camera. She looked as if she might be around Emma's age.

"When was the last time Mom saw Becky?" she asked, picking up her fork to spear a piece of lettuce from her salad.

Mr. Mercer dipped a bite of calamari into marinara sauce, frowning. "Not long after she left you with us, Sutton." He sighed. "Becky had a way of hitting her mom just where it would hurt her the most."

Emma swallowed a crouton. "Shouldn't we tell her that Becky's been in town? It's been a long time. Maybe things have changed."

Mr. Mercer shook his head. "I know it's difficult, but

we have to keep this a secret. Things haven't been easy for any of us, but your mom has taken it especially hard. Promise me you won't tell her."

"I promise," Emma said softly. She hesitated, biting her lip, then forged ahead. "I think I saw Becky the other day. She drove past me, but I know it was her."

To her astonishment, he nodded. "I guess I'm not surprised by that."

"You're not? You mean she's hung around here before, spying?"

The waitress swooped in at that very moment to ask if everything was okay. "Fine," Mr. Mercer said, giving her a clipped smile. When she vanished, he turned back to Emma. "She's come back into town a few times."

"She *clearly* saw me." Emma felt the hurt on the surface of her skin, like a physical wound. "Why did she drive off? Why did she pretend I didn't exist?"

Mr. Mercer sighed heavily. "Becky's life has never been easy."

"Sure it has." Emma suddenly felt angry. She grabbed the pile of pictures and started to flip through them. "Horseback riding. Dance lessons. Presents at Christmas. Ski vacation, beach vacation, Disneyland vacation. She had . . ." Emma swallowed hard. She'd almost said *more than I ever did.* "She had everything anyone could want. Don't make excuses for her."

She'd managed to keep her voice from climbing higher, from echoing through the entire dining room, but it shook dangerously. She pinched her forearm under the table to hold back her tears. Mr. Mercer's eyes were sad behind his glasses, and for a moment he seemed older and more tired than Emma had ever seen him.

He reached across the table and took her hand. "Sutton, believe me, I know how you feel. Your mom and I have never stopped talking about this. Wondering if we could have done more for her, wondering if any of her . . . of her behavior is our fault. But some people just have a hard time in the world, no matter how many advantages they have, no matter how loved they are. Someday you'll understand that. Not everybody is as strong as you are."

Emma pulled her hand from his. "You're talking like she's damaged. Like she's some kind of freak."

Again he hesitated. Then he turned back to his appetizer and gracefully speared another piece of calamari with his fork. "She's not a freak. You shouldn't talk about anyone that way—especially not Becky. But, honey, she has a lot of problems. Difficulties socializing or living with other people. It's one of the reasons she's moved so often, one of the reasons she keeps to herself. She can be unpredictable when she's not on her medication."

Emma's blood chilled. Becky took medication? For how long? "Unpredictable how?" she asked.

Mr. Mercer shifted in his seat. "Well, sometimes she'd be despondent for days on end. Hiding in her room, crying at the drop of a hat. Sometimes she was destructive. She broke things out of spite. She punched a hole in the wall, just because she was asked to clear the table."

"Oh," Emma said quietly. She thought about her mother's habits, things she'd always thought of as strange or irresponsible more than dangerous. Like how she'd spend a week at a time in the same pair of pajama bottoms. How she'd stolen candy by the pocketful from the corner store, or gleefully lit their unopened utilities bills on fire with a match.

Mr. Mercer cleared his throat uncomfortably. "But despite all that, Becky can also be creative and warm and wonderful. In her own way she loves you—I know she does. That's why she gave you to us, because she knew we'd take better care of you than she could. She wanted to talk to you that night in the canyon, but she wasn't ready. Maybe she's watching you now because she's trying to build up the courage to finally see you."

I wasn't so sure about that. Becky hadn't looked shy or nervous, exactly, more like caught. Or annoyed, perhaps, that Emma was running after her.

Emma was thinking the same thing. And she couldn't help thinking about what Ethan had said at the studio, about how Becky might have played a role in Sutton's disappearance. More memories started flooding back as though released from a dam, all the ones Emma usually tried not to think about. Like the night Becky caught her boyfriend Joe cheating. He was a mild-mannered guy with a goatee who watched Saturday morning cartoons with Emma before Becky crawled out of bed. Becky had intercepted a call on his phone from someone named "Rainbow" and had gone crazy, her eyes rolling madly as she paced the apartment and screamed at Joe. Emma hid under the bed when Becky picked up a folding chair to clobber her boyfriend over the head. Emma could still remember the terrible crunch of impact. She'd curled up, hugging her Socktopus for dear life and praying for everything to be over soon.

She shuddered. She wanted to be able to dismiss Ethan's suspicions, but maybe she didn't actually know what her mother was capable of.

The waitress appeared again, this time with their entrées. Just as Emma was twirling a bite of pasta, Mr. Mercer's phone jangled from his pocket. He glanced at the screen and frowned. "The hospital," he murmured. "Sorry, honey, I need to grab this."

Even through the bustle and clatter of the busy dining room, Emma could hear the crisp, calm voice on the other end of the phone. "Dr. Mercer, I'm with the University of Arizona Hospital. We have your daughter.

We have Rebecca. There's been an incident. Can you come in right away?"

Almost before the woman had finished her sentence, Mr. Mercer was scrambling for his crutches. Emma knocked over her chair as she jumped to her feet to help him. A single thought cycled in her mind again and again. *Something has happened to Becky.*

I flew behind them both as they hurried out of the club, straining my ears to hear what else the nurse had to say and bracing for whatever they'd find in that hospital bed only a few miles away.

6

THE FOURTH FLOOR

Mr. Mercer found a parking spot near the entrance of the University of Arizona Hospital and Medical Center, and they hurried into the lobby of the ER. A blast of air conditioning greeted them. "We're here for Rebecca Mercer, please," Mr. Mercer said to the woman at the triage desk.

Emma looked around, wrinkling her nose at the antiseptic hospital smell. Just one week before, she'd come here to investigate her grandfather's involvement in Sutton's disappearance, breaking into his office in the orthopedic wing and rifling through his desk—that was how she'd tracked down Becky in the first place.

The ER lobby was full of orange plastic chairs,

dilapidated coffee tables, and out-of-date magazines. A young man sat with a bloody towel wrapped around one finger, a woman who must have been his mother speaking rapidly in Spanish at his side. A man with several small children sat under a poster that showed how to sneeze in to your elbow to prevent spreading germs. A TV bolted to the ceiling was tuned to a classic movie channel— Emma recognized Jimmy Stewart and Kim Novak from *Vertigo*, which she'd seen in a class a few years before in Henderson.

Something has happened to Becky. She and her grandfather hadn't spoken a word on the drive over, both of them too terrified of what might greet them when they got here, but Emma's imagination had whipped through a thousand terrible scenarios. She pictured Becky's legs crushed under the wheels of a car, Becky sick with a mystery illness no one could cure, Becky missing limbs or plugged into life-support machines. Twenty minutes earlier she'd been angry and frustrated with her mother, but now she hated herself for even thinking it. What if she was going to lose her for real?

Even though Becky still made me feel uneasy, I was worried about the same thing.

The woman in triage said something to Mr. Mercer in a low voice that Emma couldn't hear. He nodded, then hobbled across the lobby to a gleaming bronze elevator.

With a *ping*, the doors slid open, and he got inside. Emma followed him. "Where are we going? I thought she was in the ER."

Mr. Mercer didn't answer. She could see their blurred reflections in the dented metal of the doors, but unlike in the mirror at the restaurant, here they looked warped and eerie. A Muzak version of "Bad Romance" oozed out of the speakers. The elevator crept up an inch at a time.

"Have they checked her in already?" Emma asked again. "Is it serious?"

Mr. Mercer just pressed his lips into a white line. Then the elevator dinged and the doors slid open. Gold letters spelled out the name of the ward on the sage green wall facing them: PSYCHIATRIC AND MENTAL HEALTH SERVICES.

Emma grabbed her grandfather's arm and forced him to look at her. "What are we doing here? You have to talk to me."

Mr. Mercer adjusted his crutches under his arms. "I don't know much more than you do, honey. The nurse on the phone said it was bad. Becky's had some kind of . . . episode."

"Some kind of episode?" Emma's voice sounded shrill in the quiet hallway. "What does that *mean*?"

Her grandfather opened his mouth to answer, but before he could, a thickset nurse with a stiff gray bouffant hairdo came around the corner to meet them. She glanced at her clipboard. "Dr. Mercer?" she asked, her voice brisk and efficient.

Mr. Mercer stepped forward. "Yes. How is she?"

"Follow me."

Wordlessly, they trailed the nurse through the waiting room and down a wide green hallway. The nurse's rubber-soled clogs made no sound on the linoleum, but Emma's heels clicked loudly. Otherwise, the ward was quiet. Instead of medical charts or germ prevention posters on the walls, there were soothing pastel landscapes and the kind of motivational posters you saw in a junior high classroom. One was even that gray tabby dangling from a tree limb with the words HANG IN THERE.

A strange sensation settled over me, sort of like a deep, vibrating hum. The farther we went into the ward, the stronger it became. "Be careful," I whispered to my twin, wishing she could hear me. "Something isn't right."

They passed a nurse's station, and Emma stared disinterestedly at a bulletin board that said VOLUNTEER OF THE MONTH in glittery letters across the top. But when she saw the girl's picture hanging below, she stopped short. It was Nisha Banerjee, smiling almost shyly in her candy-striper uniform. Emma cocked her head. *Nisha* volunteered here? Emma remembered that Nisha's dad worked in psychiatrics, but a stint on the psych ward seemed like a strange after-school activity.

You wouldn't have caught me volunteering here in a million years, not even if it guaranteed me admission to the college of my choice.

When Emma looked up, the nurse was escorting Mr. Mercer around another corner. All the doors on the ward had a window near the top, so the patients could be watched when the door was closed. She was too afraid to peek inside, but she could hear one man singing softly in a language she didn't recognize. Behind another door, a woman babbled something that sounded like "You have to find them in your hair, that's where they like to hide. . . . They spy on you, so you have to pull them out by the root."

Emma hurried to catch up to her dad and the nurse. "It looks like a total psychotic break," the nurse was murmuring when Emma reached them. They came to a stop outside a closed door that looked just like the others. A cheap print of Monet's haystacks decorated the facing wall. There was a stain of something red—blood?—on the linoleum floor.

The humming was louder now. The pain of everyone on this floor—their anxiety, fear, and heartbreak—vibrated through me. Each emotion had its own pitch, as though a dozen tuning forks were being struck simultaneously. But one feeling united all the patients on this floor: They were stuck, imprisoned in these rooms and in their own flawed minds. I understood how they felt, more than I cared to admit.

The nurse placed her hand on the doorknob. "Would you like to see her?"

"Yes," Emma said bravely, stepping forward.

Mr. Mercer's eyes snapped into focus, as if he'd been gazing somewhere far away and had only just realized Emma was there. He put his hand on his forehead and took a deep breath. "I don't know what I was thinking. I should have left you downstairs in the waiting room. This isn't how I want you to meet your mom."

Emma crossed her arms over her chest. "No. I'm staying."

Mr. Mercer looked like he wanted to say something else, but then he nodded. "All right," he said to the nurse.

She opened the door.

A woman in a hospital gown writhed back and forth on the bed in the room as though her skin was crawling with spiders. Her black hair was a deep tangle around her head. Her face looked hollow, and far too thin, and her skin had an unhealthy ashen hue. She wore a plastic hospital bracelet on her wrist. Emma could just make out the name written in thick black ink—Rebecca Mercer.

But this couldn't be Becky. It looked nothing like her. It didn't even look like the woman she'd seen in the car a few days before. This woman was deranged, a stranger.

Tears dotted Emma's eyes. She placed her hand over her mouth, swallowing a sob.

The woman's head whipped around. Her gaze lit on Emma, and all at once she fell still.

"Hello, Emma," she said.

Emma's mouth dropped open. She took a staggering step back, blood rushing in her ears.

The room started to spin around me, too. Usually it was some sound or image that triggered one of my memories, a flash of light or the sound of a train whistle snapping me back to the last days of my life. This time, though, the same tremulous vibration I'd felt since stepping into the ward grew louder and louder, until it became a rushing, violent ache in my ears. I knew now what that sound was—it was the sound of madness, and my mother's was the loudest of all. It attacked me like a swarm of bats, sweeping me under and pulling me down until all I saw was the darkness of my past.

7

STRANGERS IN THE NIGHT

The sound of my father's SUV fades into the distance. No, not my father. My grandfather. The thought makes my fingers curl into fists, my nails pressing into my palms until they draw blood. I wipe the tears and grime from my face and sit still until the sound of his motor dies away.

What began as a date with Thayer, the only boy I've ever really loved, has ended with him speeding toward the hospital in my sister's car, leaving me alone in the mountains with the knowledge that my entire life has been a lie. I've always known I was adopted—but until tonight, I never knew the people who'd raised me were actually related to me by blood.

The moon hides behind a cloud, and the canyon goes even

darker than before. My hands start to shake, the adrenaline turning sour in my blood. What have I done? I said horrible things to the man I considered my father, then sprinted away. I feel like I'm going to puke.

Across the street from the canyon is a suburban neighborhood, all the houses arranged on a horseshoe of streets. Porch lights float in the darkness like fireflies. I see Nisha Banerjee's house, the pool glittering in the backyard, the street lined with cars. If I hold my breath, I can hear the bass thumping in the backyard. That's where I'm supposed to be tonight, at the tennis sleepover. Maybe I should go over there. At least some of my friends will be there—I need to be around happy faces right now, people who care about me. Nisha's a pain in the ass, but she's easy enough to ignore.

I pull out my phone as I cross the street to her house. Six missed calls, all of them from Mads. Maybe the ER called her about Thayer. I try to call her but it goes straight to voicemail. I hang up before the beep, not trusting myself to speak to a recording.

I'm almost at Nisha's driveway when a creak from the house next door startles me. It's Ethan Landry's house, but I don't see any sign of him, only a big telescope on the front porch pointed at the sky. Weirdo. Any other guy would point it toward Nisha's, hoping to get a glimpse of a sexy pillow fight.

My hand is on the gate to Nisha's backyard when I hear the phone ringing inside her house. "Hello?" Nisha's voice answers. "Oh, hi, Mr. Mercer," she chirps. "No, he's not here right now. Can I take a message?"

I shift my weight. Why would my dad be calling for Dr. Banerjee? They both work at the same hospital, but as far as I know they don't interact—my dad's in orthopedics, Nisha's dad is in psychiatrics. Maybe he's calling to ask Nisha's father to keep an eye out for me. Maybe he's trying to round up some kind of dad posse.

Someone in the backyard shrieks, "Marco!" I hear a splash and then giggles. They sound so young, their voices so high and innocent, like they've never had to face anything heartbreaking or real. Suddenly all of the energy drains out of me at once, a dull ache pulling at my limbs. I can't be here right now; I can't paint a bubbly smile on my face and pretend everything's all right.

Exhausted, I walk back across the road to the canyon and plop down on a park bench, figuring I'll call a cab. Who knows where my car is after that freak drove off with it. Maybe my dad will cover for me. It's basically his fault this happened, after all.

Thinking about my parents' lies enrages me all over again. Why would they keep a secret like that from me? Was it so hard to admit that we were all related by blood? Maybe they were ashamed of me. Maybe they just wanted to make sure everyone knew the way I was wasn't their fault, that I was a bad seed from who knew where—not some monster they created. Angry tears pool in my eyes and I quickly brush them away.

The snap of a breaking branch cuts through the darkness. As I turn, I suddenly realize the crickets have gone silent. I stare into the darkness, but I can't see a damn thing.

What the hell am I doing here? A few years ago a woman got mauled while jogging through the canyon at dusk. She was training for a marathon. The authorities said she probably never even saw the mountain lion—the cats move so stealthily most people don't know they're being stalked until it's too late. After that happened, you couldn't turn on the TV without seeing a PSA warning people to hike in groups of two or more. Remember, there's safety in numbers! Don't go hiking alone in Pima County.

Don't run away from your ride when you're stuck in the wilderness at midnight, *I think. The hair on the back of my neck tingles.*

It could be a wild animal. Or it could be the maniac who stole my Volvo and ran down Thayer. He could be back for more.

I hold my breath and listen. Far away, a police siren wails.

Then, there it is again, the same sound I heard before: leaves stirring, crunching underfoot. I stand up slowly, my heart in my throat. Carefully, I step toward the path that will lead me back to the park's entrance.

That's when my eyes catch movement in the trees. Something rushes toward me. I turn on my heel and sprint up the path before I can see what it is. My body is sore from everything that's happened during this long, awful night. I can hear my pursuer behind me, crashing through the bushes. My shin slams straight into something—I don't see what—and I fall on my hands and knees. I scrabble at the dirt feebly, trying to get back to my feet.

But behind me I can hear my pursuer getting closer. I roll over just in time to see someone detach from the shadows and step into view.

It's a woman. When she sees me, she stops and stares, breathing hard. Her black hair looks almost blue in the moonlight. Her face is pitted and sunken, her eyes deep holes in her skull. She wears a dirty waitressing uniform with a tear at the hem. She steps toward me and I crabwalk backward, the dirt stinging my hands. When I turn around, I realize I've backed myself against the canyon rock. I have nowhere to run.

"Wait," the woman says, extending one of her hands toward me. When she gets close, I see that her eyes aren't black like I thought, but bright, oceanic blue. There's an eerie, predatory expression on her face, too—as if she knows I'm trapped and she likes it.

"Hello, Sutton." Her voice is soft and gravelly, and as causal as if we'd talked a thousand times before. "I'm your mother. Becky."

And then the memory collapses in on itself, and I'm left with nothing at all.

8

WHO ARE YOU?

Emma clutched the doorframe of the hospital room, her eyes locked on Becky's, the sound of her mom's voice saying her name echoing in her mind over and over. *Emma. Emma. Emma.*

Becky recognized her. In one glance, she had seen what Sutton's friends and family could not—that Emma was not Sutton. Emma wanted to believe it was because Becky was her mother, the person who knew her best. Only, Becky *didn't* know her best; Becky hadn't known her for thirteen years. But that could only mean . . .

Our brains asked the same question at the same time:

Did Becky know Emma couldn't be Sutton because she'd done something to me?

I tried to squeeze one more moment from the memory I'd just recovered, to stay in it just a little longer, but nothing came. All I could see was Becky walking toward me out of the darkness. I didn't know what it meant, but the expression on Becky's face that night in the canyon left me chilled to the soul. But what kind of woman could kill her own daughter?

"Emma," Becky whispered again. One of her front teeth was chipped, lending her smile a witchy look. Her arms spasmed at her sides.

Emma stepped away and shook her head, remembering that she wasn't Emma, not here. "N-no," she said. "I'm not Emma."

Mr. Mercer put his hand on Emma's shoulder. "Honey, this is Sutton. Remember? I sent you pictures. This is your daughter."

"Yes, my daughter." All of a sudden, Becky's twitching turned into all-out writhing. Her feet kicked off the blankets, knocking over a small dinner tray next to the bed with a loud clatter.

The nurse nodded, and two enormous, linebacker-sized orderlies stepped into the room. For the first time, Emma noticed the stained leather restraints attached to the railings on the hospital bed. An orderly with a low pony-tail leaned over the bed and pinned Becky down by her shoulders, while the other, whose hair was cut military-style, deftly tightened the leather straps around her arms and legs. They worked efficiently and quietly, as though Becky was a piece of furniture they were securing to a truck bed. Becky's eyes darted back and forth, and her mouth opened and closed like a fish's.

Emma swallowed hard, full of both pity and fear for the woman who'd abandoned her all those years ago—and who might have hurt her twin.

"Emma!" Becky wailed.

"My name's not Emma," Emma insisted, her voice loud and clear. "I'm Sutton."

"You're Emma!" Becky's voice climbed higher and higher. She sounded almost as if she were pleading. "Emma! Emma, Emma, Emma, Emma . . ." Fat tears streaked down her cheeks.

Mr. Mercer leaned in. "Who's Emma, Becky? Can you tell us?"

Becky just shook her tear-streaked face back and forth violently. Her whole body trembled and strained against the ties.

Her vacant expression triggered one of Emma's last memories of her mom. At her preschool graduation, which Becky had missed, Emma won a good citizenship award for keeping her desk cleaner than anyone else's. She'd tagged along with the families of her classmates to get ice cream afterward and had tried to pretend she didn't hear the other parents' whispers of "irresponsible" and "not all there." She'd gotten mint chocolate chip, which was Becky's favorite flavor, to help pretend that her mother was with her. Later, when she let herself into their motel room with the key she kept on a Hello Kitty lanyard in her backpack, Becky was in bed staring at the ceiling. Emma carefully put away her backpack and shoes in the closet. She crawled into bed next to her mother and nestled at her side. Becky stared at her as if she'd never seen her before.

"Which one are you again?" she asked.

Emma smiled. This was a game she knew—sometimes her mother teased her, pretending she didn't know who she was.

"I'm Emma!" she said, touching her own forehead. "Which one are you?"

At that, Becky started to cry. "I'm your mother," she whispered, hugging Emma close to her chest.

Three days later, she left Emma at the sleepover.

"Emma, Emma, Emma," whimpered Becky. Tears ran down her face, leaving tracks in the grime on her cheeks. Emma—little-girl Emma—wanted to step forward with a Kleenex to gently wipe her mother's face. But in the real world she couldn't seem to move. She didn't want to go near the deranged woman flailing on the hospital bed.

"There now, Ms. Mercer," said a gentle voice with a soft Anglo-Indian accent. A middle-aged man in a white coat stepped past the nurse, a syringe in his hand. When she saw the needle, Becky groaned. She shook her head wildly, her hair whipping across her face. "This will only hurt for a second," said the doctor, quickly sliding the needle into her arm.

Seconds later, Becky's body relaxed. Her eyes unfocused and her head lolled to face the wall.

"Thank you, Dr. Banerjee," Mr. Mercer said wearily.

Emma looked up at the doctor in surprise—it was Nisha's father, a short man with a round face, thick glasses, and a sad expression. His wife had passed away not long ago. Every time Emma had seen him, he'd looked so lost.

Dr. Banerjee ushered Mr. Mercer and Emma out of the room. "Let's go into the hall so she can rest."

"You're just going to leave the restraints on her?" Emma blurted out.

Dr. Banerjee looked at her steadily. His red-rimmed eyes were magnified behind his lenses. "They're for her own protection, Sutton. I promise, we will do our best to make her comfortable. But right now she is a danger to herself and to others."

They followed him into the hallway. A low bench ran

against the wall under the Monet print, and he gestured for them both to sit. Mr. Mercer sank onto the bench gratefully, but Emma shook her head. Dr. Banerjee turned to face them.

"This is the worst I've seen her in a long time," he said, exhaling heavily. He opened a large file that had been clamped beneath his arm and rifled through it. Becky's records, Emma realized. She glanced at Mr. Mercer questioningly.

"Dr. Banerjee has treated Becky several times over the years, when she's been in town," he explained.

She nodded slowly. "How did she end up in here today?" she asked Dr. Banerjee.

"She was arrested," Nisha's father explained.

Mr. Mercer rubbed his face, as if trying to scrub the information away. Finally, he looked up at Dr. Banerjee again. "Did she hurt anyone?"

The other man sat down across from him and took what Emma recognized as a police report from the file. "No, thankfully. She pulled a knife on a man at the mall down-town. She was confused, agitated. Several shopkeepers reported that she'd been in their stores earlier in the day asking bizarre questions. But mall security managed to get the knife from her without anyone being hurt."

I remembered the eerie look on my mother's face in the canyon the night we met. If she could wave a knife at someone, maybe she could do worse. Maybe she *had* done worse.

"When was the last time you saw her?" asked Dr. Banerjee.

Mr. Mercer shook his head. "About two months ago. She checked out of her hotel, so I assumed she'd left town, like she usually does. But then she called me from a motel just last week, so I'm not sure where she's been."

Dr. Banerjee wiped his glasses on the sleeve of his coat. "I'm sorry to tell you this, but she seems to have been living out of her car—the police found it in the parking lot. She's off her medication again. I'm not sure for how long, but you know how bad she gets."

Mr. Mercer and Dr. Banerjee continued to talk in low voices about Becky's prognosis and a potential treatment plan, and Mr. Mercer asked whether he should talk to an attorney in case anyone at the mall pressed charges. But Emma was only half listening. She glanced back to the room that held her mother, drugged and silent. Then her eyes fell on the folder on Dr. Banerjee's lap, bristling with medical records and arrest reports.

Emma imagined her two worlds, side by side like the twin images in a stereoscope. Was Becky her sad, beautiful mother, loving but tragic? Or was she a knife-wielding maniac, a woman so wild she deserved to be strapped to a bed? Her hands closed into fists. She wasn't the adoring little-girl Emma anymore, and she couldn't *afford* to be a bitter teenage Emma coming to terms with her mother's sudden reappearance. She was a different person altogether. She was the Emma who'd been channeling Sutton. She was a tough and practical Emma who had to fight to survive, who had to ask difficult questions and learn truths she wasn't sure she wanted to know. She was the Emma who was going to solve a murder, and to do that, she knew she had to find out what was in that file.

I wanted to see whatever was in that folder as badly as she did. Now she just had to figure out a way to get it.

9

WHITE LIES AND ALIBIS

It was just after midnight when Mr. Mercer pulled the car into the driveway and killed the motor. The lights were on in the kitchen—Mrs. Mercer had obviously waited up for them—but he made no move to get out of the car. He and Emma sat in silence, neither one looking directly at the other. With the AC off, the air quickly became heavy around them.

Mr. Mercer took Emma's hand in his and squeezed. "That really wasn't how I wanted you to meet your mother," he said.

"Yeah," she muttered, looking out the passenger window. She could just make out the hole Mr. Mercer had dug in the lawn before his accident. He'd been planning to plant something there, but in the dark it looked like a fresh grave.

"I'm so sorry," Mr. Mercer went on. "It must have been hard to see her like that."

Emma didn't say anything. Her body felt bruised and weak. She'd always imagined she might look for her mother someday, track her down with a private investigator or maybe by herself, with her own research skills. Sometimes in her fantasies, she told Becky off for abandoning her. Sometimes she ran to her, threw her arms around her neck, and all was forgiven. But never in all her daydreams had she pictured it like this.

After a long pause, Mr. Mercer spoke again. "I'm going to visit her tomorrow. Hopefully they'll have stabilized her a little and she'll be more coherent. Do you want to come with me?"

Emma bit her lip. She had questions she wanted to ask Becky, but nothing she could ask in front of her grandfather. And what if Becky kept calling her Emma? Someone might start trying to figure out whom Becky was referring to. In her deluded state, Becky might say anything—even that Sutton had a twin named Emma. And then what?

Mr. Mercer gave her an understanding look and squeezed her hand. "You don't have to decide right now." He undid his seat belt. "We'd better go in. Mom's probably worried."

Emma squinted in the harsh bright light in the foyer. Down the hall, she saw Laurel perched on a stool at the kitchen island, wearing her favorite terrycloth robe. Mrs. Mercer was standing behind her, pouring tea into two pineapple-shaped mugs. She almost dropped the kettle when she saw them.

"Where have you been?" she demanded. "It's after midnight. Why didn't you call? I tried you a thousand times."

Looking abashed, Mr. Mercer pulled his phone from his pocket, scrolling through the missed calls. Emma didn't have to look at hers to know that there were probably a dozen calls from her mother on the screen. "I'm so sorry, honey," he mumbled.

Laurel narrowed her eyes at Emma, giving her a long, scrutinizing look. She pointed to something on Emma's jacket. "What's that?"

Emma looked down. The hospital visitor badge was pinned to her lapel. She caught her breath. She'd been so tired on the way home that she hadn't remembered to take it off. She tried to slide it into her pocket, but it was too late.

"You were at the hospital?" Mrs. Mercer demanded.

Mr. Mercer and Emma exchanged glances. He waited a beat too long before speaking. "Look, I didn't want to bother you, but I was feeling a lot of pain in my knee. I went in to have it checked out and see if I could get some meds from the pharmacy. I'm so sorry we didn't call, honey. The signal in the hospital is awful, and we lost track of time."

The clock over the kitchen table ticked noisily. Drake, the family's Great Dane, rose from his dog bed, shook out his coat, and then lay down again. Mrs. Mercer stood with her arms crossed over her chest. Emma wondered if this was how Mrs. Mercer had spent her evenings when she was raising Becky—up late, making tea she was too nervous to drink, waiting for bad news to come in the door. She felt a flare of guilt for making her grandmother worry.

Finally Mrs. Mercer sighed and turned to Emma. "Well, it was your night to walk Drake, Sutton. It's too late for that, but the least you can do is to take him out to the yard."

Emma nodded. "Come on, boy."

The Great Dane lazily stood once more. Emma slid open the door to the backyard and followed him out into the night.

While he sniffed along the fence, Emma flopped into a wrought-iron chair and stared at the stars. As a little girl, she'd had a habit of naming the stars after things in her own life. There were the Teacher Star, a pretty twinkling one she'd named after Ms. Rodehaver, her beloved third-grade teacher. There were the Bully Star and the Brat Star, which she'd named for particularly awful classmates, stars consigned to the edges of the sky and washed out by light pollution. And then there was the Emma Star, and the Mom Star, and the Dad Star, three stars twinkling close to one another but not quite together. She had made up stories about why they had to exist apart from one another—one in Orion's Belt, another just a little left of what Ethan had told her was Venus. In her stories, they were apart because they had to break a curse or solve a riddle or go on a pilgrimage in order to reunite. They always ended up together in the end.

After seeing her mother tonight, Emma was no longer so sure her story would have a happy ending.

"So what were you *really* doing tonight?"

Emma jumped and turned, catching a whiff of tuberose lotion. Laurel stood behind her, the porch light making a halo around her honey-blond head.

"Was Dad's knee actually acting up?" Laurel asked. "Or was he covering for you, just like old times?"

Emma squinted, trying to read Laurel in the darkness. "There was nothing to cover up," she said in a clear, firm voice. "Dad's knee hurt, we went to the hospital. Why would I lie about something like that?"

Laurel shifted her weight. "Gee, I don't know, Sutton. I don't know why you lie about half the things you lie about. You only invented a whole, you know, *game* about it."

"A game you begged to be in, if I remember correctly."

"All right, all right, touché." Laurel pulled her robe more tightly around her shoulders, then sat down in a chair next to Emma's. A light breeze riffled through the wind chimes hanging over the patio. "You know you can trust me. What are these secrets about?"

In the porch light Emma could see Laurel's face, earnest and hopeful, and for a minute Emma considered telling Laurel about Becky. Maybe not the whole truth— not about Becky calling her by her real name—but what would it hurt to tell Laurel that she'd met her birth mother? Sutton might have told her adopted sister, too, once she got over the initial shock.

But if Becky really *was* responsible for Sutton's death, the less Laurel knew, the safer she'd be. Emma gazed out over the yard, where Drake was circling the birdbath.

"Okay. You've found me out," she said. "We were rehearsing for the Father-Daughter Roller Derby. His derby name is Doctor Feelbad, but I'm torn between Paris Hellton and Nicole Bitchy. What do you think?"

"Liar!" Laurel punched her in the arm, but she was laughing. The tension dissipated.

"I'm not sure we have a shot with Dad's leg in a brace, but we're going to go for it. Reach for the stars, that's what I always say," Emma went on with a smile.

Laurel grabbed a cushion from the porch swing and hit at Emma with it. Emma ducked and squealed, grabbing a pillow of her own in retaliation. By the time Drake trotted up to the patio to investigate, they were both giggling and throwing cushions at each other from opposite sides of the deck chair.

"Girls?" Mrs. Mercer's silhouette appeared in the doorway. "What are you doing? You're going to wake up the neighborhood. Drake, get inside. Laurel, Sutton, go to bed."

The door shut firmly. Emma and Laurel exchanged glances, and then collapsed into silent laughter.

I watched my sisters with a sad pang, wishing I were there between them. I marveled at my twin's ability to defuse Laurel's frustration. I'd never been able to do that.

"Sutton," Laurel whispered, pushing her away so she could look into her eyes. "Whatever's going on . . . just tell me if I can help, okay?"

Emma thought about denying that there was anything going on, but then she bit her lip. "Okay," she said.

Then they stood and strode toward the brightly lit kitchen while I, their silent third sister, trailed unseen behind them.

10

TEA FOR TWO

The next day after school, Emma skipped tennis and drove straight home. The house was quiet when she arrived, the soft ticking of the grandfather clock echoing through the foyer. When her phone beeped, piercing the silence, she jumped. She had a new text from Ethan: I DIDN'T SEE YOU AT TENNIS PRACTICE. EVERYTHING OK?

YEAH, JUST TRYING TO GET SOME REST, Emma wrote back. She hadn't gotten much sleep last night, haunted by nightmares of being strapped to a hospital bed.

HOW ARE YOU HOLDING UP?

Emma's fingers hovered over the keyboard. She'd quickly told Ethan about Becky in the hallway that

83

morning, not wanting to go into much detail because she wasn't sure who might be listening—she doubted the story of Sutton Mercer's crazy mother was something Sutton would have wanted to become common knowledge. Ethan had given her a huge hug. "I'm so sorry you had to deal with that," he'd said, and she'd felt just a little better, knowing that he was there for her.

I'M FINE, she finally wrote. BUT I MISS YOU. I CAN'T WAIT FOR OUR PICNIC TONIGHT.

ME NEITHER, he responded. SEE YOU AT 8?

After Emma texted YES, she shut the door softly. Drake loped into the foyer, his long tail waving behind him. She stroked the smooth short fur around his ears. "Hey, buddy," she whispered.

He raised his head to lick her face. When she started up the stairs to Sutton's room, he followed, his nails clattering noisily on the hardwood.

The stairwell was hung with family pictures: images of the vacations the Mercers had taken over the years to Disneyland, Paris, Maui, mixed in with snapshots of Christmas mornings and school awards ceremonies. Emma stopped absently to straighten a school picture of a seven-year-old Sutton in pigtails. Even then Sutton's smile looked mischievous, like she knew just how much she could get away with.

Emma was halfway up the stairs when Mrs. Mercer

stepped into the hall with a basket of laundry in her arms. She had changed out of the sleek, tailored work suit she'd worn this morning into a pair of dark-wash jeans and a short-sleeved cashmere sweater. When she saw Emma on the stairs, she looked startled. "Sutton!" she exclaimed. "What are you doing home?"

Emma rested her hands on the banister. "I have a headache, so I skipped tennis." It wasn't too far from the truth. The episode with Becky had shaken her to her core.

Seeing Mrs. Mercer's concerned frown, she added, "I'm okay. I took some aspirin and I'm already feeling better. Just not up to running around a hot tennis court." Then she cocked her head. "What are *you* doing home?"

Mrs. Mercer smiled. "I cut out of work early today. There was a meeting on the books that I just couldn't bring myself to sit through."

"I guess we're both playing hooky," Emma joked.

Mrs. Mercer shifted the laundry basket to one arm. "Why don't you join me for some tea? I was just about to sit down for a cup."

Emma had actually come home to try to refocus—she needed to be able to think logically if she was going to find out what had really happened to Sutton. She'd been looking forward to some time alone, relaxing in Sutton's bedroom, but she didn't feel like she could turn down the offer. "Sure."

Sun poured through the kitchen's floor-to-ceiling

windows. Emma perched at the island counter and watched as Mrs. Mercer measured loose-leaf tea into a purple-flowered teapot. "Remember playing tea when you were little?" Mrs. Mercer asked, smiling. "You would bring your stuffed animals down and sit them around the table and pretend to serve them crumpets."

"Crumpets?" Emma rolled her eyes as she imagined Sutton would have done. "I did not."

"Yes, you did. I don't think you even knew what crumpets were—you just heard the word somewhere and liked how it sounded."

Emma smiled. She liked hearing sweet memories of her sister.

I liked that my mom *had* sweet memories of me.

"How's Ethan?" Mrs. Mercer poured hot water over the leaves. Lavender-scented steam billowed from the teapot's spout.

"He's good." Emma couldn't wipe a dopey grin off her face. "We're having a picnic tonight."

Mrs. Mercer raised an eyebrow. "How romantic."

Emma ducked her head, feeling the heat rise to her cheeks. "We're going stargazing—he's really into astronomy. I was going to bake cookies this afternoon to take with us."

"*You're* making cookies?" Mrs. Mercer peered at her. "You don't even know how to turn the oven on!"

"Oh, I'm sure I can figure it out," Emma covered. It didn't surprise her that Sutton didn't know how to cook, but she'd been baking since junior high, making chocolate chip oatmeal cookies and peanut butter blossoms to try to win over her various foster families. Baking relaxed her. She liked to sit, listening to her favorite music on the used iPod she'd bought at Goodwill, inhaling the delicious smells of sugar and chocolate.

I just hoped she didn't lick the batter from the spoon. Sutton Mercer did *not* get love handles.

"Well, I'm sure he'll love them, even if they're a little burned," Mrs. Mercer teased.

"Gee, thanks, Mom," Emma groused good-naturedly. Just talking about her night with Ethan made Emma's heart speed up. It felt like ages since their date at the movie studio, and she couldn't wait to feel his breath on her ear and his lips on hers. She smiled at the thought of his cryptic text from that morning: N 32° 12' 23.2554", W 110° 41' 18.3012" = <3? 8PM? After a moment of puzzling, Emma had plugged the longitude and latitude notations into Sutton's iPhone. The coordinates were for a site in Saguaro National Park. *Sends me invitations in the form of riddles* was something else to add to her list of *Adorable Things Ethan Does*.

The teapot whistled, breaking Emma from her thoughts. "He wasn't hurt too badly in that fight, was he?" Mrs. Mercer asked.

Emma shrugged. "I think he's okay. He has a black eye that he thinks makes him look really cool."

Mrs. Mercer sighed. "He shouldn't have swung at Thayer. Boys never stop to think things through, do they? People get hurt in fights like that—and not just the people in the actual fight." Then she looked at Emma. "How are *you* doing with all of that, Sutton?"

Emma picked at a speck of lint on her skirt. "Haven't you heard? I'm Sutton Mercer. I love it when boys fight over me."

Mrs. Mercer crossed her arms over her chest. "I've never seen you get so pale as when those two started on each other."

Gratitude bubbled up in Emma's chest as she met Mrs. Mercer's eyes. No else one was willing to believe that she wasn't enjoying stringing two boys along. "I don't know what to do," she admitted. "I like Ethan, and it's completely over with me and Thayer. I just can't seem to convince either one of them of that."

Mrs. Mercer sipped her tea. "You know, Sutton, the problem isn't that you're giving them the wrong signals. It's that you're so worth fighting for. You can't blame yourself for that."

If I could have put my head on my adoptive mother's shoulder right at that moment, I would have. Ever since my death, Emma and I had scrambled around trying to figure out what I'd done to deserve getting murdered. It seemed I'd given so many people reasons to want me gone that the real mystery was why someone hadn't done it sooner. It was a welcome change to hear something nice about me for once.

Mrs. Mercer opened a package of shortbread cookies and placed a few on a plate. "Well, I for one think Ethan has been a good influence on you. Your grades have improved so much since you started seeing him, and you've been nicer to your sister." She gave Emma a motherly smile. "Or maybe my little girl is just growing up."

Emma shifted uncomfortably. "Um, where did this tea set come from, Mom?" she asked, hoping to change the subject from her personality shift.

Mrs. Mercer eyed her strangely over the silver sugar tongs. "You don't remember? This was your great-grandma's, the only thing she brought with her from Scotland. I'm not sure how old it is—I always got the impression that it'd been handed down well before then."

I suppressed a twinge of sadness—and anger. How many times had I listened to family history and felt shut out of it just because I thought I was adopted? I still didn't understand why my grandparents didn't feel that they could tell me that their stories were my stories, too, that I was related to the ancestors who had come over from Scotland with that tea set. It all came back to Becky. What had she done that had merited banishment so complete that I wasn't even allowed to know my own heritage?

Emma looked thoughtfully at the tea service, thinking the same thing I was. Wheels started turning at the back of her mind.

She looked up. "Mom, can I ask you a question? Do you . . . have any regrets?"

Mrs. Mercer looked surprised. "Regrets?"

"You know, people you don't talk to anymore, relationships you've cut off. Anything like that." She almost winced at how transparent she sounded, but Mrs. Mercer didn't seem to notice.

Her grandmother looked down into her cup. "You know, things change. People change. Sometimes you have to move on from someone you care about. It can be hard, honey." Mrs. Mercer folded and unfolded a linen napkin embroidered with a pineapple. "Sometimes you have to admit that a relationship can't be fixed. That no matter how much you want to, you can't trust some people."

Something about her words sent a little shiver up Emma's spine. She poured more tea into her cup, a few stray leaves swirling in the hot liquid. She wished she could use them to see the future. Or even better, the past.

Mrs. Mercer frowned. "What's this about, sweetheart?"

"Nothing," Emma said, biting her lip. "I've just been thinking how you've always been there for me, no matter what. I guess it just got me wondering if I've ever pushed you too far." *Like Becky did,* she thought, willing Mrs. Mercer to open up. *Come on, Grandma, tell me how Becky crossed that line.*

Her grandmother took Emma's hand across the table, her bright blue eyes wide with concern. "Are you trying to tell me something? Are you in some kind of . . . trouble?"

Emma shook her head. "No, of course not. Everything's fine."

Mrs. Mercer looked searchingly into Emma's eyes for a long moment, then let go of Emma's hand and picked up her teacup and saucer, the porcelain clinking softly together. When she spoke again, her voice was halting and careful, as if she were still forming the words in her head.

"Sutton, I love you and your sister very much. I would do anything for you two. I've been hard on you sometimes, I know that. But it's because I look at you and I think about all the potential you have, to be successful and healthy and happy." She paused. "A mother's love is unconditional, Sutton. There's nothing you could ever do to make me love you less. I promise."

Emma looked back down to her tea. An unmistakable sadness had gripped her at her grandmother's words. A mother's love should be unconditional. But Mrs. Mercer clearly hadn't felt that way about Becky. And Becky certainly hadn't felt that way about her twins.

Emma didn't know why Mrs. Mercer had accepted Laurel and Sutton and not Becky, but she knew she wouldn't be getting any information from her today. She'd just have to keep digging and find her own answers.

For both our sakes.

11

A PICNIC UNDER THE STARS

When Emma arrived at the park that evening, Ethan was already at the trailhead, his telescope in its plastic case on his back. The sun was setting behind the mountains in a blaze of red light. For a moment it gave Ethan's face an unearthly glow, as if he were illuminated from the inside.

She watched him for a long moment, adding to her mental list of *Adorable Things Ethan Does*: *#578: Carries his telescope like it's a guitar and he's a rock star.* In his beat-up jeans and white T-shirt, Ethan did actually have a James Dean thing going on. Emma's heart started beating faster as she walked over to meet him.

SARA SHEPARD

"Hey, you." Ethan held out his arms. Emma pressed her face against his T-shirt and inhaled his clean-laundry scent, feeling his chest muscles against her cheek. He kissed the top of her head. Her toes curled with pleasure inside her socks.

"Come on," he said, taking her hand and leading her toward the trail. The park was alive with the soft noises of hunting bats, the chirps of crickets and cicadas, the burrowing of small animals in the sand.

Under a breeze-tousled desert willow lay a red-and-white checkered blanket and a basket filled with grapes, strawberries, a baguette, and a wedge of Brie. Ethan had even brought a bottle of sparkling cider and plastic champagne glasses. Candles in Mason jars completed the scene.

Emma gasped and squeezed Ethan's arm. "I can't believe you did all this," she exclaimed.

He knelt on the blanket and patted the spot next to him. "I thought it might be nice to have an actual date. With, you know, romance and stuff." He opened the cider and handed her a glass, pouring himself one, too.

She laughed and clinked their glasses together. "Here's to romance, then. Though I'm not sure I'm as good at it as you are. Maybe you could give me a few pointers."

"I think that could be arranged," he murmured, leaning in to kiss her so lightly and sweetly she couldn't help but want more.

"Good lesson," she breathed when he pulled away.

They nibbled at the cheese and baguette, watching the sunset in a comfortable silence. Emma had always dreamed of a romantic night like this, but she never dared dream she'd have someone like Ethan to share it with. He was everything she could have asked for in a boyfriend, and she was finally lucky enough to get it.

"Have you thought any more about . . . you know, about what we should do when this is over?" Ethan asked, glancing up at her nervously. She blushed, remembering what he'd suggested—that they move in together if the Mercers wouldn't take her in as Emma. She bit her lip, looking away from him before she answered.

"A little." She hesitated, then went on. "I want to be with you, you know that. But moving in together is a really big step. I want to go to college. I just . . . I have to get my life back before I can even think about any of that." She tried to imagine what she would even say on her college essay. *Pretending to be my sister while I solved her murder and learned all our family secrets taught me the value of perseverance. I'm also a great multitasker.*

"Me, too," he said quickly. "I mean, I want to go to college, too. I've got early applications in. I'm just waiting to hear back."

"Early applications?" Emma was impressed. She'd be squeaking by at the last minute with hers, if she got them in this year at all. She bit the end off a strawberry. "Where are you applying?"

He shrugged. "University of Arizona, obviously. UC Davis, Carnegie Mellon, UCLA. Stanford is my long shot. It'll depend where I get enough financial aid." He frowned.

"Most of those are so far away," she said, surprised. She knew she shouldn't be shocked—Ethan was a good student, and he'd want to go to the best school he could. But she'd never imagined him leaving Tucson. The thought twisted inside her like a knot.

"Emma," he said firmly, seeming to read her thoughts. "Before I met you, I couldn't wait to get out of this place. I hated this town. It's so full of people who watch you, and judge you. But—" He swallowed, fumbling for words, and took her hand. "I'll go anywhere you want to go. If you want to stay in Tucson, we'll make it work here. If I do get in somewhere else and can figure out a way to afford it, we'll have options. And of course we don't have to move in together if you're not ready. I just want to stay close to you, no matter what."

Her head swam. His eyes were so earnest, so full of tenderness, that she couldn't find her voice. Instead she leaned toward him for another lingering kiss.

"And if the case isn't solved by then," he breathed into her ear, "maybe we can just run away. Maybe you could just come with me to school. You could work on applications while I'm in classes, and start the next fall."

Emma smiled, picturing herself strolling across the main green at Stanford, a to-go coffee mug in her hand. She'd sit on a bench and read Proust's *In Search of Lost Time*, waiting to meet Ethan after his philosophy seminar. When class let out, he'd give her a big kiss and introduce her to his professor as "my girlfriend, Emma Paxton."

"I can keep you safe, Emma," Ethan went on. "I won't let anyone hurt you."

His words brought her crashing down to earth. She pulled back sadly, shaking her head, the spell suddenly broken. "You know I can't leave Tucson, not while the person who hurt my sister is still out there." It was completely dark now, the sky bright with stars and the thin crescent of the moon. She looked out across the black expanse of the desert. "When I first started this, I was just trying to survive. But now . . . I feel like I *know* Sutton, Ethan. I know it sounds weird, but I feel like she's here sometimes, still with me, cheering me on. I love her, and I can't let her down. She deserves justice." She shook her head again. "I'm either going to solve this thing, or I'm going to die trying."

I felt my whole being fall very still. No one had ever made a promise like that for me, risked death for me. For once I was glad that Emma couldn't hear my thoughts. I wasn't sure I could find the words to tell her how grateful I was.

In the flickering candlelight, Emma saw that the color had drained from Ethan's face. "Don't talk like that," he whispered. "I don't want to think about anything bad happening to you. I couldn't take it."

His hand trembled in hers, and Emma suddenly realized that he had never really processed the danger she was in, had never really understood that a murderer was watching her. *Watching them*, she thought, remembering what had happened at the Old Tucson Movie Studios.

"Everything is so complicated right now," she said soothingly. "Let's see what happens—when the Mercers find out who I am, when you get all those college acceptance letters, when I figure out if I even have time to apply. We can't decide anything until then, anyway."

He nodded slowly. "Are there any new leads?"

She shook her head. "No, but I need to find out more about Becky." She tried to speak firmly, but her voice caught. "I mean, she can barely brush her hair. Could she really put together a scheme like this—kill one of us, make me take Sutton's place, break into Charlotte's house to strangle me, somehow trail me all over the place without my noticing? It's complicated even if you *are* all there."

Ethan spoke hesitantly. "She definitely sounds unpredictable."

Emma could hear the doubt in his voice. She thought back to all the times Becky had surprised her. One minute Becky would be doing something totally weird like crying in the middle of the supermarket over a slightly blemished grapefruit, and the next she'd be smooth-talking a waiter at the local diner into comping their dinner, or sneaking Emma deftly into a Disney movie without buying a ticket. She could be canny sometimes, even clever. She was a survivor. She and Emma were both survivors, and that meant they could be resourceful.

But that didn't mean she was homicidal. Did it? But then she thought of how Becky had smiled when she called Emma by her real name, with such an eerily calm expression, as though she knew she wasn't Sutton. As if she were sure of it.

Emma rubbed her eyes, the image of that manila folder coming back to her. "Dr. Banerjee has been her doctor for years. He had a file five inches thick on her. I bet there are session notes, diagnostic tests, all sorts of things in there. If I could get my hands on that, it might answer some questions."

When she looked back at Ethan, his spine had gone rigid and his lips were pulled in a taut, angry line. His eyes looked black in the dark, unreflective and unreadable. "Psych records are private, Emma," he said.

She recoiled at the coldness in his voice. "I know that.

Trust me, I'm not thrilled at the idea of digging into my mom's crazy past. But it could give us the answers we've been looking for. And we don't have any other leads."

He shook his head violently. "No. It's wrong."

"Ethan, this could clear Becky!" she exclaimed. A flare of irritation swept through her. Did he *want* to believe her mother was a murderer?

"You have no right to pry into someone's head that way!" he snapped. Neither one of them spoke for a moment. Far off in the desert, some coyotes barked.

Then he exhaled loudly. "I'm sorry. I just feel strongly about this."

At any other time in her life, she would have agreed with him—she didn't want to go digging through someone's private records either, particularly not her own mother's. But the people in Sutton's life protected their secrets so carefully, and Emma's safety depended on learning everything she could.

"It doesn't matter, anyway. I don't have access to the files." Emma sighed. "I don't really want to look at them, Ethan. I'm just so tired of dead ends."

He touched her cheek. "I know you're frustrated."

"I'm sorry, too." Emma smiled sadly. "So much for romance, huh?"

A small smile spread across Ethan's face. "I would say romance isn't totally off the table," he whispered into her ear. He nuzzled gently against her neck, kissing her throat softly. Emma shivered at his touch, coiling her fingers in his hair. The heat of their brief argument didn't dissipate, but it softened, morphing into a different kind of energy. Her nerve endings hummed beneath his fingertips. He kissed her, a longer, deeper kiss than before. She closed her eyes and leaned into him.

All but one of the candles had flickered out. I stared at the last tiny flame, remembering the vitriolic shouting matches between Thayer and me, and the frenzied kisses that usually followed. *That's what you get for dating a brooder, sis,* I thought. *Lots of epic fighting, lots of hot apology make-outs.*

I was glad Emma and Ethan were making up. But the question still lingered at the back of my mind: How was Emma going to find out whether Becky was innocent?

And if Ethan couldn't help her prove it, who could?

12

MONSTERS IN THE ATTIC

After a grueling tennis practice the next day, Emma stood in the upstairs hallway, staring at the hatch to the attic. During their father-daughter—or rather, *grand*father-*grand*daughter—dinner, Mr. Mercer had mentioned that some of Becky's old things were still up there. Maybe something upstairs would help her piece together Becky's relationship with her family and illuminate her motives. It was a thin lead, but it was all she had to go on.

She checked her watch. She had the house to herself—Mr. Mercer was at the hospital, Mrs. Mercer was out running errands, and Laurel was still at school for a physics project—but she wasn't sure for how long, so she had to move fast. She tugged the cord down from the ceiling. Drake, who was keeping her company in the hall, scampered backward as dust billowed down around her. For a big lug, he was quite the coward.

Emma gripped the sides of the ladder and climbed up into the darkness. The musty smell of old paper and mothballs pervaded the attic, which was cluttered with evidence of abandoned hobbies and family history. A pair of downhill skis was propped against a yellowed dress form. Translucent boxes of red and green Christmas ornaments were neatly piled on the floor. A porcelain doll with a cracked cheek sat staring blankly from a child-sized rocking chair. At one end of the attic a few beams of sunlight fought through a small, dirty window that looked out over the backyard.

The attic gave me that same frustrating feeling of déjà vu that I got from all the objects and places of my former life. Some of the objects—a child-sized vanity with a padded pink stool, a North Face frame backpack, a pile of old board games laced with cobwebs—drew me toward them like magnets. I knew they'd meant something to me, but I couldn't remember what.

Emma stood still for a moment, wondering where the Mercers would have stored Becky's things. It wasn't as if there would be a big box in the corner labeled OUR ESTRANGED SECRET DAUGHTER'S STUFF. But she knew that

Mr. Mercer had been up here recently for the pictures, so she looked around the attic for areas that seemed recently disturbed. Her gaze fell on an ornately carved Chinese chest. A bunch of graying shoe boxes were sitting next to it, as if they'd been recently shifted off the top. The patterns on its rosewood lid were clean and dust free. She braced herself and opened it.

The inside of the chest smelled like tobacco and old newspapers. A stuffed rabbit with one ear was nestled in the leg of a purple Dr. Martens combat boot. Under that she found a silver-plated hand mirror wrapped in a scarf, a bunch of shattered CD jewel cases, a dog-eared copy of Sylvia Plath's *Ariel*, and a crumpled pack of cigarettes. It looked as if someone had swept up all the contents of Becky's room and shoved them in the chest. Then, tucked near the bottom, under a pile of faded magazines, she found a composition book covered in doodles. Her heart lurched. She knew a journal when she saw it—she'd certainly kept enough herself. She just never knew her mother had.

Girl Finds Mother's Old Journal, Contents Change Everything, she hoped, looking at the book's cover. Then she flipped the journal open.

The handwriting was painfully familiar, the same untidy scrawl Emma remembered from childhood birthday cards and from the note Becky had left for her at the diner just a few weeks earlier.

At first, the journal's entries were neat and tidy, dated even down to the time of day:

Today I woke up at five and could not sleep any more so I climbed out the window and went to Denny's. Mom and Dad panicked and thought I had run away when I did not come down to the table and when they saw my shoes were missing. Can't a person enjoy her Grand Slam breakfast in peace around here?

A few days later:

I got $200 for the cheesy diamond studs Mom got me for "sweet sixteen" last year. Part of me thinks I should feel bad for selling them but I'm not sweet at all and she should know that. Between that & the $150 I've saved babysitting for the Gandins, I almost have enough to get out of here.

Emma looked up from the book, a strange ache piercing her chest. She felt as if she was spying on her mother, never mind that almost twenty years had passed. But spying or not, this was her only lead. She turned another page.

The entries went on and on, one every few days. Sketches filled some pages, mostly elaborate abstract designs or flowering vines. An Emily Dickinson poem filled a sheet, with colored-pencil illustrations all around the text. Becky complained about school and her parents. She broke up with one boyfriend and hooked up with another one. She cheated on a third. She was always lonely, even when she was surrounded by people. She sounded surprisingly, almost disappointingly normal—creative and sullen and rebellious, but not crazy.

But about halfway through the composition book the entries started to change. The language became disjointed, the thoughts scattered. *Dog next door keeps barking and if he doesn't stop soon I may snap*, she'd written one day. *This town is poison. Even the clothes on my back hurt my skin.* And then, one day, just the words *Mama, I'm so sorry.* The writing ran sideways in some places or curled around in weird spirals of text.

Emma turned another page. Her breath caught in her throat. Printed across two facing pages, in enormous block letters, was *Emma*.

On the next page it was repeated in long lines across the paper—*Emma, Emma, Emma, Emma*—in different sizes and scripts, ornate calligraphy and cartoon block letters and colorful sketches sprinkled with stars. She flipped through the pages, faster and faster. The rest of the book was filled with nothing but that one word, EMMA, scrawled wilder and wilder, in Sharpie, in pencil, sometimes written so hard the letters tore through the paper.

The book fell out of her trembling hands and hit the

floor in a cloud of dust. The attic spun around her like a strange, shadowy carousel. She knew Becky was sick, but this . . . this was obsession.

I was afraid, too. What was going through our mother's mind? Had she written this before or after we were born?

The garage door rattled open, and Emma jumped. She quickly slid the journal into her pocket and stood up. As quietly as she could, she went down the ladder, closing the hatch door after her.

The house was silent again when she reached the hall. She frowned and padded down the stairs to the entryway. "Hello?" she called. No one answered. She opened the front door and looked out on the lawn.

She had to blink her eyes several times to clear her vision. For a moment it looked as if an enormous agave plant was wobbling around the Mercers' yard on uncertain human legs. After the quiet, dim attic, her eyes had to be playing tricks on her.

A moment later the walking plant was replaced by a tall, broad-shouldered boy carrying a giant succulent. She peeked around the plant's prickly leaves. Thayer.

I swooned. What's hotter than watching a gorgeous boy carry heavy things? At that moment I would have given anything for hands, just so I could run them over his shoulders and up into his damp, tousled hair.

"What're you doing here?" Emma asked.

Thayer stopped and grinned at her, balancing on his good leg. "Laurel said your dad's bummed out that he got hurt in the middle of landscaping the yard," he explained. "I figured that since it's partly my fault he got hurt, I should come and help him finish. Besides, I know all about knee injuries," he said, nodding down at his own bad leg.

A flush of pleasure swept over Emma's cheeks. She understood what Sutton saw in Thayer. He had so much more depth, and warmth, than she'd realized at first. "Here, let me help you," she said, grabbing one side of the heavy plant. Together they wrestled it out of the plastic and into the hole Mr. Mercer had dug.

"Careful with the spines, they can hurt pretty bad," Thayer warned.

"I'm used to cactus spines," Emma answered. She laughed when they stood up in a shower of dirt. Their arms, even their faces, were covered with it. "It's really nice of you to help my dad out," she added, walking toward the willow tree to get out of the hot sun.

Thayer shrugged. "I'm just trying to put things right. As much as I can, anyway." He glanced at Emma, then blinked, as if he was seeing her for the first time. "Is everything okay? You look kind of pale."

Emma looked down, thinking about what she'd just found in the attic. "I saw my mom again two nights ago," she admitted.

Thayer's long-lashed hazel eyes opened wide with concern. "Where?"

Suddenly the whole story was pouring out of her—the hospital visit, the discovery that her mother had a history of mental illness. The fact that she'd pulled a knife on someone. Emma left out the part about Becky calling her by her real name, but as she told him the rest, she felt the compression around her heart relax ever so slightly. She breathed deeply.

Thayer let out a low whistle. "Damn."

"I know," she said. Talking to Thayer was so easy—she already felt calmer, more focused. "The worst thing is that I can't really tell anyone. Mom—I mean, my adopted mom—doesn't know, and my dad won't let me tell her. He says it'd destroy her. I can't tell Laurel either, and I can't tell any of the other girls because they'd tell Laurel. The whole thing is awkward and stupid."

"Keeping secrets for your parents sucks," Thayer agreed, his expression darkening. He leaned back against the tree, and frowned. Emma watched him from the corner of her eye. Thayer knew all about family secrets. He rarely talked about it, but part of the reason he'd run away from home was to escape his father's violent temper.

When he spoke, his voice was low. "I never told you this, but I caught my dad having an affair last year."

Emma's jaw dropped. "Seriously?" She imagined

hotheaded, strict Mr. Vega. His brow was always furrowed, his spine stiff and straight, and he seemed to disapprove of everything. Who would even want to have an affair with him?

Thayer nodded. "Yeah. I caught his girlfriend or whatever leaving our house when my mom was away visiting my aunt. I tried to talk to him about it, but he just blasted me for messing with his business. Acted like he could do no wrong." Thayer gritted his teeth. "My mom didn't factor into the equation at all."

"That sucks," Emma said softly. She reached over and squeezed his hand. When their skin touched, an electric hum started at the point of contact. Realizing what she'd done, she pulled her hand away, blushing. Thayer looked away, too.

They sat together in silence for a moment. Emma's hand still tingled from touching his. She felt a little guilty confiding so much in Thayer, as if she were sneaking around behind Ethan's back. But it wasn't like that at all. She and Thayer were just friends, and friends were allowed to confide in each other when something was on their minds. Besides, the only reason Thayer was even interested in her was that he thought she was Sutton—his ex-girlfriend.

I hoped she was right about Thayer still being in love with me. Of all the things my death had taken away from me, Thayer had been the hardest to lose.

He stood up carefully, testing his weight on his bad knee. "I should go. I've got physical therapy in thirty minutes."

"How's that going?"

"Better," he said. "If I keep working on it, I might even get to play soccer next year."

Emma beamed. "That's great!"

"Yeah." When Thayer smiled, a dimple appeared in his left cheek. "Anyway, tell your dad . . . well, whatever."

"I'll tell him you said hi," Emma said.

Thayer saluted her, then turned and headed unstably to his car. For a moment, Emma wanted to run to him and hug him good-bye . . . but something told her that wasn't a great idea.

Maybe that something was me. I hovered next to her, and together we watched as he started his car and drove away.

13

NEVER UNDERESTIMATE THE POWER
OF A LITTLE RETAIL THERAPY

Emma was still standing on the porch when she heard something creak behind her. Her heart skipped a beat. What if it was Becky, escaped from the hospital? The journal pages covered with *Emma* swirled in her mind. But when she spun around, she came face-to-face with Laurel.

"You scared me," Emma accused, her hand over her heart.

"Geez, you never used to scare so easy." Laurel laughed, looping her arm in Emma's elbow. "Dating a nice boy is making you soft. Now come on, we need to go." She checked her lipstick in a Chanel compact, then pulled Emma toward the door.

"Where are we going?" Emma asked, grabbing her purse.

Laurel gave her an incredulous look. "Duh, space cadet. Only the biggest Saks sample sale of the year?"

Emma blinked. "Right," she said. She had no idea what Laurel was talking about, but no doubt Sutton would have had this marked on her virtual calendar for months. She mock-slapped herself on the forehead. "It's that time again?"

"Uh, it's the same time every year." Laurel rolled her eyes. "I think all that time at the hospital the other night must have affected your memory."

She opened the door to her Jetta, and Emma climbed in. They drove past an emerald green golf course, vivid against Tucson's tawny fall colors. Usher crooned softly on the stereo. Emma tipped her head up and felt the wind on her cheeks.

Laurel chattered happily as she drove. "I want something really special for Char's party next weekend. I'm so tired of everything in my closet."

"Tell me about it," Emma lied. Sutton's closet was, in a word, *amazing.* She had a zillion pairs of jeans. A bag for every pair of shoes. Racks of party dresses, some of them with tags still attached. A whole drawer of belts and scarves. A single outfit of Sutton's cost more than Emma's entire wardrobe from her former life. In a strange way, though, she kind of *missed* thrift stores—digging through the bins for buried treasure, laughing at the hideous pairs of shoes no one in their right mind should have bought the first time around, let alone the second, and picking up a knickknack from the housewares department just because. Not that she'd ever tell Laurel that.

Yeah, my friends aren't exactly the Goodwill type. Emma had dragged Mads into a thrift store when she first arrived. And even though she'd scored a sweet pair of Chanel shades, poor Mads had backed away from the place as if everything was crawling with lice.

As the Saks Fifth Avenue sign glittered into view, Laurel gave Emma an awkward glance. "Um, I invited Nisha to meet us," Laurel blurted. "Is that okay?"

Emma blinked. "Nisha?"

Laurel angled the car into a parking space and turned off the ignition. "It's just—it seems like you guys are getting along better now. . . . She really put Celeste in her place at tennis, you know? We've been working together on that physics project and I just thought . . ."

"Sure, it's fine. I was just surprised," Emma said.

A relieved smile crossed Laurel's face. Emma remembered how nervous Laurel had been when Emma discovered she'd been at Nisha's slumber party the night Sutton died. Poor Laurel had closed her eyes, almost as if to brace herself for some kind of punishment. She wondered why Sutton had cared so much about who her sister had spent time with. The Lying Game girls were extremely invested in managing each other's social lives.

Watching from this distance, I wasn't sure why myself. I remembered the rush of power, of strength, when I drove people together or apart, when I told my friends who they were allowed to like, or date. Now it just seemed . . . small.

Nisha stood outside the Saks entrance, her straight, shiny hair loose around her shoulders. She lifted her hand almost shyly as they approached. The light was fading fast, the sky a pale silvery blue overhead. Magpies flitted through the parking lot, screaming from the tops of light posts and swooping down to get the crumbs trailing from the food court to the cars. The three girls stood awkwardly for a moment, looking at each other.

Then Emma grinned and gestured toward Saks. "You girls ready for combat?"

Nisha's dark brown eyes lit up. "Born ready. Thanks for inviting me."

"Of course," Laurel said, pushing through the wide glass door. "Let's do it."

The scene inside the store was a madhouse. Women swarmed like angry bees, grabbing clothes off hangers and out of bins. Two girls Emma recognized from her German class were actually yanking a pair of jeans back and forth between them, arguing loudly over who'd seen them first. Older women reeking of Chanel No. 5 pursed their lips in disdain at the disorder, but snatched at hats and bags just as eagerly when they found the labels they were looking for. Salesgirls tottered around on five-inch heels looking harassed.

Emma ran her hand over a cashmere T-shirt left rumpled on a table. When she flipped over the tag, she burst into a fit of coughing. Even with the price reduction, the shirt was four hundred dollars. Laurel grabbed her elbow.

"Ralph Lauren? Who are you shopping for, Grandma? Come on." She steered her toward a cluster of cocktail dresses. Nisha was already sorting through a rack of jewel-toned Oscar de la Rentas. Laurel whipped her sweater off and pulled a strapless yellow minidress over her camisole and jeans, then, frowning, tugged off the jeans underneath. It would have been strange if all the other women in the store hadn't been doing the same thing. Laurel studied her reflection in a full-length mirror on a pillar, then looked enviously at Emma. "I wish I had your shoulders." She pulled off the minidress and handed it to her. "You try it on."

Emma tugged the dress over her head. She pivoted back and forth in the mirror, scrunching up her face. The color was way too banana.

Come on, I wanted to tell her. Didn't she know yellow was *the* color this year? And she and I actually have the skin tone to pull it off.

Now Laurel was wearing a gold lace Dolce & Gabbana number that made her skin glow. "So you're talking to Thayer again, huh? I saw you guys in the front yard."

Emma shrugged as she took the dress off. "Yeah. It's been kind of awkward between us, but I don't want to lose him as a friend."

Laurel scoffed. "Well, what'd you expect? I don't know what happened between you or why you decided to break it off with him, but he's not over it."

Emma eyed her carefully. Laurel had forgiven her sister for coming between her and Thayer, but her tone was still tinged with wistfulness. She grabbed a short red Alice + Olivia dress.

"You would look drop-dead in this," Emma said, holding the dress out to Laurel. "Every guy at the party will be drooling over you."

"Really?" Laurel said, looking touched.

"Promise." Emma grabbed more dresses from the rack and held them up to her body without trying them on. Tucking a black sheath under her chin, she used both hands to pull her hair away from her face to see what the dress would look like in an updo.

Laurel glanced at her and made a jealous snort. "You and your cheekbones. It's so unfair. Who was your birth mom, some Russian ballerina?"

Emma's eyebrows shot up. She and Laurel had never

talked about Sutton's birth mother before. Had she and Sutton? She appraised Laurel's face out of the corner of her eye. Their coloring was completely different—Laurel had the peachy skin and sandy-blond hair of Mr. Mercer's side of the family, while Emma had inherited Mrs. Mercer's dark hair and porcelain skin. At first glance they looked nothing alike. But the longer she looked, the more she noticed the things they shared: the arching brows, the same small, delicate earlobes, the same hairline. She wondered if Sutton and Laurel had ever noticed or commented on it growing up.

"Thayer's still got it bad for you, you know," Laurel went on. "He looks at you the same way he did two summers ago at that county fair. Remember that? He spent three hours to win you that giant Scooby-Doo prize in the ring toss? *That's* dedication. That kind of feeling doesn't go away overnight."

Emma hid a smile. That *was* dedication. No one had spent three hours doing *anything* for her, but it was the kind of goofy romantic gesture she loved. She imagined the two of them sharing a funnel cake, riding the Ferris wheel. But then she stopped in confusion. Who was she picturing in this memory—Sutton, or herself?

Watch it, Emma. Like I said, I don't share well, especially with sisters.

Nisha appeared beside them, wearing a paper-thin

purple dress that made her skin look radiant. She'd already been through the register and carried two black Saks bags over her shoulder. "So how are things with you and Ethan?" she asked.

"Good," Emma said. "He's such a romantic."

Nisha nudged her. "And he's got a pretty fierce right hook, too."

Emma rolled her eyes. "How stupid was that fight? I could have strangled them both."

Laurel laughed from the depths of a black peplum dress she was in the process of tugging on over her head. "Like you haven't been playing him and Thayer off each other. Seriously, Sutton, everyone knows how you work. You like keeping them jealous."

"I do not!" Emma insisted, crossed her arms over her chest and glaring. "Why can't they just mellow out and accept that I'm not in the market for more drama right now?"

"I wouldn't worry. Ethan's obviously nuts about you. If he can't handle a little competition, he can't handle dating Sutton Mercer." Laurel gave her a playful body check, then ripped off the dress without even glancing at it in the mirror. "Let's check out the shoes."

Emma ditched a sequined Badgley Mischka dress and followed Laurel across the store. Shoe boxes, tissue paper, and crumpled disposable nylon socks were strewn all over the footwear section. A blond woman with skin so tan it looked like leather modeled a pair of leopard-print six-inch heels, while a balding middle-aged man in an Armani suit held her purse. A gaggle of preteen girls giggled and took pictures of one another in Lanvin platforms they clearly weren't going to buy.

Laurel reached out hungrily toward a pair of velvet Louboutins. She slid them onto her small feet and cocked her hip critically.

"Mom and Dad would kill me," she said, looking at the price. "But at least I'd die happy."

"They look . . ." Suddenly Nisha trailed off and grabbed Emma's arm. "Uh-oh," she said under her breath.

Emma followed her gaze across the store. Just twenty feet away, standing in front of a rack of silk scarves, was Garrett Austin, Sutton's ex-boyfriend.

Emma stared back. Garrett was wearing a crisp, striped oxford shirt and a pair of perfectly broken-in J Brands. He'd grown out his sandy blond hair, trading the preppy cut he'd had while dating Sutton for a longer, more tousled look. All in all, he was pretty cute . . . except for the fiery expression on his face.

Emma recoiled and looked down, surprised to see him so angry. She knew that Garrett harbored a lot of ill will toward her, both for rejecting him the night of Sutton's birthday party and for breaking up with him soon afterward. He'd practically attacked her at the Halloween dance. If it hadn't been for Ethan interrupting them, who knew what would have happened.

At that moment, two girls approached Garrett, their arms full of overstuffed shopping bags. "We're all done," said a girl in a fedora and black lace miniskirt. Emma was pretty sure she was Louisa, Garrett's little sister. The other girl was Celeste.

"Thanks so much again for the ride, Garrett," Celeste cooed, touching Garrett suggestively with her long, multi-ringed fingers. "It's so sad that people in Tucson waste gas going in separate cars. In Taos, everyone carpools every-where."

Nisha made a noise at the back of her throat.

Garrett blushed, smiling bashfully at the new girl. "I totally agree. We've got to, like, preserve the earth's resources. But some people are selfish, I guess."

I snorted with laughter. This, coming from the guy who begged his dad for a gas-guzzling Hummer.

Emma looked at Nisha. "I guess this means you and Garrett aren't together anymore?" she murmured.

Nisha looked like she was choking down laughter. "*Please.* We weren't ever really together. He's still kind of hung up on you, but he won't admit it. Even I got tired of hearing about what a bitch you were."

Emma poked her. "How charitable of you."

Nisha grinned. "Plus, he's kind of a crybaby."

Emma eyed Garrett and Celeste again. "That's exactly right," Celeste was saying, squeezing Garrett's hand. "There are *a lot* of selfish people around here." She glanced back at Emma, Laurel, and Nisha, shooting them a pinched smile.

"Excuse me!" Laurel said, stepping forward, her shoulders tense.

Celeste blinked innocently. "Oh, I didn't mean you, obviously." She brightened when her gaze landed on Emma, as if noticing her for the first time. "Sutton! Hi!" She eyed Emma's empty arms. "What's the matter? Can't find anything that fits?" Garrett snickered.

Emma jerked back, like she'd been slapped. "As a matter of fact, she was just about to buy this," Laurel jumped in, holding up the yellow dress Emma had tried on earlier.

"Oh, no," Celeste pouted, her large eyes blinking dopily. "But yellow *so* clashes with your aura. I wouldn't wear it, if I were you."

Nisha scowled. "Who died and made you the new age fashion police?"

Garrett frowned, crossing his arms over his chest. His sister looked between all the girls and took a tentative step back.

"Oh, please." Celeste laughed, all innocence. "I would never claim to be the police of anything, let alone fashion. I don't believe in anything so . . . *fleeting*. Meaningless."

"Then why are you here?" Laurel asked, not bothering to hide her sarcasm.

Nice one, little sister, I cheered silently.

"Just to keep my *friends* company and pick up a few gifts," Celeste explained, draping an arm around Garrett's shoulders suggestively. "But you're right, it's time for me to leave. My chakras are extremely sensitive to all this consumerism." She sniffed and turned toward the door.

"Um, right," Garrett said, hurrying to catch up. He shot Emma one more venomous look before disappearing from view.

Emma slumped against the shoe rack, feeling drained. "She's so weird."

Nisha waved her hand dismissively. "Don't let her get to you."

"Oh, she's not," Emma said in her best Sutton voice.

"And don't let Garrett bother you either," Laurel said quietly. "He's just jealous."

Emma nodded, turning back to the shoes, but she wasn't so sure. Garrett had seemed more than jealous at the Halloween dance. He'd seemed angry—violent, even.

I couldn't stop thinking about the look on Garrett's face either. My memories of my ex were hazy, but I could still see his sweet smile, the gentleness in his eyes when he looked at me. I'd never thought he was capable of that kind of hatred. Was all that anger just because Emma wouldn't sleep with him? The idea broke my heart a little. I had thought I'd known him better than that.

But obviously I didn't know anyone as well as I'd thought I did, as Emma kept proving again and again.

14

THE SCHOOL OF BITCHCRAFT

Friday morning, Emma plopped Sutton's red Kate Spade purse on the table in the pottery studio and slid into the seat between Charlotte and Madeline. A misshapen vase sat in front of Madeline. Charlotte turned over a bulky mug. Across from them, Laurel toyed with two tiny espresso cups. Pots of glaze were strewn across the table alongside paintbrushes of varying sizes, and paper towels.

"That looks awesome, Char," Emma said after she collected her own long, footed pot from the rack. She pointed to the swirl Charlotte was painting on her mug.

Charlotte flushed with pleasure. "It's just like putting on eyeliner," she said.

"Okay, girls," Madeline interrupted. "We have party details to figure out. It's a week away, and we're running out of time."

Party? Emma almost said out loud, then remembered that Charlotte's parents were out of town next weekend.

Charlotte propped her chin on her perfectly manicured hand. "I know a guy who can get us a few kegs. That and my parents' liquor cabinet should be enough."

Emma tilted her head. "Won't your parents notice if anything goes missing?"

Charlotte snorted. "Please. They go through Tanqueray like water."

"What about food?" Madeline asked.

Charlotte shrugged. "We'll get some platters at AJ's. I've been jonesing for their Brie en croûte, anyway."

Emma reached for the container of blue glaze, thinking about the parties she'd attended in her old life, where party snacks pretty much consisted of Doritos, Oreos, or a big bowl of Starbursts. She tried to picture Sutton's friends at one of those parties and nearly burst out laughing.

Suddenly, the telltale jingle of silver on silver made her look up. Celeste stood at the door to the studio in a long loose tunic embroidered with shiny metallic thread, Garrett at her side. She leaned up and planted a wet, lingering kiss on his lips, then shot a pointed glance at Emma, as if to rub in the fact that she was with Sutton's ex.

"Thanks for walking me to class," she cooed, her voice low and dreamy.

Garrett touched one of her braids. "See you soon," he said huskily. She hung on the doorjamb after he left, watching him until he disappeared around the corner.

Madeline's jaw dropped open. Charlotte threw her brush on the table in disgust, then peered at Emma. "Um, why aren't you more pissed?"

Emma shrugged, unscrewing the lid to the glaze. "I saw them last night at Saks. Apparently, they're a thing now."

Charlotte balled up her fist. "Well, he's clearly going out with her just to get back at you, Sutton. There's no way he actually likes her."

Laurel cleared her throat. "Apparently, a lot of the guys think she's really cute." All heads whipped around to face her. She shrugged. "Thayer says they're all talking about her, anyway."

"Does *Thayer* think she's cute?" Emma asked, wrinkling her nose. Celeste didn't seem like his type.

Laurel rolled her eyes. "He says, and I quote, 'She's got a celestial body.'"

"Ew!" I said aloud, though no one heard me. That didn't sound like Thayer at all.

Celeste entered the room, drifted to the rack of fired pottery, and removed a bowl, the bells at her ankles jingling with every move. On her way back to her seat, she paused at Emma's table. She looked at Emma searchingly, as if she were trying to make her out through a dense fog.

"Can I help you?" Emma said acidly, suddenly on the defensive. She wasn't ready for another baffling Celeste confrontation.

"I just wish *I* could help *you*," Celeste breathed. Madeline and Charlotte exchanged glances, arching their eyebrows. "Laugh all you will," Celeste said to them, "but Sutton's aura is in *dire* need of healing energy. Somewhere along the way, maybe in a past life, her spirit has been fractured. That's why it's so hard for you to be emotionally generous," she said to Emma in a sickly sweet tone.

"I hear you're getting pretty emotionally generous with Sutton's ex," Charlotte spat. "Hope your birthday's coming up. He gives pretty good presents."

Madeline and Laurel both snorted with laughter.

Celeste just smiled knowingly, her gaze still on Emma. "Secrets will out, Sutton Mercer. You've been warned." With that, she drifted past them in a wave of patchouli.

The words hit Emma like a brick. Secrets were the only thing keeping her alive.

"What's her problem?" Charlotte whispered.

"Yeah, did you hurt her in a past life or something, Sutton?" Madeline joked.

"I don't know," Emma said, feeling uneasy. "But she definitely has it in for me."

They stared at Celeste, who'd found a spot at a table full of boys, all of whom were now surreptitiously ogling her. One of them, a junior who wore his hair in an emo shag over his left eye, leaned over to inspect the bowl she was painting, using the opportunity to look down her shirt.

"You know what I've been thinking?" Madeline said, her voice dropping low. "I think we're overdue for a Lying Game prank. And I think our next victim may have just fallen right in our lap."

The other three girls all leaned imperceptibly toward Madeline, eyes flashing in breathless excitement. But Emma still felt torn. The Lying Game's pranks sometimes made her uncomfortable—she'd been on the receiving end of popular kids' cruelty too many times back in Nevada. She couldn't shake a feeling of guilt whenever she participated.

"This school's cafeteria is totally disappointing," Celeste was saying to an athletic boy across the room. "In Taos, my school only sold organic produce, and all of the entrées were farm-to-table."

"Cool," the boy said. As if he really *cared*.

"And there are so many snack machines in this place," Celeste went on. "It's disgusting. You know those things are full of toxins—plus, they make you overweight." Her gaze slid to Beth Franklin, a sweet but slightly heavy girl who was munching on a bag of vending machine pretzels at the next table. Beth turned purple and shoved the pretzels back into her bag.

Then again, Emma wasn't sure she *would* feel guilty about this prank. Maybe Celeste deserved it.

I was thinking the same thing.

"So what should we do?" asked Laurel. "Write some love letters from 'Garrett' and send her on an embarrassing fake date? Like, with a mime or a clown or something?"

"We've done stuff like that already." Charlotte shook her head. "We need something special for this girl."

They all fell silent, brainstorming. A low, cool voice came from behind Emma. "Hold a séance."

They all turned at once to see Nisha, who hadn't even looked up from the clay cat she was painting. Her hair was pulled into a ponytail that spilled down over one shoulder. As she carefully lined whiskers onto the cat's face, she continued. "Fake a bunch of ghosts. You know she believes in all that crap. She'll totally fall for it."

The girls exchanged a glance. Emma could tell they were impressed. Finally, Madeline spoke up, an indignant huff in her voice. "We don't accept suggestions from people outside the Lying Game."

Nisha shrugged. "You don't usually have such good ideas."

"Have you forgotten about the locker room murder?" Madeline shot back, referring to a prank they'd played on

Nisha several months earlier, creating a mock crime scene at Nisha's locker. "You were ready to pee your pants."

Nisha opened her mouth to argue, but Emma jumped in before she could. "Nisha's right," she said. "A fake séance would be an amazing trick." It also seemed more harmless than some of the other Lying Game ideas, which had included things like nearly choking Sutton into unconsciousness or parking Sutton's Volvo on the train tracks.

Emma looked around at the others. "C'mon, guys, this idea rocks. And Nisha, since you thought of it, do you want to help?"

Madeline, Charlotte, and Laurel whipped their heads around to stare at her. "Are you crazy?" hissed Madeline, leaning close. "She's not an official member."

"Gabby and Lili will be so pissed," Charlotte added. "It took them years to get in."

"Since when do we make decisions based on what Gabby and Lili think?" Emma asked.

Madeline crossed her arms over her chest. "I wanted Samantha Weir to join two years ago and you were a mega-bitch about it then, Sutton. I don't see what's changed."

"Nisha's way cooler than Samantha Weir," Emma argued, channeling her inner Sutton. "But if you have a better idea, we won't use Nisha's and we won't let her in on it. Anyone?"

They looked back and forth at one another. No one said anything. Finally, Madeline blew out a loud breath. "Okay. But this is a one-time-only deal. We don't need any associate members."

"Nisha?" Emma asked.

The other girl gave them a long, appraising look over the clay cat. Then she grinned. "Why not," she said. "Count me in. I've always wanted to see a Lying Game prank from the other side."

Across the room, Celeste painted astrological symbols around the rim of her bowl. An electric jolt charged down Emma's spine as the new girl looked up and met her eyes. A slow, languid smile spread across her face—as if she had just caught Emma in a lie and couldn't wait for the chance to expose her.

Or, I thought with a shudder, as if she'd just seen me, floating behind my twin.

～ 15 ～

HOPES AND SCHEMES

On Monday morning, Emma, Laurel, Madeline, Charlotte, and the Twitter Twins were perched on the low stone wall in the courtyard, enjoying the sun before the first bell rang. Emma felt a bit more rested after the weekend. She'd tried to regroup, spending a lot of time watching reality TV with Laurel on the couch and going on a bike ride with Ethan. Mr. Mercer hadn't brought up the subject of Becky once, and she hadn't asked.

Swarms of students moved through the quad on their way to lockers or classrooms, many of them casting the girls surreptitious looks and trying not to look too desperate. Word had gotten out that Charlotte was having a party on Saturday, and everyone wanted an invite.

"I can't wait for your party, Char," Laurel said, ripping the cover off a Chobani yogurt container.

"It's going to be amazing," Charlotte agreed. "I've got Poor Tony playing at ten." She leaned back and took a sip of her iced latte, seemingly oblivious to the horde of would-be attendees.

"The DJ from Plush?" Madeline looked impressed. "How'd you swing that?"

"Money talks, girl." Charlotte's eyes glinted behind her aviator shades. "Mom and Dad left me an envelope of cash for the weekend, to buy food or whatever. They must be feeling guilty for something, because they went pretty overboard this time."

A girl with blue streaks in her hair and a flowered romper suddenly appeared next to the wall. "Hey, Charlotte. I made all these blueberry scones for the drama club bake sale, but I ended up with way too many." She gave a flustered little laugh, her round cheeks flushing. "Do you guys want some? They're really good."

Lili's hand snaked out toward the plate of treats, but Charlotte swatted it back. "Thanks, but we already had breakfast." Charlotte gestured toward the Starbucks cups and empty yogurt containers scattered around them.

The girl's face fell. "Oh. Right." She scampered away, cheeks blazing.

Madeline snorted in her wake. "Trying too hard, much?"

"The scones, or that outfit?" Charlotte asked.

"She's not so bad, you guys," Lili piped up. "I'm in P.E. with her and she's actually pretty fun."

"Whatever," Charlotte said. "You can invite her when you see her this afternoon, Lili. Just tell her not to wear a whipped cream dress or something insane, okay?"

Emma sipped tentatively at her own coffee and winced. Sutton drank hers black, with just a hint of Splenda, and she still wasn't used to the bitterness.

Madeline nudged her. "Someone's quiet this morning."

"Yeah, what are you planning?" Charlotte lowered her shades and peered sternly out at her over the tops of the frames. "I do *not* want pig blood anywhere near my parents' Persian rug, Sutton, so don't even think about it."

Emma tossed her hair with what she hoped was convincing hauteur. "Relax, Char, I'm not planning anything for the party. Except showing the rest of you up, that is."

"That's not a plan, that's just your terrible personality," Laurel teased.

Before Emma could come up with a retort, someone placed an icy hand on her shoulder. "Ladies," said a cool female voice.

Emma yelped in surprise. Her balance swayed violently, and before she knew it she was on the ground splayed out

135

next to the low wall, looking up at Nisha's startled face.

Everyone burst into hysterics. Tears of mirth poured down Laurel's face. Charlotte and Madeline were paralyzed with laughter, clutching their stomachs. Lili and Gabby had fallen into each other's arms. Nisha was the one to lean down and help Emma to her feet. "Sorry," she said, sounding mortified. "I didn't mean to scare you."

Emma's face burned. "Don't worry about it," she said, trying to shrug it off. "I just . . . thought you were someone else, that's all."

Yeah, my murderer. But Emma needed to keep her wits about her. The killer could be watching her right now. Not to mention that she was making me look bad.

The others stopped laughing long enough to catch their breath, and Nisha stepped forward. "I just wanted to show you what I made," she said, pulling a piece of paper out of her coral messenger bag and handing it to Emma. The others leaned in over her shoulders to see what it said.

Across the top of the flyer, twenty-point Gothic script read CONFERENCE OF THE DEAD. Below it was a clip-art picture of a tombstone.

"'Penetrate the mysteries beyond the veil of the living,'" Charlotte read out loud. "'Join us Sunday evening in Sabino Canyon as we call upon the spirits to reveal themselves. Masks and cloaks required for entrance.'"

There was an e-mail address at the bottom for an RSVP. Charlotte grinned.

"Oh, that's too perfect," Madeline said. "She's going to eat it up."

"Who?" Gabby asked, staring at it.

"Celeste," Charlotte said. "She's our next victim."

Lili looked confused. "That hippie chick? Since when?"

"Since she started seriously creeping me out," Emma explained. "And Nisha is helping us. It was her idea."

Gabby and Lili raised their eyebrows, but neither said a word. For once, their fingers were still hovering over their phone keypads.

Laurel pointed at the invite. "What's with the masks?"

"That way she won't recognize us and leave right away," Nisha explained. "Plus, masks are scary, right? All part of the smoke and mirrors."

"We'll meet at Sutton and Laurel's on Sunday to finalize everything," Charlotte said, tossing her cup in the garbage and standing up.

"We're doing it in Sabino Canyon?" Emma couldn't keep a note of dismay out of her voice. The less she had to be at the scene of her sister's murder, the better.

"It's close to my house," Nisha explained. "I thought that afterward we could order takeout and celebrate our success. If you guys want to, that is," she added.

"Sabino is totally perfect," Madeline said, squeezing

Emma's elbow. "It's so spooky out there, it'll be the perfect place for a séance. That freak is going to be sorry she ever tried to mess with you."

Emma's gaze traveled across the courtyard to where Celeste sat in a half-lotus pose. Today she was wearing hemp pants and knotted rope sandals, with a five-point Wiccan star on a chain around her neck. For a moment, Emma felt almost bad about the prank—Celeste reminded her of a weirder version of Erin Featherstone, a girl at her school in Henderson who was a devout Buddhist and cried whenever bugs died. But then Celeste looked up and met Emma's gaze. A slow, dreamy smirk came to her lips, and her eyes narrowed dangerously. It didn't matter what *Emma* thought, she realized—right now she was Sutton Mercer, and no one messed with Sutton.

She turned to the others. "Let's do this."

Damn right, I agreed.

Everyone got up and headed to Celeste's locker, which was in the fine arts hall between the auditorium and the dance studio. They nominated Charlotte to shove the invitation through the ventilation slats, then ran behind a corner and waited breathlessly for Celeste to appear, choking back their laughter.

The cacophonous warm-up of the school orchestra crashed out from the music room down the hall. The smell of turpentine was pungent in the air. "She's coming!"

Laurel whispered, and they all craned their necks around the corner to watch.

Celeste drifted toward her locker. Even her walk was dreamy, as though she wasn't entirely touching the ground. She swung open the locker door and the flyer fluttered out. Laurel bit down on her knuckles to stifle her giggles as Celeste leaned over to pick it up.

"She's reading it," hissed Lili.

Charlotte slapped her shoulder. "That's what we *want* her to do, idiot."

Celeste looked up and down the hall, then carefully folded the sheet of paper and slid it into a book. She shut her locker and started down the hall toward them.

"Quick!" Gabby shrieked.

The girls ran down the hall into the pottery studio for cover. A few moments later, Nisha's iPhone vibrated. "She RSVP'd," she announced, locking eyes with Emma and grinning. "Ladies, it's time to raise the dead."

If only she meant it literally, I thought. But a prank on a girl who deserved it was almost as good.

16

EVERY DAY SHOULD BE SENIOR SKIP DAY

The next day, before third period, Charlotte and Madeline swooped in on either side of Emma and steered her toward the door to the student parking lot. "Guys?" Emma asked as they passed her classroom. "I have English next. I have to turn in a paper on *Jane Eyre*."

No matter how important it was for her to pretend to be Sutton, Emma hadn't been able to give up her own study habits. She'd finished *Jane Eyre* for the second time and loved it, not that she could ever admit it to Sutton's friends. She doubted Sutton would have gushed over angsty Victorian literature.

Um, no. I would have been more likely to browse the

Wikipedia entry ten minutes before class and hope no one called on me. But good for my sister. It was nice to know that one of us was a brainiac.

Madeline snorted. "So turn it in at the end of school. Anyway, who wants to talk about some weird old book by a chick who obviously never got laid? I gave up after the first page. We totally deserve a mental health day. *And* we need new clothes for the party."

Emma paused. In her old life back in Nevada, she wouldn't have dreamed of skipping class. She'd always been a good student—she knew her only shot at going to college was to land a top-notch scholarship, so she'd worked hard. She'd also *liked* school—it was an escape from the more depressing living situations in which she found herself, a place she could slip anonymously into the crowd and disappear from the eyes of creepy foster siblings or eccentric guardians and just be a normal kid.

But a mental health day did sound like just what she needed right now. "Okay, I'm in," she agreed, linking arms with Madeline and walking out into the sunshine.

The girls climbed into Charlotte's Jeep Grand Cherokee and blasted a Kelly Clarkson song as they turned out into the street. Emma felt the weight on her shoulders lightening for the first time in days. This *was* better than sitting in class.

"So, I ordered dessert for the party from Hey, Cupcake!" Charlotte said as they drove past a comic book shop with a life-sized fiberglass Spider-Man attached to the outside wall. "Do you think seven dozen will be enough?"

"I love their red velvet," Madeline said, her eyes fluttering back in her head in bliss. "Maybe you'd better request another dozen."

"If I have to watch you eat a dozen cupcakes, I'm going to kill myself," Charlotte complained, eyeing Madeline's lithe dancer's frame with envy.

"Are you bringing a date, Char?" Madeline asked, in what Emma suspected was an attempt to change the subject.

Charlotte applied NARS peach gloss in the rearview mirror at a stoplight. "John Hokosawa," she said. "I wasn't going to bother, but we were talking after Calc yesterday, and he's looking amazing."

"Oh my God, I love his new haircut," Madeline agreed. "He looks like he should be racing motorcycles." They both giggled.

"Wait, rewind," Emma said, cocking her head at Charlotte. "What did you mean, you weren't going to bother with a date?" As far as she knew, the Lying Game girls didn't go stag to anything.

Charlotte shrugged. "There's no one to date anymore."

"Ugh, tell me about it." Madeline leaned back against her seat, sticking her lip out in a pout. "I'm so tired of high school boys. I keep looking around the halls and thinking, this is it? They're all such children."

"So are *you* going alone?" Emma asked.

Madeline looked at her like she was crazy. "Of course not. I'm taking Jake Wood. I'm not going to go without for the next six months just because there are college guys on the horizon."

Emma had never heard Madeline or Charlotte talk about college, but she probably shouldn't have been shocked. College *was* on the horizon—at least for them. Everyone seemed to be looking ahead, ready to move forward with their lives, while she was stuck in someone else's. What would happen if she couldn't solve this case before college applications were due? Would she submit them as Sutton, or would she be stuck here in limbo, chasing dead leads and spinning her wheels?

I wondered, too. What if she got sick of wondering who'd killed me? What if she figured out a way to abandon my life without getting hurt? *Then* what would happen to me?

They pulled into the La Encantada parking lot. Young mothers in Lululemon yoga pants and diamond earrings pushed strollers through the sunny arcades. A group of senior citizens power walked past the girls, swinging their arms cheerfully. Upbeat jazz filtered through the PA speakers, and the smell of bread and frying things wafted through the air from AJ's Market. As they walked toward the main shopping area, Emma's phone chimed. ANY MORE THOUGHTS ABOUT BECKY? Ethan wrote.

NOT REALLY, Emma responded.

MAYBE WE SHOULD RESEARCH WHAT HER CONDITION IS, EXACTLY, Ethan suggested. IF IT'S SOMETHING HARMLESS, THEN WE CAN RULE HER OUT.

THAT'S A GOOD IDEA, Emma agreed. GOTTA GO.

ENGLISH IS THAT INTERESTING? Ethan joked.

Emma stared at the gleaming storefronts in front of her. What would Ethan think about her cutting class? She knew that he considered Sutton's friends frivolous and superficial. TOTALLY INTERESTING, she wrote back, deciding not to tell him.

They hopped on the escalator up toward the Bebe store. Emma looked at the girls out of the corner of her eye. Charlotte's gaze was hidden behind her aviators, while Madeline was texting furiously. A decal that said SWAN LAKE MAFIA covered the back of her iPhone—some kind of ballet inside joke. Once they walked through the doors, Madeline beelined straight for a rack of cropped sweaters, while Charlotte started leafing through dresses. As she studied a short, fringed dress that made her think of flappers and the Roaring Twenties, Emma had a sudden thought: Tons of people would be at Charlotte's house, the very place she'd been attacked late one night during her first week in Tucson. The party would be unsupervised. What if Sutton's killer was there?

She shuddered, remembering those strong hands at her throat, tightening the chain of Sutton's silver locket against her skin until she could barely breathe. If only she'd been able to see her attacker's face.

"Char?" Emma tried to look casual as she flipped through a rack of belts. "Are you going to disarm the security system for the party?"

Charlotte looked at her strangely. "Um, yeah? I don't exactly want the cops showing up before the party's even had a chance to start. The last thing I need is for some drunk moron to trip the switch."

"Have you seen anyone, like, prowling around your house lately?"

Charlotte narrowed her eyes. "Is this the build-up to a Lying Game prank? Lame, Sutton. No repeats allowed, remember?"

"Repeats?"

"Oh, please. Don't pretend you forgot about the guy who crashed my tenth-grade birthday with a chain saw and a Jason mask."

I laughed silently. I wished I remembered that one.

Emma held up her hands. "I'm not planning anything, honest. I'm just curious. I mean, why do you guys even have such a serious alarm system? Has anyone ever broken in?"

Charlotte shrugged. "I don't know. I don't think so, Detective Mercer."

Shooting one last look at Emma, she threw a few dresses over her shoulder and headed off to the fitting room. Emma stood there thinking. She could see puddles of fabric pooling around her friend's perfectly pedicured toes. What she really wanted was to know who had access to the security codes—but Charlotte already thought she was acting weird.

The door opened a half inch, and Charlotte's face appeared in the gap. "Oh good, you're still here. Can you help zip me up?"

Charlotte turned around and lifted her hair out of the way. Emma tugged at the zipper, but it wouldn't move. The jade green dress was pulled tight across Charlotte's midsection. "Um," Emma said uncomfortably, not wanting to say the words *I think you need a bigger size.* Charlotte was sensitive enough about her weight already.

Unfortunately, that was the moment Madeline chose to come bounding out of an adjacent fitting room, a midriff-baring sweater stretched tight over her slender torso, exposing her toned abs and narrow waist. She did a quick pas de bourrée in the mirror, landing in a graceful half curtsey. "What do we think, ladies?"

Charlotte tore away from Emma and slammed the door shut.

Madeline froze, her eyes wide. "*What the hell?*" she mouthed silently at Emma.

Emma gritted her teeth, not knowing how to answer. How could she tell Madeline she'd picked the wrong moment to dance around looking like a Victoria's Secret model?

Then she turned to Charlotte's dressing room. "Char?" she called softly, laying her cheek against the door. "Are you okay?"

She heard a sniff inside the dressing room. "I'm fine."

Madeline shifted her weight uncomfortably. "Did I do something?" she whispered. She wrapped her arms around her waist as if she suddenly felt naked. Emma shook her head. "No, I did." She turned back to the fitting room door.

"Let's go," Emma said. "This place sucks. Plus, I saw an amazing bronze dress down at Castor and Pollux that will look perfect with your skin tone."

The door flew open. Charlotte's cheeks were blotchy and her eyes were wet, but she'd conjured up a blasé expression. Behind her, dresses lay in unkempt piles on the floor. Normally Emma would have hated to leave a mess like that for the shop assistants to clean up—she had, after all, been a working-class girl herself in her former life— but now she just laced her arm through Charlotte's and led her toward the door. Madeline rushed behind them, but

Emma twisted around and gave her a look that said, *She's cool, just give me a little time alone with her.* Madeline nodded, waiting a beat so she was a few steps behind them.

"So, Castor and Pollux?" Emma asked.

Char shrugged. "Whatever."

Emma watched Charlotte carefully as they stepped onto the down escalator, trying to read her. Char always carried herself with alpha-female confidence, but it must have been hard to run around with Madeline the Prima Ballerina and Stone-Cold Sutton Mercer, both of whom wriggled into the lower sizes on the racks with ease. Then there was Charlotte's mother, who ate nothing but grapefruit and who looked as if she could be Charlotte's older sister.

She placed a hand on her friend's shoulder. "Char. You know you're gorgeous, right?"

Charlotte's face didn't budge from its cool, aloof mask. She watched three elderly women on the lower level as though they were the most fascinating people in the world.

"Seriously," Emma persisted. "You've got an awesome body. I'd give anything to be able to fill out a V-neck the way you can."

Charlotte's face whipped toward Emma, her lips curling angrily. "Spare me, Sutton. If my body was so great, that stupid prank with my tags wouldn't have worked."

"Tags?" Emma blinked.

"Last year, when you guys spent a whole month switching tags on my clothes so I thought I was gaining weight?"

Emma's lips parted. They'd seriously *done* that?

"I got a real kick out of spending half my junior year thinking I was too fat for a size fourteen," Charlotte spat angrily.

"That was an awful joke," Emma said seriously. "I'm really sorry, Char."

The apology seemed to knock Charlotte off kilter for a moment, but then her expression became impassive once more. "It doesn't matter."

"Yes it does," Emma insisted. "It was a mean thing to do."

Charlotte sniffed. "It was your idea."

Emma winced. Of *course* it was Sutton's idea. "Well, it was a bad move, and I'd take it back if I could. I'm sorry."

Charlotte stopped in front of Williams-Sonoma and lifted up her shades to peer at Emma from under them. "Okay, I'm starting to think Celeste might be right. You've been replaced by a pod person or something."

Emma smiled. "No pod person here. I've just . . . well, I realized that I sometimes take you guys for granted. I hope you know how much you and Madeline mean to me. You're my best friends."

I hovered by my sister in silent agreement. Being dead had given me an entirely new perspective on the way that I had lived. I guess even ghosts could grow up.

"Wait a minute," Madeline said, stepping forward to join them for real. "Sutton, having a heart-to-heart? Is this the influence of Mr. Sensitivity?"

Charlotte grinned. "Mads, I think you're onto something. Are you going to start writing poetry now, Sutton?"

Madeline and Charlotte both giggled, startling a nearby pigeon that sat perched on top of a pretzel. "What about bottle-feeding kittens?" Madeline teased.

"Donating your hair to cancer kids?" Charlotte giggled.

"Taking up the guitar and going to open mikes?" Madeline added.

The tension had broken. Emma wrinkled her nose in mock irritation while Madeline and Charlotte leaned into each other, laughing. "You're both hilarious," she said haughtily.

"We know," Charlotte said, gulping down another giggle. She grabbed their hands. "Come on. I have to find a dress that can handle my hot body." Her voice was sarcastic, but the bitter edge was gone. "And Sutton . . ."

"Yeah?"

Charlotte shook her head. "Nothing. Thanks. Or . . . you know . . . I forgive you. Both of you." She looked at Madeline, too.

"Hey, I didn't apologize," Madeline joked, looping her arm through Charlotte's.

"That's because you're a bitch," Charlotte said lightly. "You can't help it. But I still forgive you."

They started down the mall together, my best friends and my sister. "Thank you," I whispered to Charlotte. "Thanks for forgiving me."

Everything changes. Sooner or later, we all grow up.

∽ 17 ᔐ

RESEARCHING AND REMINISCING

During free period on Wednesday, Emma slipped into the school library. The library was a bland, beige room lined with metal shelves and hung with posters of celebrities holding books. The librarian's name was Ms. Rigby, a youngish woman who wore cat-eye glasses and vintage cardigans. She had a perpetually aggravated air, as if she simply could not believe teenagers would turn down a chance to use actual research materials on a daily basis, but if she caught sight of a student perusing the stacks voluntarily, she immediately softened. Emma had been in the library a few times since her arrival in Tucson, first to check out materials for an English paper and again to get some books for pleasure reading. The librarian had treated her with skepticism at first—she seemed to know Sutton by her bad-girl reputation rather than by actual library attendance. But over the past few weeks she'd seemed to accept that Sutton Mercer had taken a bookish turn.

Emma had decided to follow Ethan's suggestion and do some digging into her mother's illness. It might not help her solve Sutton's murder, but at least it'd give her some insight into what Becky was going through.

"Hi, Sutton," Ms. Rigby said, smiling up at her from the reference desk.

"Hey, Ms. Rigby." She looked around to make sure no one could overhear her, though the library was mostly empty. "I'm doing some research for a presentation."

"What's the topic?"

"Uh, mental illness."

Ms. Rigby leaned back in her chair thoughtfully. "That's a pretty big subject to tackle all at once. Anything specific you're interested in?"

"Well, I'm interested in . . . violent cases." Her pulse quickened mildly just saying the words out loud.

The librarian nodded. "The violent ones are always the most interesting, aren't they?" she said. "I have to admit, Abnormal Psychology was one of my favorite subjects in college. Follow me."

The librarian led her to an aisle in the middle of the

nonfiction stacks. There were four and a half shelves full of titles like *An Idiot's Guide to Personality Disorders* and *Case Studies in Mental Illness*. A lot of the books looked outdated and moldy.

Ms. Rigby surveyed the shelves for a moment, then found what she was looking for. "*The Devil's Playground*," she said cheerfully. "It's about criminal insanity. It's a good read, and it should give you a good place to start your research if you're interested in that sort of thing."

Emma liked Ms. Rigby, but it was a little chilling to hear her talk about violent insanity as if it was a source of entertainment. "Um, great."

"The school board obviously doesn't let us keep anything too disturbing in the library, so you might also check the university. They'll have tons of stuff."

The librarian returned to her desk, and Emma looked back at the shelves. She grabbed a few more books and went to a table hidden behind the science fiction section, a little out of sight of the front desk.

She started to leaf through the first book. It contained lots of pictures, from woodcuts of the Salem witch trials to before-and-after pictures of lobotomies in the 1960s. She flipped to the index and ran her finger down the list of entries, unsure what she was even really looking for. Then she remembered something the nurse had said in the hospital: *It looks like a total psychotic break.*

She found the entry for *psychotic break* and flipped to the page indicated. *Psychosis is marked by a complete removal of the patient from reality*, it said. *Delusions, hallucinations, disordered thinking or behavior, and poor impulse control are all indicators of a psychotic break.* Then the book went on to describe a bunch of serial killers with names like the Night Slasher and the Dallas Axe Killer who had received instructions from the voices in their heads to kill and kill again. They murdered people they loved. Parents. Sisters. *Children.* All because a voice told them to.

Emma's stomach turned. Becky had been taken to the hospital because she'd pulled a knife on someone. Had a voice commanded her to do that? What might she have done if the security guards hadn't intervened?

"Good reading?"

Thayer stood over her, his dark hair falling shaggily into his hazel eyes. Emma slapped the book shut and placed it at her side, face down. A book on criminal psychosis didn't seem like typical Sutton Mercer reading material.

Thayer flopped down across from her, and suddenly a package of Twizzlers manifested itself in front of her nose. The sweet strawberry smell made her mouth water. "For you!"

"These are my favorite!" Emma exclaimed, taking a large bite of the sticky, sugary candy. Emma had always kept a package of the candy in her purse back in Nevada, hiding it from foster siblings with personal-space-and-property issues. "How did you know?"

His brow crinkled. "Because I used to bring them to you every day?"

Emma smiled at the thought that she and Sutton had the same favorite candy. So much about their lifestyles seemed so different, but maybe there had been some tastes they'd shared after all.

"What are you reading, anyway?" Thayer asked. He grabbed at the book and let out a low whistle of surprise. "Whoa. You have a dark side I didn't know about."

"Is that why you're here? To find out about my dark side?" Emma asked.

Thayer nodded. "Obviously. I'm stalking you."

Emma felt her cheeks getting warm under Thayer's gaze. *He thinks he's looking at Sutton, not me*, she reminded herself. A tickle of curiosity stirred in the back of her mind. Thayer had seemed so unhappy and brittle when she first met him, and it still surprised her to see this friendly, sweet side of him. Then she remembered something and cleared her throat.

"Do you remember that day at the fair when you won me the big Scooby-Doo?" she asked.

His eyebrows shot up in surprise. "How could I forget? I only threw rings at bowling pins for three hours to get the stupid thing."

"Laurel reminded me about it the other day," Emma said softly. "It was really . . . *sweet*."

Thayer frowned. "You said it was stupid. You said carnival animals were full of lice."

"Oh please, I loved it," Emma murmured. For a moment she imagined herself as Sutton, receiving the stuffed animal, rolling her eyes to keep her diva reputation intact but later laying her cheek against the cheap plush toy and smiling at the thought of Thayer. She felt sure that her sister had secretly swooned over the gesture.

An image came to me of the Scooby-Doo sitting on my bedspread. Thayer and I had loved each other so intensely, but we'd only been together a short time. It just wasn't fair.

Thayer reached across the table for Emma's hand. For a split second she let him curl his fingers around hers—but then she pulled quickly away.

He flushed. "Sorry," he said. "Old habits die hard."

She was spared having to say anything else when Celeste, idly shuffling a deck of cards, emerged from behind a bookshelf. She was wearing a green lace jacket over a short, shapeless gray dress, and a large purple stone on a lanyard hung around her neck. The rings on her fingers glittered as she played with the cards. She stopped when she saw Sutton and Thayer. "Hell*oooo*," she said, drawing out the word.

SARA SHEPARD

"What do you want?" Emma asked, frowning. She wasn't in the mood to hear more about her damaged aura today.

Celeste smiled at Thayer, her expression looking like it was somehow filtered through a soft-focus camera lens. "I don't know if I've met you. Are you Sutton's boyfriend?"

Thayer coughed and glanced at Emma awkwardly. "I'm Thayer," he said, holding out his hand.

Celeste didn't shake it. She slid next to Thayer and looked at Emma unblinkingly. "Sutton," she said finally, "I think I've been sent here to give you a message."

Thayer widened his eyes, clearly enjoying this. Emma remembered he'd said that Celeste had a *celestial body.* Typical guy. "A message?" she challenged. "Really? Who from?"

"From the universe." Celeste's gaze was distant. "I was heading toward the Student Center to meet Garrett when I felt an undeniable urge to come in here. I don't know why—I wasn't planning to visit the library. But something guided my steps, straight to you." She leaned even closer. "I think I should read your cards, if you don't mind."

Emma stopped. She'd had her tarot read once before, when she and Alex had snuck into a New Age convention at the Cosmopolitan in Vegas. The psychic had been a slender woman with long dark hair and an accent that seemed to waver between Jamaican and Southern.

She'd told Emma that she saw family difficulties on the horizon—secrets and lies exposed, a death—but that in the end Emma would gain financially. She and Alex had laughed about it. At the time it'd seemed like a good joke, since Emma didn't have a family.

But she did now. And that family had difficulties in spades.

Emma chewed on her lip. She wasn't sure she believed in fortune-telling. But she was out of ideas. And maybe, just maybe, the cards could tell her something. "All right," she said. "Go ahead."

Celeste said nothing, just started shuffling the cards. Emma couldn't help noticing that, in spite of the faraway expression on her face, her hands moved with the speed and confidence of a seasoned cardsharp.

Celeste laid out the first card, which pictured a woman blindfolded and tied up in front of a row of swords. The drawing was simple and colorful, the woman's face mostly obscured by the scarf around her eyes—but Emma's skin crawled just looking at it. The woman was trapped, surrounded by blades.

"The Eight of Swords," Celeste said carefully. "It indicates that you are incapacitated. That your options are limited and you cannot see a way out."

Emma's hands started to tremble, and she hid them under the table. Celeste drew another card. Two dogs stared up at the man in the moon. The face in the moon looked strange and unfriendly.

"The Moon." Celeste turned her gaze up to meet Emma's, her face serious and sad. "There's madness around you, Sutton Mercer."

The words sent a shaft of ice through Emma's heart. The way she'd said it made it sound like it was Emma's fault, like she'd generated insanity. She shook her head almost imperceptibly as Celeste turned over the third card. She didn't need to have that one explained to her. The dark, skeletal rider carrying a black banner. That one was obvious.

"Death," Celeste whispered.

Emma realized she'd squeezed her fists tight against her thighs, and she concentrated on releasing them. She willed herself to open her mouth and say something cutting, to sneer at the whole process. But her entire life seemed laid out before her in cardboard. She couldn't bring herself to move.

The hint of a smile played across Celeste's lips. "The cards don't lie," she whispered. With that, she gathered up her deck and swept away.

Emma kept staring down at the table as if the cards were still there. Had something . . . *supernatural* just happened?

Thayer touched her elbow. "Don't tell me you believe in that crap."

Emma swallowed. "She was right, Thayer. About my mom."

He rolled his eyes. "She just saw what you were reading and made some guesses. She's trying to mess with your head."

Emma blinked hard. Of course. The books scattered around her were titled things like *Clinical Insanity* and *A Guide to Psychosis*. Celeste had played her. She breathed out, relieved. "Now I feel even stupider."

"You're not stupid," he murmured. "You're scared. But it's all going to be okay."

If I crowded as close to my twin as possible, I could almost believe he was speaking to me. That it was my face he looked at like that.

Emma shoved the books away from her and gritted her teeth.

We both knew what she needed to do: find out more about Becky, one way or another, and discover what our mad mother was capable of.

18

MOM, INTERRUPTED

As soon as tennis practice ended, Emma drove straight to the hospital and rode the elevator to the fourth floor. The pungent smell of air freshener stung her nostrils, along with a harsher, antiseptic odor. The hallway was eerily silent, as if the whole ward was bowed under the pressure of its own secrets and delusions. She tightened her jaw and strode to the nurses' station, her heart beating like a drumroll in her chest.

The young male nurse, bespectacled and prematurely balding, looked up from his computer screen. The reflection from his monitor made twin glowing squares in the lenses of his glasses. "Can I help you?" he asked.

She clenched her fist around the strap of her messenger bag. "I'm here to visit Becky—I mean, Rebecca Mercer."

He gestured to a sheet of paper attached to a clipboard. "Sign in."

The page was depressingly blank. Emma printed Sutton's name neatly. The nurse stepped out from behind the desk and read the inscription with a raised eyebrow. "You're the daughter, right?"

What was the right answer? *Sort of. Used to be. Just genetically.* Instead she just nodded.

"She's been asking for you," he said, jerking his head to indicate she should follow. Emma trailed behind him. "That's all any of us can get out of her. 'I want my daughter.'"

Which one? Emma wondered.

There was a large social room on their left, a half dozen people visible through the windows. Their eyes were trained on a TV tuned to *Dancing with the Stars*. A bathrobe-clad girl only a little older than Emma stood swaying in time to the music. A middle-aged woman sat by the window, her head in her hands. One of the patients in front of the TV, a man with gray, greasy hair curling down over his neck, looked into the hall and gave Emma a wink. His grin was missing several teeth. Emma hurried after the nurse, swallowing her almost palpable fear. For a moment, she wanted to run back to the elevator, back to

Sutton's car, back home. But she had to do this. She had to talk to Becky.

I drifted behind Emma, wishing I could warn her to be careful. This was not a good place. Maybe I was more sensitive now that I was dead, or maybe I was just feeding off of Emma's anxiety, but all around me I could feel sadness and rage and fear. It was even stronger now than the first time we'd come here—emotions buffeted me from all sides. I felt like a raw nerve.

"Sutton?"

A hand curled around Emma's bicep. A scream caught in Emma's throat. For a split second she was sure it was the gray-haired man from the social room, and a shudder of revulsion swept through her. But then her eyes refocused.

"N-nisha?" she asked.

Nisha's red-and-white striped uniform was immaculate, and her thick hair had been pinned up in a French twist. A few feet away rested a cart loaded with outdated magazines and beat-up paperbacks. Her lips parted in surprise. "What're you doing here?"

Emma swallowed hard. She hadn't planned on being seen by anyone she knew. How could she have forgotten that Nisha volunteered here? Ahead of her she could see the balding nurse waiting impatiently for her outside Becky's room. She leaned toward Nisha's ear.

"I'm . . . visiting a friend. But this has to be a secret.

Please don't tell anyone you saw me here. I'll explain later."

Nisha nodded. She opened her mouth as if to say something else, then seemed to change her mind. Emma turned back toward the male nurse, acutely aware of Nisha's eyes on her as she walked away.

Becky's room hadn't changed, except for the addition of a small vase full of irises and yellow roses on the side table. Emma wondered if Mr. Mercer had brought them. A fluorescent light flickered and buzzed overhead, and from the tiny attached bathroom came the erratic *plink* of a dripping faucet. A tray of mushy food sat untouched on the counter.

Becky sprawled across the bed, asleep. She was wearing flannel pajama pants and an oversized Arizona Wildcats T-shirt instead of the hospital gown, and her hair had been washed and combed, her fingernails scrubbed. But her complexion was still ashen and marked with deep shadows. Emma noticed that she wasn't tied to the bed— that had to be a good sign, right?

I felt a low boil of emotion roiling off Becky's mind. It was hard to sense what she was feeling—everything was all mixed up in her head. But through the confusion, one burning thought came through louder than anything else, repeated over and over like a chant. *I'm so sorry. I'm so sorry for what I did.*

"You have thirty minutes," said the nurse. He nodded at Emma and retreated down the hall.

Emma pulled out Sutton's iPhone, opened the voice recorder app, and pressed RECORD, then gently nudged the door shut with her foot. Becky's eyes fluttered open when she heard the *snick* of the latch falling in place, her gaze darting around like a wild animal's. She tried to sit up, but she seemed weak and uncoordinated. Then she saw Emma. Her eyes bulged.

"It's you," she croaked. "Emma."

"No," Emma said softly. "No, my name is Sutton."

"Oh." Becky's eyes went glassy as she laid her head back against the pillows.

Emma took a step toward the bed. A chemical, medicinal odor came off her mother's body. She bit her lip. "How long have you been in town?" she asked, keeping her voice low and controlled.

"A while," Becky slurred.

"What have you been doing here?"

A slow, strange smile crept across Becky's face. "Watching you, of course."

I shivered, looking down into that ravaged, slack face. Watching her because she knew she was Emma? Watching her to make sure she played me? Watching her and putting threatening messages under Laurel's windshield, choking her in the Chamberlains' kitchen?

Emma clutched the rail. "When was the last time we talked?" she asked. "When did we see each other last, I mean?"

Becky's mouth twisted downward. "When you were five years old, Emma."

The fluorescent light flickered again, its electrical hum deafening in the silence. Emma leaned over the bed. "My name is Sutton," she insisted softly.

But Becky's head rolled from side to side on the pile of pillows, her eyes far away. "You used to love doing my scavenger hunts when you were little. Did you like the one I left you at the hotel, Emma?"

"I'm Sutton," Emma said again, but Becky ignored her.

"Remember the princess dress I bought you at Goodwill? You used to dance around the motel room." Becky raised her hands as if she were directing music only she could hear. "You'd twirl around and around and around . . . so pretty."

Emma focused on breathing slowly, carefully. If she didn't, she might scream, or burst into tears.

"You were a good little girl, Emmy, but a bad little girl, too. You were too much to handle." A single tear rolled down Becky's sunken cheek.

Emma gritted her teeth. "I'm Sutton," she said. "My name is Sutton. So one more time. When was the last time you saw me?"

Becky edged up on the pillow. "At the canyon," she said, her voice suddenly steady, the words no longer slurred. "That night at the canyon."

Her hand grabbed Emma's forearm, her nails cutting into Emma's skin. A scream tore from Emma's throat as she tried to pull away. Becky's fingers clenched, her face staring and blank. Bubbles of foam gathered at the corners of her lips and trickled down her chin.

"Help!" Emma screamed. She fumbled to pry Becky's fingers away, but it was like a bad dream—Becky's grip just got tighter and tighter. The door flew open and nurses quickly flocked into the room. The man who'd escorted Emma earlier helped release her wrist. "She's convulsing," he shouted at the others as he pushed Emma back toward the doorway. Emma saw one woman deftly preparing a syringe, flicking it with her forefinger.

The place where Becky had squeezed Emma's arm throbbed, and I could feel it, too. Then, without my willing it to happen, the heat of my birth mother's touch blossomed into a memory. A memory of that night in the canyon, when I'd met Becky for the first—and last—time . . .

19

MOMMIE DEAREST

The woman's smile broadens as she reaches out her hand to help me to my feet. "Hello, Sutton. I'm your mother. Becky," she singsongs again. "It's so nice to meet you."

I stare at her outstretched palm. Something tells me not to take it. I try to get up on my own, but I stumble again, my shirt snagging on a branch behind me. I immediately curse my decision to come back here to this pitch-black, end-of-the-earth place. Why didn't I go to Nisha's, or call a cab to take me home?

I sneak a peek at the woman who claims to be my mother and take in her tangled hair, her glowing eyes, her jittery mouth. My stomach tightens the way it does when Thayer and I watch horror movies. The air crackles with tension.

"It's okay," Becky croons softly, kneeling down to me. Sticks and leaves cling to her torn clothes, as if she's been wandering in the desert for days. Then I see a shallow gash across her forehead and a smear of blood on her cheek.

"What happened to you?" I ask, pointing. My voice is pitched too high, like a scared little girl's.

Becky's hand flies to her wound. "Oh. Just an accident." She giggles cagily. "A little stumble." But it doesn't look like a cut from a stumble to me. It looks like the type of gash a steering wheel might make if one's head were to bash into it after ramming into a seventeen-year-old boy.

Down in the subdivision, the thumping party music stops abruptly. It's suddenly so silent I can hear my heart pounding in my ears, the quick and panicked sound of my breathing. The woman in front of me shuffles a little closer. "Sutton," she whispers, and reaches out an arm to stroke my cheek. "Look at you. You're so beautiful."

I want to jerk away, but I feel paralyzed. Her hands are cold, sandpapery. I can smell her sour breath. "You're so beautiful," she says again, the woman who thinks she's my mother. But she isn't. She can't be. My mother is someone else, someone beautiful and soft and tragic. Not this dirty mountain woman, this freak. For whatever reason, my father—or whoever he is—lied to me. Maybe he just wanted to mess with my mind.

Finally, my muscles cooperate, and I pull away. "I—I have to go," I say, climbing to my feet. "My ride's waiting."

Becky chuckles. "You don't have a ride." She's on her feet in an instant. She's quicker than I would have expected. "I saw your grandfather drive away."

I blink. "You've been watching me?"

She nods. "Oh, sweetheart, I've been watching you for years." Her voice is soothing, as if she's singing a lullaby, but her words are twisted. "I watched you when you were learning to swim, when you were a little girl. Wearing Mickey Mouse water wings for the longest time. I saw when you dyed your hair blond in junior high. I was at the regional tennis meet last year—I saw you play. You're amazing. And I saw you run off with that boy tonight—Thayer? Is that his name?"

The world feels unsteady under my feet. She knows everything. All this time, this weirdo has been a face in the crowd, an unwelcome guest in my life. White anger surges through my whole body. "You had no right," I hiss.

Becky recoils as if I've shoved her. "Of course I do. I gave you life."

There's something so matter-of-fact about the way she says it, that in that moment, I realize she's telling me the truth. I let the idea wash over me. It just makes me even sicker. "That gives you even less of a right," I growl. "You watched me instead of caring for me. And now you just show up randomly, in the desert, in the dark, alone, and drop this on me? What the hell is wrong with you?"

Becky squares her shoulders defensively. "This isn't how I planned it," she pleads.

But I'm riled up. I want to hurt her. I want my words to burn. I'm furious at everyone who lied to me—my dad, my mom, and this woman most of all. "You're no mother," I spit, the words dropping into the silence with a sizzle, like acid. "You're a liar, and I hate you."

"You don't understand," she whispers.

"You're damn right I don't understand, and I don't want to understand," I say. "I don't want to see you ever again."

"Don't you dare say that!" she screams, grabbing my arm.

I freeze. No adult has ever screamed at me like that, from the depths of her soul. Now her chest is heaving. She clamps down hard on my wrist and brings her face close. "They only told me there was going to be one of you," she growls, her mouth within biting distance. "Not two. You weren't supposed to be here, Sutton. You weren't supposed to come."

I stare at her. "Who told you?"

But she doesn't answer. "I was so afraid I'd break you. I break everything I touch." She's launched back into that chanting, lullaby voice. "But I guess it's too late. You're already broken."

"Get off me," I protest, straining against her, trying to push away. But she's so much stronger than she looks. Her wiry arms tighten around me until I can't breathe. "Stop it!" I scream. I can smell the sweat on her body and feel the hard bones under her skin. My gaze searches around me. I see the dark, open mouth of the canyon below.

She hugs me tight, but it feels as if I'm being embraced by a

*snake, squeezed and squeezed and squeezed and then swallowed
whole. I wriggle some more.* "Let. Go!"

But Becky doesn't let up. "My little girl," *she says close to my
ear. I open my mouth wide, trying to gulp some air, but all I get
is a mouthful of T-shirt. As her arms clench tighter and tighter, I
hear her words once more:* You weren't supposed to be here,
Sutton. It's too late. You're already broken.

My mother is here to kill me, *I think in terror.*

And then the memory evaporates into darkness.

20

THE ESCAPE

Becky writhed in her hospital bed, her eyes rolling back and her limbs flailing. She let out a keening groan. Emma staggered backward into the hallway. She felt something wet on her arm. Her wrist was dotted with half-moons of blood where Becky's nails had broken skin. Her cheeks were wet, too—not with blood, but with tears. Something had broken inside of her: The love, the hope, had withered away. Maybe Becky *had* killed Sutton. It didn't seem so difficult anymore, to conceive of her mother as her sister's killer.

I trembled from the memory I'd just recovered, fearing she was right. The crushing way Becky had squeezed me, the sad way she'd looked at me, as though saying good-bye for the last time. *You weren't supposed to be here. They told me.* She *was* hearing voices in her head—voices that told her to kill me.

Emma watched through the doorway as two nurses and an orderly surrounded Becky's bed. "Get her strapped down," said one of them, a middle-aged woman wearing pink-heart-print scrubs. The silvery tip of a needle flashed in her right hand.

A hulking, crew-cut orderly leaned over Becky, grunting as he fixed the leather straps around her wrists. But Becky was too quick for him. Like a cat, she slid away from under his grip, sinuous and fluid. When he grabbed her shoulders, she let out a shrill, tortured scream. The orderly glanced over his shoulder. "A little help?"

"On it," the nurse said, dropping the syringe on a tray. She grabbed Becky's bare feet. Suddenly, there was a horrible crunching sound, and then a scream. The nurse flew back, blood pouring from her nose. It took Emma a second to realize that Becky had kicked her. The orderly's grip loosened for a split second in surprise, and Becky sprang to her feet. She grabbed the syringe off the nightstand and wielded it like a weapon.

"Stay away from me," she hissed, her voice hoarse and raspy.

The orderly raised his palms. "It's going to be okay, Ms. Mercer. No one's trying to hurt you."

Becky looked wildly around the room. The nurse was still lying on the ground in a fetal position, clutching her nose. The orderly had taken a few careful steps toward Becky. She held up the needle higher, pointing it at him. "I'll do it. I swear I will." The orderly stopped and took a step back.

Emma froze. The hallway was empty and quiet. She was the only one here who might be able to intervene, to take Becky by surprise. She couldn't allow her sister's killer to escape.

Taking a deep breath, she lunged forward and made a grab at Becky, wrapping her arms tightly around her mother's skinny shoulders. Becky shrieked and threw Emma's arms off her, body checking her with surprising force. Emma fell to the floor. She scrabbled away as Becky appeared in the doorway, the syringe still in her hand. Becky paused for a moment, staring down at Emma with wide eyes.

"Sutton . . . ," she whispered, her eyes shifting to just above Emma—to *me*. Neither Emma nor I knew which of us she was talking to anymore.

Emma's lips parted. She wanted to move, but her limbs hung heavy and useless. Becky leaned toward her for another moment, then spun on her heel and, with a scream, ran toward the stairwell at the other end of the hallway. A confused babble broke out from the social room. One of the ward's inhabitants yelled, "Run!"

"Someone call security!" spat the nurse in pink-heart scrubs, staggering to her feet.

She and the orderly rushed past Emma in the hallway. The patients who had been watching TV were shouting, some of them crying and others bellowing curse words. An old man in a nightshirt went running out of his room toward the stairwell in his own bid for freedom. He was pinned by a muscular orderly and wrestled back toward his room. A siren started to whoop through the linoleum halls.

"That night at the canyon." Emma repeated Becky's words out loud. Just thinking about Sutton's last night alive had sent Becky into some kind of fit. Had it been guilt she'd seen on her mother's face, or something more like . . . excitement?

She thought about Mr. Rochester's wife in *Jane Eyre*, sneaking into Jane's room and destroying her things, setting the house on fire. Becky was a madwoman, and the Mercers had tried to hide her away just like Mr. Rochester had hidden his wife. Now, it seemed, she was getting revenge on all of them.

I break everything I touch, Becky had said to me at the canyon.

"Girly all alone in the hallway?" asked a creaking voice. Just a few feet away stood the leering man from the social room, the one who had winked at her. His stringy hair fell heavily into his face, and the white T-shirt he wore was blotched with stains. He grinned, revealing yellowed and chipped teeth, and started toward her.

Emma looked around frantically to see if anyone had noticed him, but the orderlies and nurses were in a froth of activity, running down the hall or yelling into the phone at the nurses' station. Emma shook her head mutely. He chuckled and stepped close to her. A ripe smell rolled off him. Up close she could see his eyes were almost black. They glittered malevolently.

"Girly shouldn't be alone in a place like this. She's too sweet. She gets everyone all excited."

Emma's back was to the wall. His breath was hot and rancid on her face as he leaned toward her. She turned her face to the side, squeezing her eyes shut. She could picture him, his face coming closer and closer toward hers with those horrible teeth bared . . .

"Mr. Silva, please step back. Ms. Mercer needs some space to breathe."

She opened her eyes to see Mr. Silva wobbling in front of her, looking up the hall to where two people had come in off the elevator. Nisha Banerjee strode purposefully toward them, followed by her father. Dr. Banerjee's white lab coat fluttered behind him like a cape as he hurried down the hall. Mr. Silva took a step back, looking abashed.

"I was helping," he mumbled.

Dr. Banerjee gently propelled him up the hallway toward the TV room. "We have the situation under control now, thank you. Go back to your room, please."

Nisha rushed over to Emma. Her eyes were wide, her uniform rumpled. A stray wisp of hair had fallen down her cheek. She looked like she'd been running. "I heard the commotion and went to get Dad. You okay?"

Emma nodded mutely. She swallowed, fighting to keep the hot tears just behind her eyes from spilling down her cheeks.

Dr. Banerjee turned to the girls. "Nisha, can you please go and page Sutton's father? He should be in orthopedics."

Nisha gave Emma another searching look, then stood back up and walked briskly away.

Dr. Banerjee held out a hand to help her to her feet. All around, Emma could still hear the shrieking of the patients, the quick steps of nurses in rubber soles. A walkie-talkie crackled. A nurse held the receiver a few feet away. Her face was pale as she stared at the device.

"I repeat, we can't find her anywhere," said the voice on the other end. "We've called the cops."

"This one has been a problem before," said the nurse. "Tell them to be careful."

Emma looked at Dr. Banerjee. "Will they find her? She hasn't gotten *out*, has she?"

The doctor cleared his throat. "Let's go somewhere quiet to wait for your father, okay?"

Weak-limbed and shaking, Emma followed Nisha's father into a conference room around a corner. Dr. Banerjee guided Emma to a vinyl love seat under a window. "Would you like some tea? Or a glass of water?" Emma just shook her head. Then he pulled a wooden chair from the conference table and sat across from her. Beneath his lab coat, which was spotless, she could see that he wore a rumpled oxford shirt with a coffee stain on the breast pocket. She wondered how many household chores he forgot to do—or just didn't feel like doing—now that his wife was gone.

"Your father has told me a little of your family situation," he said softly. "For therapeutic purposes, of course. So that I can understand what Becky is going through. I'm very sorry that you had to see your mother like this."

Emma nodded, glancing at the clock. Becky had been gone for five minutes. "She didn't *leave* the hospital, did she?" she asked again. "You have the place on lockdown, right?"

Suddenly, the door burst open, and Mr. Mercer limped in, looking terrified. He made a beeline for Emma and took her hands. "My God, Sutton. Did she hurt you?"

"No. I'm okay," she whispered.

He hugged her tightly. "I'm so sorry." Then he turned to Dr. Banerjee. "What could have triggered this? Sutton? Something else?"

Dr. Banerjee twisted his mouth awkwardly. "Well, I cannot violate doctor-patient confidentiality, but sometimes patients like Becky are at their most high risk just after making an important breakthrough. We have made excellent progress in our sessions in a short amount of time. She seems to be carrying a lot of guilt for something she deeply regrets. I believe Ms. Mercer might have brought on some of that extreme emotional distress by her visit tonight."

"Guilt?" Mr. Mercer frowned. "For what?"

Dr. Banerjee shook his head. "That I can't tell you. I'm sorry, Ted."

"But you're saying she was doing better? That she was making some kind of progress?" Mr. Mercer seemed confused. "Then why would she . . . escape? It doesn't make any sense."

"I did this," Emma said, her voice barely above a whisper. Both men looked at her. She looked down at her lap so she wouldn't have to meet their eyes. "I made her angry. I set her off."

Dr. Banerjee frowned. "Ms. Mercer, this is not your fault. Your mother is a sick woman. Her behavior is not normal. To be honest, I'm the one who failed. I shouldn't have allowed her to see visitors who I thought might distress her."

"He's right, Sutton," Mr. Mercer said. "I should never have encouraged you to come see her. She was here because she attacked someone—she's obviously unstable."

Emma appreciated their comforting words, but she knew they weren't the truth. They didn't know the whole story. They hadn't seen the expression on Becky's face when she mentioned the canyon.

More of Becky's words haunted me: *I've been watching you.* And now she was watching Emma. Watching her be *me.*

Mr. Mercer took Emma's arm and helped her stand. "Thank you, Sanjay. I think I need to get my daughter home now. She's had a rough day."

"Of course." Dr. Banerjee looked from Emma to her grandfather. "I don't wish to scare you, but I feel I should warn you. Becky is in a very precarious position right now. If we don't locate her soon, she may find her way to you, and I can't promise what condition she'll be in."

"You *have* to find her," Emma said. The thought of Becky loose, wandering the streets alone, coming for her, made her tremble.

"Don't worry, we will," Dr. Banerjee assured her. "But Sutton, please don't blame yourself. Often, for those with such severe isolation and mental disturbance, the ones they lash out at are the ones they love the most."

Emma didn't know what to say. Love? Love couldn't be a part of this. Becky hadn't looked at her lovingly. She'd looked as though she'd seen a ghost.

And maybe she had, I thought.

21

CALM IN THE STORM

Mr. Mercer walked Emma to her car in silence. Dusk had fallen while she was in the hospital, the last of the day's sunlight playing across the distant mountains. The parking lot was half empty under the yellow light of the streetlamps, but police cars surrounded the perimeter. A news van rolled up and reporters jumped out. Emma could just imagine the headline: *Crazy Woman Escapes from Hospital, Threatens Pedestrians with Syringe.* What sort of hospital allowed a madwoman to just walk out?

"Should I drive you home?" Mr. Mercer asked as Sutton's Volvo came into view. "You could leave the car here overnight."

Emma shook her head. "It's okay. I'll follow you."

Mr. Mercer nodded, pressing the keyfob to his SUV. Two short *bleeps* rang out through the darkness. "I never thought she'd try to hurt you," he said in a low voice.

"I know." She didn't blame Mr. Mercer for what Becky had done. He had just wanted what was best for Becky, and for Sutton, too. He'd probably had fantasies of his own about his daughter and granddaughter reuniting; of Becky finally coming home, healthy and happy and ready to be part of the family again. He'd been blinded to just how dangerous Becky really was. But he wasn't the only one who'd been misled.

"I don't know what's going to happen now," Mr. Mercer said, frowning. "Becky's unpredictable. She might skip town again. But Sutton, if you see her, if you even *think* you see her, tell me right away. All right?"

"Of course." She clutched her car keys so tightly they dug into her palm.

Emma drove slowly on the way home, following his taillights. Her head pounded and her muscles still twitched anxiously as the adrenaline of the past hour dissipated. She passed under a pedestrian bridge designed to look like a giant rattlesnake arched high over traffic, its fangs bared. Usually the installation amused her, but today it felt ominous, as if any minute it would lean over and swallow her whole.

Becky could be anywhere by now. And even though the cops were on the lookout for her, she had always been good at not getting caught. Emma had seen it dozens of times as a little girl—the way Becky could disappear in a crowd, the way she slipped past prying eyes. She could become a ghost as easily as snapping her fingers.

Somehow I didn't think she'd skip town. I had a feeling she would stay close. *Too* close.

Porch lights throughout the subdivision cut through the darkness that filled the streets. Emma had never noticed how many shadows there were, how many places for someone to hide. As they pulled up to the Mercers' two-story adobe house, she made out a tall, broad-shouldered form moving in the yard.

Thayer, wearing hiking boots and cargo shorts, was raking smooth river stones into one of the new beds Mr. Mercer had built before his accident. A deep white scar spread across his knee from his surgery. As the cars pulled into the driveway, he straightened up and waved.

Mr. Mercer waved weakly back at him before heading inside. Thayer leaned on the rake, watching Emma as she slowly got out of her car.

"You're really dedicated," Emma said, trying to hide the strain from her voice. "Almost done, huh?"

Thayer frowned in concern and put his hands on her shoulders. "What happened?" he asked.

Emma looked away. "Nothing."

"Come on, Sutton. I *know* you. Something's going on. What?"

Emma's lip started to tremble. Before she could stop herself, she leaned into his arms. The tears that she'd been holding back broke free and rolled down her cheeks. "It's my birth mother," she began.

And then the whole story came pouring out—Becky's attack at the hospital, her escape, her tendency toward violence. Thayer turned her arm to look at the marks from Becky's ragged nails and winced, then met her eyes.

"And they think she might come here?" he asked, looking stricken. "That she might attack you again?"

Emma took a shuddering breath, wiping her eyes with the back of her hand. "They don't know what she'll do."

"Why is she attacking you at *all*? You're her daughter." Thayer still hadn't let go of her wrist. His fingers were warm and reassuring.

"She's . . . sick," Emma fumbled, not sure how much to admit. "It's hard to explain. I know it doesn't make any sense."

Thayer narrowed his eyes at the street. "She'd *better* not come here."

Gratitude coursed through Emma's veins. "You're such a good friend," she murmured, squeezing him around the neck in a hug. Thayer held her close, his hands traveling

SARA SHEPARD

up and down her spine. When Emma stepped back, they laughed awkwardly and then fell into a silence. The tinny laugh track of a sitcom came through a neighbor's open window. Somewhere a few blocks away a dog barked.

Thayer shifted his weight. "Anyway. You should go get some rest." He glanced back at the yard. "I'm gonna finish up here and head home. And, Sutton?" he added, suddenly serious. "You know you can always call me if you need anything, right? I mean, no matter how awkward things are between us, I'll be here in a heartbeat if you need me. Okay?"

Emma looked into his deep-set hazel eyes, which had lit up with a soft intensity. "Okay," she whispered. Then she slung her bag over her shoulder and went into the house.

I tried to linger behind as long as I could, watching the boy I loved turn back to his work. Soon, though, the cord between me and my twin pulled taut, and I was dragged along after her.

22

IN HOT WATER

The next night, Emma and Ethan pulled into the parking lot of the Clayton Resort. The sprawling hotel was situated against the mountains on the outskirts of Tucson, far away from highways and city traffic and surrounded by the natural beauty of red boulders and flowering cacti. A thick forest of ironwood and mesquite enclosed the resort, protecting its patios and pools from any prying eyes—and providing the perfect cover for anyone who wanted to sneak into the hot springs.

I had broken into the hot springs dozens of times with the Lying Game clique. It was where some of our best pranks had been planned. It was also where my wonderful friends had grabbed me from behind, thrown me in the trunk of Laurel's car, and driven me to the desert to choke me with my own locket chain.

Ethan had been asking to go for weeks, and after the scene at the hospital the day before, Emma's need for relaxation had finally outweighed her reluctance to break the rules. Her body ached all over. The stress of the last few weeks had settled around her shoulders like a weight, leaving her back full of knots and her neck sore. The only thing she wasn't so eager about was traipsing off into the desolate, scary desert, but Ethan was with her.

"You ready for this?" Ethan asked as they walked across the parking lot.

Emma hugged Sutton's straw beach bag to her chest. She glanced around, trying to ignore the feeling that she was being watched. Every time she left the house she became hyperaware of all the hiding places around her, all the places Becky could be. "Uh-huh," she said uneasily.

Ethan, who was in a pair of red swim trunks and a T-shirt printed with an old Japanese Godzilla movie poster, grabbed her hand comfortingly. Emma looked around to get her bearings, then led Ethan down a narrow, unlit deer trail. The resort's lights twinkled occasionally through gaps in the trees, but otherwise it was dark. Scraps of clouds hung in the sky, concealing patches of stars. Emma's skin felt prickly.

"I hate not knowing where Becky is," she whispered.

Emma had filled him in on everything shortly after arriving home last night. Ethan had wanted to come over, but Emma put him off, claiming exhaustion. It was only partially true. She also didn't want Ethan coming over when Thayer was still in the front yard. She hadn't mentioned that Sutton's ex was helping Mr. Mercer out, and she didn't need Ethan getting all weird and jealous about it.

Ethan nodded. "Me, too. But I won't let her hurt you," he said firmly, taking her hand.

Emma bit down on her thumbnail, remembering the night at the movie studio when the note had appeared on her car. Whoever had left it had been listening to them talk—she was sure of it. That meant the murderer—Becky—knew that Ethan was in on her secret. Would Becky even hesitate to get rid of Ethan if she needed to?

The thought ripped through her like a bullet, and she stopped in her tracks. "Promise me that you'll be careful," she said urgently. "If you see Becky, don't do anything brave or stupid. She's dangerous. And I can't bear the thought of losing you."

"You won't lose me," he said. "It's going to be okay. As long as we're together, she can't hurt us."

Emma swallowed hard. With Ethan's arms wrapped around her so protectively, she almost felt safe. "Okay," she whispered.

Careful, I thought. *You can't afford to let down your guard. Becky is stronger and smarter than she looks.*

"Do you want to talk about it?" Ethan asked. "About . . . suspects? What to do about Becky?"

Emma felt a pang of guilt. As much as she needed to focus on the investigation, she had let it consume their relationship. Ethan deserved a night off from playing Nancy Drew. "Let's just be us for a little bit," she said, and her heart warmed at the sight of his face lighting up.

"Sounds good to me," Ethan said, kissing her lightly and melting the tension in her limbs. She leaned into him, loving the way their bodies fit together.

"Come on," he murmured, taking a step back and pulling her along the path.

The springs were in a small clearing, landscaped with red rocks and lit by floodlights positioned discreetly in the surrounding trees. Steam rose invitingly from the surface. "It's beautiful, right?" Emma said, turning to Ethan.

But he wasn't looking around, admiring the landscape. Instead he was staring at her so intently that she blushed.

"*You're* beautiful," he whispered.

She stepped forward silently and touched his cheek, falling under the spell of the still, peaceful evening. Ethan closed his long-lashed eyes, and she traced the line of his jaw, the perfect cupid's bow of his lips, his cheekbones.

He pulled her into his arms and kissed her, more

urgently this time. Her lips opened against his as his hand coiled into her hair. All other thoughts were swept from her mind. She ran her hands beneath his T-shirt, up the rigid V of his stomach muscles, before pulling the shirt off over his head. He tugged at the tank dress she'd thrown on over her bikini, leaving it on the ground with his shirt.

Their breathing was shallow and quick. She took him by the hand. Slowly, gazing into his eyes, she led him into the springs. The water roiled against her, too hot, almost painful at first. They sat on the stone bench, backs to the side of the pool.

"You're amazing, you know that?" Ethan finally whispered.

She rested her cheek over his heart, feeling its strong pulse in his chest. "So are you," she said. "I've never met anyone like you before."

"Guys like me are a dime a dozen," he teased. "What boy doesn't love poetry and astrophysics?" She laughed softly, but then his eyes became serious. "Emma, you're the special one. I can't believe I've found you. I can't believe you're mine."

"I'm glad you did," she murmured. "And I *am* yours."

He rested his forehead against hers, gazing directly into her eyes. He took a deep breath. "Emma . . . I love you."

Emma's lips parted. She pulled back, cupping his face in her fingers. "I love you, too," she whispered. It was all she'd ever wanted—to be loved, to find someone who understood her. To find someone she could share everything with.

They stepped into deeper water. Emma wrapped her legs around Ethan's waist, and he held her up, carrying her toward the source of the spring, where the water was warmest. She kissed him playfully—his neck, his shoulders, his mouth. His hand traced along the back of her head, moving restlessly in her hair, then drifted downward to find the knot tying her bikini behind her neck. He fumbled with it for a moment before she realized what he was doing.

"Wait," she gasped, catching her breath. She put a hand on his chest. Suddenly she felt exposed, and nervous.

Ethan bit his lip. "Sorry," he said, looking ashamed. He pulled his hands away from her. She stroked a damp curl out of his eyes.

"Ethan, I just mean . . . I want to, but not now. It's too public."

His eyes darted around the clearing, studying the rocks, the surface of the water—anything but her face. "Too public for . . . *what*?" he asked shyly. "What I mean is . . . do you want to . . . are you thinking of . . . I would love to—"

"Yes," Emma interrupted him. "I would love to, too." She'd been imagining her first time with Ethan ever since they started dating, though she hadn't been brave enough to confess it until now. She hadn't known if she was ready either. But now, knowing that he loved her, knowing that she loved him, she was suddenly sure.

"I want to share that with you," she went on. "I've never . . . never done that before."

"Neither have I," Ethan said. He cupped her chin in his hand, and she looked up into his eyes. "When the time is right, it'll be special for both of us."

They kissed a little more after that, but slower, without the same frenzy. Between the warmth of the water and the feeling of Ethan's embrace, Emma had completely relaxed. Overhead, stars shimmered in the clear desert sky. A chorus of crickets serenaded them from the nearby tree branches. *This was a perfect idea*, Emma thought. To let go of her fear for a few minutes, to forget about all of the heartbreak and fury and terror that Becky brought with her. What would she have done if she hadn't been able to share any of that with Ethan?

But as much as I hoped that Ethan could protect my sister, I was far from certain. Becky was unpredictable and dangerous—and she was out there somewhere in the darkness. If she had tried to run down Thayer that night in the canyon, would she try to get rid of Ethan, too?

23

HELP FROM AN UNEXPECTED SOURCE

Ethan's house was dark when Emma dropped him off. Some of the other homes on the block already had their Christmas lights out, the red, green, and white glowing colorfully against the adobe walls even though it wasn't even Thanksgiving yet. One family had a herd of fake reindeer on their lawn, complete with a red-nosed Rudolph and a sleigh full of poinsettias. But Ethan's bungalow was undecorated, even neglected. Paint flaked off the siding, and the porch had one rotten step Emma almost always forgot about. It creaked ominously under her feet.

"When can I see you again?" Ethan asked, his arms coiled around her waist.

"Tomorrow at school?" she teased. He kissed her on the nose playfully.

"Saturday?" he asked, hopeful. "We could rent a movie, or just look at the stars . . ." Emma smiled. That's how they had met—Emma caught him stargazing while she was at Nisha's party, the first night she was pretending to be Sutton.

"We have Charlotte's party, remember?" she said. He wrinkled his nose a little, and Emma laughed. "Come on, Mr. Wallflower, don't make me face it alone." Ethan had never been big on parties, but she'd been hoping that getting to know Sutton's friends better would warm him up to the idea.

"For you, anything," he whispered. He gave her another lingering kiss, and then slipped through the door. She heard the lock snap shut behind him.

Across the street, the Catalina Mountains loomed. She couldn't see it in the dark, but the entrance to the Sabino Canyon recreation area was in sight of Ethan's porch. Just the thought of it made her skin crawl. It was where she'd waited for Sutton when she'd first come to Tucson, full of anticipation. It was also where her sister had spent the last night of her life. She shivered, feeling as if the canyon itself were watching her, a dark and malevolent presence. She didn't believe in ghosts, but something about the area felt menacing. Maybe Becky was out there.

The sound of footsteps interrupted Emma's thoughts. She froze, her hand on her car door. Just as she was getting ready to jump in and slam the locks down, Nisha stepped into the light. She was dressed in Hollier High sweatpants and a tank top that showed off her muscular shoulders. Her hair glinted almost purple in the darkness. She wore a pair of tortoiseshell Guess eyeglasses and no makeup. It looked as if she'd been getting ready for bed.

"Hey," Nisha said. "Sorry. I didn't mean to scare you."

Emma exhaled, then laughed nervously. "You didn't. I'm just a little on edge, I guess."

"From hanging out with Ethan?"

"Yeah—I mean, *no*, of course not. For other reasons. But yeah, Ethan and I were hanging out." Just saying his name brought a smile to her lips.

Nisha shook her head. "You guys are the weirdest couple of all time."

"Why do you say that?"

The motion-sensor light in the Banerjees' driveway shut off, and they were left in the dark. Nisha cleared her throat. "Sorry. Forget I said it. Anyway, I saw your car and just wanted to make sure everything was okay. I mean, after all the craziness at the hospital."

Emma stared down for a moment, picking nervously at the fabric of her still-damp tank dress. "The woman who escaped yesterday is my birth mom. Your dad's been treating her." She shifted her weight and blurted out the thought that had been bothering her more than any other. "Nice genetics, huh?"

Nisha's eyes were soft behind her glasses. "What's wrong with her?"

"I'm not really sure," Emma replied. She was grateful for the darkness. It would have been too hard to talk about this if Nisha could see her face. "I mean, she's obviously crazy. You don't end up in the psych ward unless you're crazy, right?"

"Crazy's not exactly the word I'd use," Nisha said carefully. "People have all kinds of problems that land them in treatment."

"Well, whatever her problems are, I'm apparently one of them." Emma sighed. "Nisha, would you mind not telling anyone about this? No one knows any of it—that I've met my birth mom, or what she's like. It's a secret between me and my dad."

"Of course," Nisha said. She paused, a shallow frown wrinkling her forehead. "Why did she call you Emma?"

Emma fidgeted, her pulse surging. "Um, it turns out Emma was the name she gave me as a baby," she said, thinking quickly. "My parents changed my name when I was a few days old."

Nisha nodded. "You got lucky. Emma sounds like an old maid. Sutton's way better."

Emma pursed her lips, but I couldn't help it. I burst out laughing.

"Anyway, I'm sorry if I was prying," Nisha said. "The whole thing just seemed really scary, and I wanted to make sure you were okay. It's not the same, but . . . I understand what you're going through. It's tough to watch your mom not acting like herself."

Nisha's mother had died of cancer last year. Emma had gotten the sense that it had been fairly quick, but surely Mrs. Banerjee had undergone treatment—radiation, chemo—that would have made her unrecognizable.

"What's it like, volunteering up there?" Emma asked. "I mean, isn't it hard, being around all that . . . insanity?"

Nisha took off her glasses and polished them on the edge of her shirt. "To be honest, I signed on for the psych ward because my dad works there," she said bluntly. "It's the only way I ever get a chance to see him anymore. He's always been a workaholic, but it got way worse after Mom died." She slid the glasses back on, making her eyes look bigger and somehow more vulnerable. "It's actually not so bad. I mean, there's lots of creepy stuff that happens there. But sometimes you get to watch someone getting better. It's like they come back to themselves or wake up from a really bad dream. It's pretty inspiring." She cleared her throat. "That sounds so cheesy."

"No, it doesn't," Emma said softly. "I think it sounds amazing."

The floodlight snapped back on. Emma flinched, squinting into the sudden glare. Nisha looked back toward her driveway. "Don't worry, it's probably just the neighbor's cat."

Emma exhaled heavily. "I've been jumpy ever since my mom escaped from the hospital. I just wish I knew exactly what was wrong with her. No one will tell me anything. What if she's . . . violent?"

Nisha nodded slowly. "Is there anything I can do to help?"

Emma bit her lip, glancing at Ethan's house.

"Do you know a way I could look at her records?" she asked. Nisha recoiled slightly. "I would never ask you to get them for me," Emma said quickly. "I know they're confidential. But if you knew *how* to get them . . . it would mean a lot. Maybe I could figure out where she's gone. Maybe I could find her."

Nisha tilted her head back and looked up at the sky. She fidgeted with a gold initial pendant on a chain around her neck, the letter *D*. Emma suspected it must have belonged to Mrs. Banerjee.

"I think I might be able to help you," Nisha said. She ran her fingers through her hair. "Can you wait here for a second?"

"Sure."

Nisha padded back across the driveway to the house. Emma heard her door open and shut. She leaned against her car, counting the seconds. Somewhere in the canyon a coyote was hunting, its short, shrill barks bouncing off the desert rock. The sound sent a shiver up her spine. She stared into the darkness in the direction of the park, trying to convince herself she had nothing to be afraid of.

A few minutes later, Nisha's footsteps sounded on the gravel driveway. "My mother's birthday is September seventh," Nisha said cryptically. Then she slid something shaped like a credit card into Emma's hand.

Emma opened her fist. It was a small white electronic passkey. The University of Arizona Hospital logo was stamped on the front.

She immediately pulled Nisha into a hug. For a few seconds, Nisha stood rigid and surprised in her arms. Then Emma felt her body relax as she tentatively hugged her back.

"Thanks," Emma whispered, stepping away.

Nisha nodded. "I've gotta go. See you at the party, okay?" She went back into the house. Emma imagined her going into the Banerjees' silent foyer, walking past all the things that her mother had bought for their household—a vase, a picture frame, a throw. The house must feel almost haunted.

I wondered about that. Did Nisha travel with her own invisible passenger? Did Mrs. Banerjee hover around her, cajoling and comforting a daughter who couldn't hear her anymore? Somehow I doubted she had the same kind of unfinished business I did.

Emma opened the door to the Volvo. As she was getting in, she saw a curtain flutter at a window in Ethan's house. A moment later, a light snapped on in the front room, and his mother passed by the window in a worn gray bathrobe. Emma watched for another moment, wondering if she'd been eavesdropping on her conversation with Nisha. Then she climbed in the car.

Emma sighed. Maybe asking Nisha for help with the files was unethical. But if it helped clear Becky, it would be worth it. And if it didn't—it might help her finally catch her sister's killer.

I agreed with Emma. With Becky on the loose, we needed all the information we could get.

It was time to learn some of our mother's secrets.

24

MEET ME AT THE PLAZA

Emma opened her eyes, blinking slowly in confusion. Her body felt strangely heavy, her arms like lead at her sides. She stared up at an unfamiliar tiled ceiling dotted with industrial fluorescent lights. The room smelled like floor wax and medicine. Strange monitors loomed over her bed, beeping and winking down at her.

She tried to sit up, but her body still wouldn't budge. She looked down, and her heart began to hammer. Instead of Sutton's polka-dot pajamas, she wore a thin white hospital gown. A plastic bracelet stuck to her wrist. Her arms and legs were strapped to the bed with stained leather restraints.

"No!" Emma screamed, pulling against the restraints. She thrashed back and forth, but that only seemed to make them tighter.

"I've been waiting a long time for this," said a familiar voice. Emma gasped. Becky. "I'm so glad you could finally join me."

A rustle of the sheets and a creak of the mattress springs indicated that her mother had crawled out of bed. Emma turned her head so hard that her neck felt like it might snap off, but she still couldn't see her. "Mom?" she whispered.

"They tried to keep us apart," said her mother. "But you and I are supposed to be together always, Emmy. And now we can be."

"This is a mistake," Emma said, struggling again. "I don't belong here."

"Of course you belong with your mother," said Becky soothingly. "Don't worry. You're here now, and I'll take care of you. Then you'll realize."

"Realize what?" Emma asked. Becky didn't answer. "Mom?"

"It was so hard to watch you bounce from foster home to foster home." Her mother's voice sounded sad, tremulous. It was closer now. "I hated to see you so lonely. So miserable. All you ever wanted was a family."

Emma lay in breathless silence.

"You thought that I abandoned you, but I was watching over you all this time. And I know. A mother always knows. I had a plan, and it worked. You waited patiently like a good little girl, and now you have a family."

Emma shook her head frantically, straining against her bonds. "I didn't want to get a family this way," she insisted. "I never wanted to hurt anyone."

"People get hurt every day," Becky whispered into her ear. "Do you have any idea how much it hurt to give birth to twins? I never knew there was going to be two of you. There wasn't supposed to be two. But that's okay. I've corrected the mistake."

"Mom, stop," Emma said, writhing again. "Please tell me you didn't do this."

Becky's face suddenly appeared in front of her, more skeletal than ever. Her eyes were sunken and hollow, her lips thin and bloodless. She smiled down at her daughter sadly. A gnarled hand reached down to stroke Emma's hair off her forehead, a gesture Emma remembered from when she was a little girl.

Then Becky picked up a pillow from the bed next to Emma and cradled it almost like a baby.

"Honey, you don't always get what you wish for," she said. Then, still smiling, she pushed the pillow down onto Emma's face.

Emma screamed into the pillow. She tried to shake off

Becky's weight, but the cuffs on her wrists and ankles cut into her skin. Multicolored spots danced against the backs of her eyelids. Her lungs burned, and her mind went fuzzy, until the world around her became shiny and transparent. And there, in that surreal space somewhere beyond vision, she saw a girl around her own age. The girl was shouting something. She was pretty, with long brunette hair and blue eyes. Was she seeing . . . herself?

No. She was seeing *me*. "Emma," I yelled.

Emma saw the girl's lips move, but she couldn't distinguish the words. Somehow, though, she knew that this was Sutton. Emma gazed at her sister's face, so like her own. Then she felt a peaceful sense of detachment, as if she was deep underwater. *Wait for me, Sutton*, she thought. *I'm coming*. At least she would be with her sister now. Becky had seen to that.

Her lungs gave a final, desperate heave. Then she sat, bolt upright, in Sutton's bed. In Sutton's pajamas, in Sutton's house. It was Saturday morning. The sheets had wound around her arms and legs so tight she could barely move. Daylight streamed in through the window.

Still breathing heavily, she grabbed Sutton's robe and stepped into the bathroom connecting her room to Laurel's. Locking the door, she turned on the water as hot as it would go. Steam filled the little pink-and-white room. She pulled the shower curtain aside and stepped in.

It was just a dream, she kept repeating to herself. But didn't scientists always say that dreams revealed the truths that the waking self couldn't face? Had her dream shown her the real truth about Becky? She wished she could talk to Sutton, just for a minute, so that her twin could tell her the name of her killer.

But I don't know either, I thought sadly.

Emma scrubbed angrily at her skin with a pink loofah, trying to wash away the memory of the nightmare. By the time she'd dried her hair and decided on fire-engine red skinny jeans and a white T-shirt, she was feeling a little better, though the dream still clung to the back of her mind like a piece of cellophane. She trotted downstairs to the kitchen, hoping that a glass of orange juice and some breakfast might help clear her head.

Mrs. Mercer sat at the table, sipping a cup of tea and reading the wedding section like she did every lazy Saturday morning. Mr. Mercer was finishing the dishes while Laurel dried them and put them away.

"There you are," Mrs. Mercer said, glancing up over her reading glasses. "I was just about to knock and see if you were moving."

"We saved you a waffle," Laurel added, sliding a plate toward Emma.

Laurel and I had always had a tacit agreement not to talk about carbs or calories on Saturday mornings, when our parents would make pancakes or French toast or my mom's special cream cheese blintzes. Emma smiled and reached for the syrup.

"We thought we'd go to the farmers' market after breakfast," Mr. Mercer said. "I'll throw together a ratatouille tonight if I can find some decent vegetables."

Emma took a bite of her waffle, considering. She had wanted to go straight to the hospital today to find Becky's records. But after the nightmare she'd just had, she didn't think she could face it quite yet. The sun shone in through the window, and a crisp fall breeze ruffled the curtains. It was a beautiful day for a family excursion. "Sure," she said. "Let's do it."

Half an hour later, the family piled into the SUV. Mr. Mercer turned the radio to a fifties station as he drove along the back roads toward the market. The weekly Tucson farmers' market was in a stone plaza adjacent to an old, mission-style church. Eucalyptus trees perfumed the air, and a fountain splashed musically at the center. Booths covered in checkered picnic cloths were overflowing with fresh produce—zucchini and summer squash, apples and oranges and pears, a rainbow of bell peppers. A young couple with a double stroller stood outside a carpenter's booth, examining the hand-painted wooden toys on display. The line for the organic coffee shop across the courtyard snaked almost to the church steps.

Mr. Mercer immediately approached a man in a Grateful Dead T-shirt selling tomatoes on the vine and began haggling over prices. Mrs. Mercer sampled various eco-friendly cosmetics, chatting happily with the saleswoman, who reminded Emma a bit of an older, friendlier version of Celeste with her all-linen outfit and her stacks of rings.

"We shouldn't have had breakfast," Laurel said, eyeing a booth of mini crackers and cheeses. Emma examined a jar of fresh olive tapenade, thinking back to her picnic with Ethan. The memory made her smile. "Um, hello? Earth to Sutton?" Laurel said, waving her hand in front of Emma's face. "What planet are you on?"

"Just thinking about Ethan," Emma confessed.

"Cute." Laurel nudged her playfully. "So I was wondering, can I borrow your liquid eyeliner for the party tonight? I want to do a retro cat-eye thing."

"Of course," Emma said. "Are *you* taking anyone to the party?"

"Yeah, Caleb and I are trying again," Laurel said, turning pink. "I kind of dropped him when Thayer came back. But I told him that was all over."

"He seems really sweet," Emma offered. Laurel and Caleb had started dating right before Halloween, and Laurel had been really into him—until Thayer reentered the picture.

"He is." Laurel smiled. "I'm glad he forgave me."

"I wish Ethan would get over the whole Thayer thing, too," Emma said, hoping it wasn't too weird to talk about this with Laurel. "I really do want to be friends with Thayer, but whenever I talk to him, it feels like I'm sneaking around behind Ethan's back."

Laurel adjusted the gold tennis bracelet on her wrist. "That's because you and Thayer can't be friends," she said matter-of-factly. Emma blinked. "Oh, come on," Laurel pressed. "Just because you first dated him as a prank doesn't mean we don't all know that you two were crazy about each other. And Thayer's *still* in love with you. Those kinds of feelings . . . they don't go away easily. Maybe ever."

Emma shook her head, sputtering. Sutton had first dated Thayer as a Lying Game prank? That was news. "You're crazy. Thayer's not still in love with me."

"Whatever you say." Laurel reached for a plastic bag and filled it with a few pomegranates. Emma looked away, out across the plaza, so she wouldn't have to meet Laurel's eyes.

And that was when she saw a woman with wild black hair, too-skinny arms, and a threadbare T-shirt sitting on a park bench on the other side of the plaza. Becky. A large family passed in front of Emma, and by the time they moved past, Becky had vanished.

Without thinking, Emma jumped to her feet, threw

her purse into Laurel's arms, and took off into the crowd. She passed a man wearing bright purple suspenders selling homemade ice cream in flavors like salted caramel fudge and ginger pear, then tore through a group of teenagers.

"Hey, watch it!" A girl riding a bike with yellow streamers swerved to avoid Emma, but Emma barely even flinched.

"Sorry," she mumbled, still turning frantically around, trying to see where Becky had gone.

There. She was walking toward the farthest row of booths. Her sneakers were held together with duct tape and didn't match. Her hair was in pigtail braids, just how she used to do Emma's hair before school every morning. Emma felt a pang in her chest. Becky looked so helpless—and innocent. Could she really be capable of murder?

Emma pushed through a group of college girls in front of a vegan candy booth, almost stepping into the open guitar case of a stubble-chinned street performer. "Mom!" she yelled. Several women looked her way but then turned back when they realized it wasn't their daughter yelling. "Becky!"

Emma knew this was her last chance. She broke free from the crowd, running past an upscale pizza restaurant and a gallery that sold Hopi artwork, almost colliding with Becky from behind. She grabbed her mom's arm and yanked her back.

"What are you . . ." The question died on her lips. The woman Emma had stopped was only a few years older than herself. She had a safety pin through her nose and deep purple shadow on her eyelids. Her T-shirt advertised a band called the Pukes, and up close Emma could see tattoos through the cigarette burns in the fabric.

She let go of the stranger's arm.

"I'm so sorry. I thought you were someone else," Emma muttered.

"Clearly," the woman said, her voice ragged with hostility. "Keep your hands to yourself."

Emma turned dazedly away in time to see Laurel running to meet her. The punk girl swore under her breath and stalked away.

"Who was that?" Laurel asked when she'd caught her breath.

"It was . . . I thought it was Rose McGowan." Emma stood numbly in place. "I wanted to get her autograph."

Laurel gaped at her in disbelief. "Why would Rose McGowan be wandering around the Tucson farmers' market in November?"

"Well, obviously, she wasn't," snapped Emma. Her throat ached and she felt as if she was choking—it took her a minute to realize she was fighting back a sob. She took her purse back from Laurel. "Come on, we'd better get back."

She turned on her heel and strode back to the plaza without another word. Laurel chased after her.

"I think you're cracking up," Laurel muttered.

Emma was starting to agree with her. She put her hand in her purse and felt the outline of the hospital key card. Nightmare or no, she had to act. If she sat around waiting any longer to see what Becky might do, she'd end up going crazy herself.

She had to keep it together. Her life depended on it—and any hope I had for justice depended on it, too.

∽ 25 ∾

FILE M FOR MURDER

Emma stepped off the elevator into the psych wing that afternoon for the third time. This time, though, she had a plan. She'd stopped on the basement level first, using Nisha's passkey to get into the laundry so she could borrow a volunteer's uniform. The only one she could find was a size too small, so it looked more like a naughty nurse costume, the red-and-white fabric clinging to her curves. She'd tied her hair back in a tight bun and wiped away all her makeup in the hope that the nurses wouldn't recognize her as the girl who'd caused so much trouble earlier that week. Last but not least, she put on a pair of black-framed reading glasses she'd found on Mr.

Mercer's bedside table. If it worked for Clark Kent, it'd work for her.

None of the nurses reacted as she passed the station, barely even glancing up from their filing and typing. The ward was as quiet as ever, a silence heavy with drugged sleep and barely suppressed panic. Emma heard a voice in one of the bedrooms chanting a children's rhyme. "Ring around the rosy, a pocket full of posies. Ashes, ashes . . ." The person trailed off into garbled laughter, or maybe it was sobs. Emma couldn't tell. She forced herself not to walk too quickly away from the sound. She was supposed to look like she belonged here.

The now familiar pulse of the ward's emotions thudded dully around me. It felt like quicksand, pulling me down. I hovered close to my sister, clinging to her thoughts and feelings, trying to stay afloat.

As she passed the common room, she saw the same blank faces angled toward the television set, the same dark-haired woman rocking herself violently in the corner. Mr. Silva sat in the armchair he'd occupied two nights earlier. His eyes met hers and narrowed suspiciously. She held her breath, half expecting him to get out of his chair, to come toward her sniffing like a dog.

But after a moment, he turned back to the television set, his black eyes losing focus. She wiped the sweat off her forehead and kept moving.

Around a few more corners she found it: a wooden door labeled RECORDS. She swiped her card against the reader and heard the lock click. Glancing up the hallway to make sure no one had noticed, she slid in and shut the door behind her.

The light fluttered on, revealing a narrow closet filled with dusty metal cabinets reaching from floor to ceiling. Carefully typed alphabetic labels were affixed to the front of each drawer. Emma took a moment to listen to the room's deep silence, her blood pounding in her ears. For better or worse, she was moments from finding out the truth about her mother.

She traced her fingers over the letters on the cabinets until she found a drawer labeled L–N. She gave the drawer a firm tug. It didn't budge.

Then she noticed the LED screen blinking on the top of the cabinet. PLEASE ENTER CODE, read the message. She stared blankly at it. What was it Nisha had said? *My mother's birthday is September seventh.* Emma reached a trembling finger up to type 0907 on the keypad. The drawer slid smoothly open.

Inside, it bulged with files, each one packed with documents, forms, and even photos. Emma scanned the labels quickly, trying to get her bearings in the dense forest of alphabetized folder tags. Her eyes darted over a particularly fat file. Then she did a double take. Her gaze shot back to the file. "Landry," she whispered.

She thought of Ethan's mother shuffling past the living room window, wearing a threadbare robe. She'd had cancer . . . but did she also have psychological issues? Before Emma could stop herself, her fingers reached for the file and pulled it out. Her breath caught in her throat when she saw the patient's first name printed precisely on the cover. It wasn't Mrs. Landry's file at all. It was Ethan's.

Emma's fingers tightened around the edge of the manila folder. Maybe it was a different Ethan Landry. It had to be a common name. There had to be an explanation.

Deep in her gut, though, she knew. This was Ethan's file. *Her* Ethan.

Ethan had told her not to come here, and now she knew why. What was in it? What had he hidden from her? Suddenly Emma felt angry and deeply hurt. She had shared *everything* about herself with Ethan—things she'd never told anyone, the worst stories from her foster homes, stupid childhood fantasies, her most private secrets.

Emma took a shuddering breath, then slipped Ethan's file back where it belonged. She couldn't betray his privacy, no matter how betrayed she herself felt.

"It doesn't matter," I told her. "It's not why we're here. Now hurry," I said, as we both heard footsteps approaching. Emma tensed. But whoever it was walked past the records room, and she let out a breath of relief.

Emma shook her head quickly to clear it, then flipped to the back of the drawer. MELVILLE, MENDEL, MENDOZA—there it was: MERCER. She pulled out the file and laid it flat across the drawer. On top was Becky's most recent admittance form and a scrawled copy of her prescriptions. Behind that were her session notes, stapled into a clear plastic folder like a kid's book report. They were written in Dr. Banerjee's neat, slanting cursive.

Patient is despondent and unresponsive, was all that was written under one day. Another note read:

> *Patient refers constantly to some "terrible act" she has performed. Have cross-checked with her police record, but nothing seems to correspond with her guilt complex. She will suffer these delusions of persecution until she is able to confess.*

Some of Becky's sketches were included in the notes, the same intricate and abstract filigree that filled the notebook Emma had found in the attic. *Patient's art shows both incredible creativity and crippling level of compulsion*, Dr. Banerjee had written on the back of one of them. *Increased dosage recommended.*

None of this was anything Emma didn't already know. She turned a few pages.

*Patient talks frequently about the daughter who was taken
from her. She seems convinced the child is being brainwashed
and fantasizes about stealing her away.*

The paper rattled in Emma's hand as she started to
tremble. A daughter taken from her? Did that mean
Sutton? Had she come back to Tucson in August to take
Sutton away from the Mercers? Had Sutton fought her—
and lost? Emma kept reading.

*The little girl was born twelve years ago this month. It seems
to bring back bad memories for Ms. Mercer and exacerbates
her episodes.*

Twelve years ago this month. That couldn't mean
Sutton or Emma.

There'd been another baby.

I inhaled sharply. Becky had *another* daughter?

The world spun around Emma. She clung to the file
cabinet, feeling as if she might fall and bring the whole
room crashing down on top of her. Rapid calculations
shot through her mind. Becky had left Emma when she
was five—thirteen years ago exactly. Right around the
time she would have realized she was pregnant again.

Jealousy and excitement fought for control in Emma's
mind. Becky had traded her in for this new baby. But the

note said that the girl had been "taken" from Becky. What if her second sister was suffering through the foster care system just as Emma had?

Emma and I had the same questions: Where was she now? Could Emma track her down? Was she safe?

Then Emma took a deep breath. She could think more about her other sister later. Right now she had to keep looking for answers. Flipping rapidly through the notes, she found the most recent session at the back of the folder. Something had primed Becky for that fit.

> . . . *finally, we are making progress in processing Ms. Mercer's guilt and grief. She admitted to me today that a few short months ago she actually met her first daughter in Sabino Canyon. It apparently did not go well. She still won't tell me the entire story, but something happened between them that triggered this most recent episode.*

Dr. Banerjee didn't seem to have gotten anything more specific than that. There were a few more scribbled notes, including several medication adjustments that looked increasingly dire to Emma's eye. She pawed through the pages, desperate for more.

A door banged loudly down the hall. She jumped and fumbled the folder, sending pages fluttering in every direction. Distant chatter grew louder as Emma lunged to gather the scattered forms. She shoved the folder back in the drawer and slammed it shut.

"I'll grab Mr. Lindon's file," said a female voice in the hallway. Emma took a deep breath, then cracked the door and peeked out. A short dark-haired nurse was coming around a corner. Emma couldn't leave now without getting caught. She looked around wildly, but there was no place to hide in the cramped space. Then her eyes landed on the door hinges and she realized the door opened inward. She flattened herself against the wall, silently praying the door wouldn't open hard enough to hurt her. With a soft click, the door swung back against her. She held her breath. She could hear the nurse humming softly to herself. Dust tickled her nose—the urge to scratch it was almost painful. She clenched her fists tightly at her sides.

A drawer slid open, and Emma heard the sound of paper rustling as the nurse shuffled files.

Go away, Emma and I thought together. *Get the files and go.* But the nurse seemed to be taking her time.

The door pressed back against her as another nurse stopped in the doorway, leaning against it. "Hey, Marliz, there's cake in the break room. It's Huong's birthday."

"Someone's got these files all jumbled," complained the first voice. Emma gritted her teeth. She must not have put Becky's file back where it belonged.

"Well, if that's the worst thing that happens today, we're in good shape."

Marliz laughed. Her voice was high and girlish. "I guess it's nothing compared to a breakout."

Emma could hear the second woman step into the records room, lowering her voice. "Did you hear the latest about the Mercer woman?"

The words sent Emma's body rigid. She bit down on the inside of her cheek.

"I heard that when they cleaned out her room they found a photo of her kid," continued the second voice. "You know, the girl who was visiting when she flipped out? Anyways, they find this picture tucked away under her mattress. Except she had scribbled all over the girl's face with a ballpoint pen, over and over until she ripped through the picture. Like she was trying to scratch her out or something."

"Oh my God. Do you think she's actually violent?"

"Who knows? I tell you what, Mar, I've been working on this floor for almost thirty years, and Rebecca Mercer is one of the worst I've ever seen. I don't understand why her family can't just keep her on her meds. Every time she gets off, it's worse and worse. We couldn't even get a complete sentence out of her this time around."

"Don't you think the daughter should know she's at

risk? A woman that crazy, there's no telling what she'll do."

"I agree, but supposedly scribbling on a photo isn't violent enough to merit breaking doctor-patient confidentiality." The woman sighed. "Found that file yet?"

"Got it," said Marliz. "Now let's get some cake before it's all gone."

The door swung closed. Emma kept her back to the wall and slid slowly down to sit on the floor, her heart racing.

The nurse's words echoed in her ears. *Like she was trying to scratch her out or something.* If the folder had been ambiguous, the photo made everything clear.

I had been a mistake, and our mother had finally figured out how to erase me.

26

YOU BETTER GET THIS PARTY STARTED

"That looks amazing," Madeline said, watching Emma smudge slate gray eyeliner along her lid. "I love that color on you."

The girls were in Charlotte's enormous bathroom getting ready for the party. The room was decorated in gray stone tile and Caribbean blue glass. Fluffy white towels hung from the racks. Collages of the Lying Game girls hung in heavy frames on the walls—Sutton, Madeline, and Charlotte mugging in front of a giant fiberglass cowboy, the Twitter Twins making ironic gang signs in cocktail dresses, Laurel carrying a laughing Sutton piggyback.

Emma blinked at herself in the mirror, her eyes

transformed into those of a smoldering starlet. Gabby sat at the vanity while Lili stood behind her, wrapping one of her sister's long blond locks around a curling iron. Through the open door to Charlotte's bedroom she could see Laurel zipping Nisha into her dress, the hot pink silk perfect against Nisha's dark skin. Madeline stood next to Emma in her bra and panties, applying a fiftieth layer of mascara to her already long eyelashes. Charlotte was downstairs, putting the finishing touches on the decorations.

"I could live in this bathroom. Like, just in this bathroom and never leave," Gabby said, looking around. Emma privately agreed—the room was bigger than some of her old foster homes. A Jacuzzi-style tub occupied a pedestal at one end of the bathroom, a mini sauna next to it. A shower with six different heads took up the opposite corner. The bathmats were thick and soft, and the whole room sparkled pristinely with the cleanliness only a full-time housekeeper could maintain.

"Ew," said Madeline, wrinkling her nose. "Who wants to live in a bathroom?"

"Well, maybe I'd build a separate bathroom off the bathroom," Gabby admitted.

I perched on the edge of the counter, filled with a wave of longing as I watched my friends. How many times had we done this before parties, gossiping and plotting pranks while we helped one another get ready? Watching my life through Emma's eyes, I'd realized how much we teased and undermined each other. It was nice to be reminded that we'd done things like this, too.

"Hold still," Madeline said, turning Emma to face her. She held up an eyelash curler and pressed the trigger a few times threateningly. Emma tried not to move as Madeline fixed her lashes.

"Is everything okay?" Madeline asked quietly as she pulled the curler away, looking curiously at Emma. "You seem tired."

Emma sighed. She'd felt shell-shocked and hollow since the hospital, unable to fully process everything she'd discovered. Becky had another daughter. Becky had defaced the picture of Sutton—or was it of Emma? And the most hurtful of all, Ethan had lied to her, had hidden something huge and important. What could Ethan have done to end up in the psych ward—and for a while, if the size of the file was any indication? Was it for something so awful he was afraid she'd be scared off?

She tried to smile at Madeline. In spite of everything, Emma was determined to have a good time tonight, to shut off the part of her mind that was stressing and just enjoy a few hours with her friends. More than anything she wanted to stop wondering what Ethan was hiding. She picked up the red plastic cup she'd left on the counter and took a long, slow sip of cranberry juice and vodka. The alcohol stung the back of her throat.

"I'm great," she said. "Getting greater by the second."

"Okay, then," Madeline said, though she clearly wasn't convinced. "To greatness!" She lifted her own cup in a mock toast.

Laurel peeked her head around the bathroom door. She looked stunning in the gold bandage dress she'd bought at the Saks sample sale. "Are you ladies almost finished? Some of us still need to do our makeup."

Emma stood up. "I'll go downstairs and check on Char."

On the way through the bedroom, she stopped to check herself out in the full-length mirror. She'd decided on a pale pink halter dress that gave her skin a rosy glow. It was maybe on the sexy side for Emma and the sweet side for Sutton, but it felt perfect for the tenuous in-between that Emma lived in now. She pulled on a pair of strappy gold Miu Miu heels and headed for the stairs.

Of everything in Sutton's luxe life, Charlotte's house was probably the *most* over-the-top thing Emma had seen. A sprawling adobe villa, it had an Olympic-sized pool, a six-car garage, and a bell tower that had been transplanted stone by stone from a two-hundred-year-old mission south of Yuma. Stunning views of the city were visible from every window. The marble stairs curved elegantly down into an entryway the size of a ballroom, where the girls had spent the afternoon hanging crisscrossing strings of globe lights from the high ceiling. On the top landing Emma ran into a guy wearing a leather vest over his bare chest who was setting up turntables. He didn't even look up as she stepped over the cords onto the stairs.

She found Charlotte in the kitchen, where they'd covered a table with Mrs. Chamberlain's best linen and sprinkled glittery confetti across the surface for an accent. Platters of food covered every inch—a sun-dried tomato and pesto torta, prosciutto-wrapped asparagus, garlic-stuffed olives, and fresh-baked pita wedges. She picked up a mini quiche and popped it in her mouth.

Charlotte glanced up when Emma came in. "You look mahvelous, dahling," she said, air-kissing Emma's cheek.

"So do you!" Emma exclaimed. Charlotte's emerald-green dress brought out her eyes. She'd had her hair done by a stylist that afternoon, in a classic updo with a few ringlets artfully arranged around her face. Her crystal dangle earrings caught the light and made her positively glow.

Emma held up her cup. "I seem to be empty."

Charlotte gestured toward the bar, which was almost as big as Sutton's bedroom, complete with four different wine refrigerators across the back wall. Dozens of glass bottles were lined up on the counter, along with mixers, limes, and even a blender. Emma fixed two cosmos, one for herself and one for Charlotte. She did it properly in a shaker, the way a cool older foster sister had once taught her. Through the French doors to the back patio, Emma could see the big-bellied keg by the light of the tiki torches.

Tucked into an alcove next to the walk-in pantry, the security system control panel flashed green. Disarmed. Not that it mattered if it was on or not, since Becky had gotten past it before. Emma's heart picked up speed at the memory of Sutton's killer strangling her in this very kitchen. Her hands shook. Couldn't she have one night off from worrying for her life? She deserved it.

"Bottoms up!" she yelled to Charlotte, then finished her drink in a single gulp.

A few hours later, Emma wasn't worried about anything at all. She and Brian Lloyd, cocaptain of the basketball team, had just beat Charlotte and Mark Bell in a heated game of beer pong out on the patio. When Brian challenged her to a victory tequila shot, she hadn't even flinched, just tossed back her head and downed it quickly, without salt or lime. "That's the Sutton Mercer I know and love!" Charlotte trilled, throwing an arm around Emma's shoulders affectionately. "Where have you been hiding?"

Emma shrugged and floated past Tim Sullivan, whose

father owned a string of sporting goods stores across Arizona and who was doing a keg stand as the entire football team cheered him on. Inside, a Jay-Z song was playing on Charlotte's sound system. Girls in tiny dresses were dancing in groups, or with their arms entwined around boys in button-downs and jeans. Emma smiled and waved at everyone, reveling in just how much *fun* it was to be Sutton.

She passed the Twitter Twins holding court in the kitchen, taking turns telling a juicy story to a group of rapt junior girls. Madeline was draped across Antonio Ramirez's lap on an overstuffed chair, whispering into his ear. Caroline Ellerby, an overeager freshman, came in the front door holding a tray of premade Jell-O shots. "Want one, Sutton?" she asked with a tentative smile. Emma grabbed a tiny cup of red Jell-O and slurped it carelessly.

Her phone kept vibrating in her snakeskin clutch, but she ignored it. It was probably just another text from Ethan saying he was on his way. She didn't want to see Ethan right now. She didn't want to talk to him. Or did she? Did she want to talk to him right away so she could tell him just what she thought of his little secret? She shoved the thought away and went back to the bar. Another drink might help her make up her mind.

Nisha stood in front of the array of bottles, measuring a precise amount of gin into her glass. She looked up just as Emma stumbled into her, grabbing her to stop her fall. "Whoa, girl. You okay?"

"I'm Sutton Mercer," Emma said, striking a pose. "I am fabulous." She reached for the vodka, but Nisha took the bottle before she could pour herself another cup.

"Slow down there, champ." Nisha laughed and poured Emma a glass of water instead. "Where's Ethan? Isn't he supposed to be here?"

Emma sipped the water slowly. The room spun pleasantly, pretty and bright, like a children's carnival ride. "Who knows? He's probably watching a meteor shower or something."

Nisha put her hand on Emma's arm. "Hey, is everything okay with you two?"

Maybe it was the alcohol, but before Emma could stop herself, words started spilling out. "Remember how you helped me find that . . . information about my mom?" Emma whispered. "Well, Ethan had a file in there, too. A huge one."

"Whoa," Nisha said, her eyes widening. "Have you talked to him about it?"

Seeing the alarm on Nisha's face made Emma's vision spin even faster, and she suddenly realized what she had done. Yes, Ethan had betrayed her, but that was between him and her. "Forget it. I'm sure it's nothing," she mumbled, pushing her way back through the crowd.

"Hang on, Sutton," Nisha called, but Emma kept going until she made it onto the patio. A couple of the boys were playing water volleyball in the pool, wearing nothing but their mesh shorts. Laurel and another girl were sitting by the hot tub, trailing their feet in the water. They beckoned her over, but Emma sank into a chaise longue instead. She leaned back and closed her eyes. When her phone vibrated again, she didn't even bother checking it.

At ten, Poor Tony, the bare-chested DJ Emma had run into earlier, started to play from the upstairs landing. The entryway flooded with screaming partygoers. Emma wandered into the crowd, the heavy bass vibrating through her body like a second heartbeat. She spotted Madeline and started to head in that direction, then realized that Mads was with a boy and probably wouldn't want to be bothered. She squinted—the boy definitely wasn't Antonio. Mads moved fast.

Emma took a step backward, stumbling right into a tall guy with perfectly gelled blond hair. He gave her a withering look as she caught her balance. Garrett.

"Sorry," she yelled over the music. He just rolled his eyes and leaned over to Celeste, who was standing next to him, wearing an ikat-print baby-doll dress and velvet stockings. She shook her hair, which was curled into thick ringlets, and laughed. Then she wrapped her arms around his neck and danced close to him, staring pointedly at Emma.

The world started to tilt dangerously. Suddenly, Emma wanted nothing more than to escape, to go somewhere away from all the noise and chaos. The music was starting to feel less like a heartbeat and more like a hammer pounding at her skull. She tripped toward the front door, ducking as she passed Gabby and Lili to avoid being pulled into their hyperactive dance circle. She slipped out onto the porch and sighed in relief at the feel of the cool night air on her skin.

Even with the massive oak door shut, she could still hear the rumble of the music and the screams of the crowd. But compared to the rest of the party, the porch, tiled in elegant stone and covered with enormous potted plants, was an oasis of calm. Moths threw themselves again and again at the lights in antique iron sconces, battering them with their tiny bodies.

Emma closed her eyes and rested her head against one of the pillars. Garrett's expression had shattered her good mood, and she suddenly felt sober.

Then she heard it. A soft rustle, the sound of someone moving nearby. She froze, rooted to the spot. Someone was on the porch with her.

"Mom?" she whispered, peering into the shadows where the noise had come from.

"Go back inside!" I hissed at her. "Hurry!"

But it was too late. A tall form moved out from the darkness, laughing softly. Both Emma and I screamed, my voice inaudible to everyone but me, hers swallowed by the noise from inside.

No one would hear us.

27

A VOICE IN THE DARK

Emma scurried backward into a terra-cotta planter. Her pulse thudded loudly in her ears. Should she run out toward the street, or back inside? The alcohol slowed her thoughts, keeping her in dangerous indecision. She took another step backward. This was it. She was about to die.

"I didn't mean to scare you, Sutton. It's just me," said a male voice from the shadows.

Thayer stepped forward into the light. He looked gorgeous in a blue Hugo Boss button-down and khaki shorts.

Emma exhaled in relief.

I watched enviously as he reached out to take Emma's

arm and led her over to the porch swing. They sat down next to each other in friendly silence.

"What were you doing out here?" Emma finally asked. Her heart still hadn't slowed down to its resting rate.

Thayer smiled sadly, holding up his Coke can. "Turns out being in recovery makes you kind of a buzzkill."

Emma thought about what it must be like for Thayer, showing up to a party like this. It wasn't easy resisting that kind of pressure, listening to drunken teenagers wreaking havoc inside, knowing he couldn't really be one of them.

Thayer pushed them gently back and forth on the swing, his feet on the floor. Overhead Emma could hear the squeaking call of hunting bats. The slow rocking of the swing calmed her nerves. She had to get a grip. What if he *had* been Becky? Screaming and tripping over furniture wouldn't exactly do her any good. She needed to always be ready for anything. She shouldn't have let her guard down, even for one night. She sighed. It just wasn't fair. She was so tired of being constantly alert. She wanted to be vulnerable, to be *normal*, just once.

"You feeling okay?" Thayer asked.

"Everyone keeps asking me that tonight," Emma said. "Don't I look okay?"

"You look perfect, as always. I asked how you *felt*."

She turned toward Thayer. It struck her that he was

probably the only person who would have pressed her on that point, forcing her to distinguish between appearance and reality. He gazed back at her seriously, his eyes bright against his tanned skin. She didn't know how to begin to answer. She hadn't felt like herself in weeks. Or maybe she had never felt so much like herself? The alcohol softened the edges of all her thoughts, so she wasn't quite sure what she meant until she said it out loud. Nothing made sense anyway tonight—not her and Thayer, sitting here on this bench in the cool November evening; not her friends; not even Ethan. Especially not Ethan.

She tucked a lock of hair behind her ears. "Do you ever feel like no one is really what they seem?"

Thayer's lips twisted ironically. "All the time. Why do you think I didn't tell people I went to rehab? I knew half of the people I thought were my friends would turn their backs on me." He gave a short bark of laughter. "I knew I'd end up alone on the porch drinking soda while almost everyone I knew pretended they hadn't seen me there."

Emma suddenly felt self-conscious. Here she was, smelling like beer while she sat next to a boy who'd won a hard-fought battle for sobriety. She fidgeted with Sutton's clutch, opening and closing the clasp.

"I just don't know who I can count on anymore," she said softly. "I keep getting hurt by people I think I know."

Thayer looked out over the wrought-iron porch

railing. The Chamberlains' sprawling front lawn looked like an elephant graveyard in the darkness, cars parked haphazardly across it. Someone had angled their Miata right into one of Mrs. Chamberlain's prize rosebushes. Emma wondered distantly how Charlotte would talk her way out of that one.

"That sucks," Thayer said, playing with the pop-top on his Coke can. It broke off in his fingers and he set it on the swing's armrest. "Maybe you need some new people in your life."

Emma bit her lip and gave an awkward little laugh. "The problem is some of them are related to me."

"Ah," he said. "Yeah, I know that story, too. Wouldn't it be awesome if you could pick your family?"

"I'll take Steve Carell for a dad and Tina Fey for a mom," she joked.

"Bart Simpson for a brother."

"Wednesday Addams for a sister."

Thayer smiled. He leaned back into the porch swing, his expression thoughtful. "You know, one of the things I learned in rehab that turned out not to be a total cliché is that you can't control other people. The best you can do is be honest with the people you love and hope that they'll care enough about you to listen. But you can't make someone be something they're not."

"That sounds very . . . adult," Emma said.

"Well, a lot of addicts act like children," he said, shrugging. "I'm just saying—you can't prevent other people from disappointing you. It's bound to happen at some point. We're all only human. What you *can* do is decide how you're going to respond to it, how you're going to deal with it."

Emma nodded slowly. It was good advice—she just wasn't sure it really worked in her situation. This was a murder investigation, and she had to fight fire with fire. She couldn't play a defensive game, not anymore. "It's all just so complicated sometimes," she said, wishing she could tell Thayer everything.

"Yeah, I know." He exhaled loudly. "Believe me. Living with my dad, there's so much I have to let go of. Sometimes I want to hit him, to punish him. I've done that, you know—before I went to Seattle, I took a few swings at him." He shook his head. "But that's just me thinking I can change him somehow. Make him sorry. I can't, obviously."

They sat there in the shadows, rocking back and forth, Poor Tony's music still shaking the house. Emma was sobering up quickly thanks to the cool air and the rush of adrenaline from thinking Becky was on the porch. But she was still tipsy enough to admire Thayer without feeling self-conscious. She kept sneaking glances at his profile, studying the curve of his cheek, the small scar along his jawline. She wondered if that, too, was a reminder of the accident in Sabino Canyon.

"Thayer," she whispered. He turned to face her, and the intensity of his eyes made her lose her breath for a moment. She coughed into her hand. "I never said this, but . . . I'm really proud of you." It was true: She admired Thayer's resolve, his strength. Even though she hadn't known him before, she felt that he wasn't the boy from the MISSING posters any longer. The boy who'd vanished without a word. He'd come back a new person. More than anyone else here tonight, he knew exactly who he was and what he believed. It was refreshing—especially after all the lies and pretending she'd been piling up.

"Really?" he asked.

"It takes guts to change," Emma said quietly. "To start telling the truth to everyone, and mostly to yourself. I know it's been hard for you. But the people who really care about you—we're here to support you."

She felt Thayer's warm hands, calloused from all the yard work he'd been doing, wrap around her fingers. "The people who really care about me, huh?"

Her cheeks burned. "You know, Mads, Char, Laurel. Your dad, even. We all care about you."

"Glad to hear it," he said softly, drawing her closer. And then, before she knew it, his lips were on hers.

For a split second, she leaned into the kiss. Thayer's

mouth was so soft and inviting. All she'd wanted to do tonight was let go of being Emma and become Sutton, even if it had to end at the stroke of midnight like a fairy tale. And in this moment, tasting the sweetness of vanilla Coke on Thayer's lips, the line between her and Sutton felt especially blurry. She moved unconsciously toward him on the swing, and his fingers slid around her waist.

As strange as this was for me, I understood Emma's complicated feelings, about the line between us getting more and more confusing. We were both sinking deeper into each other, in danger of losing ourselves in the process. Watching Emma live my life and feeling the thrill of Thayer's kiss on her lips was the next best thing to actually kissing Thayer myself. I couldn't even decide whether I wanted to throw the Coke can at their heads or cheer them on.

But then Emma pulled away from Thayer with a jolt. What was she doing? Just because everyone called her Sutton didn't mean she had turned into her twin. Guilt stabbed her like a knife. She'd betrayed Ethan and misled Thayer. All she'd done was break things right and left. *Just like Becky*, she thought bitterly.

"What the hell?"

An angry voice tore through her thoughts, and she looked up to see Ethan on the steps to the porch.

His eyes blazed in fury. His jaw was tight and clenched,

his fists opening and closing as if he couldn't figure out if he wanted to hit something or strangle it. Emma's hands flew to her mouth.

"Ethan," she exclaimed. "It's not what you think—"

"You," he snarled, ignoring her. His eyes were locked on Thayer. "You're dead."

Thayer barely had time to get to his feet before Ethan was on him, his fist landing square on the taller boy's chin. He gripped Thayer by his shirt and slammed him against one of the porch's pillars.

"Stop it!" Emma screamed. Blood trickled from a cut on Thayer's head. He rammed an elbow into Ethan's rib cage and Ethan leaned over, wincing. Thayer tackled him off the porch.

Poor Tony chose that exact moment to finish his set. Emma's cries pierced the sudden quiet, and the doors quickly flew open, the confused and rowdy crowd spilling out onto the porch.

"Fight!" someone yelled, catching on to what was happening, and everyone took up the chant. "Figh! Fight! Fight!"

The spectators divided almost instantly into two sides. Most of the boys cheered on Thayer with cries of "Kick his ass, Vega!" and "Take that, Landry!" It was a testament to Sutton's power and popularity that the girls, especially the younger ones, all started screaming for Ethan.

The two boys in the yard kept fighting, seemingly unaware of the crowd that had gathered. Blood pooled in the dirt and smeared muddily over them both. Someone's shirt ripped audibly.

Emma locked eyes with Charlotte in the crowd, shooting her a pleading look. Charlotte understood, and quickly turned to Mark Bell, who hurried back to the house and yelled at someone Emma couldn't see. A few moments later, two other boys—both of them on the varsity basketball team—hurried down the steps. Ricky Parker, the shooting guard who'd just been handed a full ride to Duke, latched onto Ethan and held his arms back while Andrew Collins and Mark Bell pulled Thayer in the opposite direction. Ethan and Thayer struggled to break free, staring at each other with open hostility.

"Nice one, Science Fair," Thayer said, the ironic smirk back on his lips. There was a nasty cut over his eye. "Looks like you finally beefed up."

Ethan's breath heaved as Ricky let go of his arms. His jeans were smeared with grass stains and dirt. For a moment Emma thought he'd fall on Thayer again. Instead, he turned to her.

"You haven't changed at all, *Sutton*," he spat. "You're a selfish slut, just like you've always been."

With that he turned and strode across the lawn toward his car.

28

SCENIC OVERLOOK AHEAD

"Ethan, wait!" Emma called, but he didn't turn around. She hurried down the porch steps and ran after him, ignoring the curious looks of everyone behind her. She stumbled on the flagstones and kicked off her heels in frustration, abandoning them on the grass. Ethan's beat-up Honda was almost at the gates, since he'd been one of the last people to arrive at the party. She reached the car just as he was getting in and climbed stubbornly into the passenger seat.

The spring-loaded hula girl Ethan kept on his dashboard swayed as he slammed the door. "Stop," she panted. "I can explain."

"What is there to explain?" Ethan snarled in disgust. His fists clenched dangerously, as if he wanted to hit something again. In the dark she could see a streak of blood trickling down his forehead into his eye. "You told me not to be jealous, Emma. You said Thayer was Sutton's thing, not yours. You're such a liar. As big a liar as your sister was."

"Don't you dare say that about my sister!" Emma spat. "And please. You're one to talk about lying." She felt completely sober now, her anger filling her with its sharp edges so that everything stood out in clear relief.

"What are you talking about?" Ethan's fingers curled tightly around the steering wheel, even though the car wasn't on. She gritted her teeth.

"I'm talking about the file in the psych ward with your name on it," Emma said, her voice dangerously calm. "Sound familiar?"

Ethan's face hardened. "You went? How?"

"Nisha gave me the keycard," Emma said softly.

He inhaled sharply. "I thought we decided you weren't going to pry into your mother's private records."

"No, *you* decided that. And you didn't care about my *mom's* privacy, you just didn't want me to find out about your deep, dark secret. Isn't that right?" Suddenly, Emma felt drained and hollow, the anger deflating. She blinked back tears. "Ethan, I love you. I shared everything with you. And now it feels like I don't even know you at all."

The muted sounds of the party drifted toward them on the cool night air. Crickets chirped hopefully around the car. But inside, everything was deathly silent.

"Did you read my file?" Ethan asked. His voice had gone low and calm. She looked sideways at him. He sat very still, his mouth pulled into a straight, stoic line.

She shook her head. "No. It didn't feel right."

The rigidity left his body, his shoulders collapsing helplessly. He shoved his shaggy hair back with one hand. "I should have told you," he admitted, his lips crumpling miserably. "I wanted to tell you. But it's not a part of my life I'm proud of, okay?" He slumped back into the driver's seat, his face twisted in anguish.

Emma stared straight ahead, into the dark knot of mesquite in front of the car.

"This was a couple years ago." Ethan's voice was so quiet she had to hold her breath to hear him. "My dad came back to town after a long business trip. The house was a total mess. Mom was too sick to clean, and I was, like, fifteen, so I was kind of useless about housework. Dad flipped out about it. I mean . . . really flipped out. He started beating the hell out of my mom, pushing her from room to room, shoving laundry into her arms, and throwing dirty dishes at her. In the dining room he broke a broomstick across the backs of her legs, he hit her so hard.

He was punishing her for being lazy, he said." Ethan's face tilted away into the shadows. "So I clocked him over the head with a beer bottle. I didn't know what else to do. It didn't break, but it knocked him down pretty hard. He was out cold for a few minutes. Woke up later with a concussion."

"Oh my God," Emma breathed. She reached her hand out and touched Ethan's arm, but he didn't move. She knew he was reliving that awful night, in some dark corner of his mind.

"That's not the most screwed up part. My mom called the cops on me. When they got there I was upset, kind of incoherent about the whole thing, so instead of jail they took me to the hospital. I ended up spending a night strapped to a bed, pumped so full of haloperidol I couldn't even remember my name. I guess I was lucky—jail would have been much worse. When they evaluated me the next day, they concluded I was acting to defend my mom, and because I was a minor they just dismissed the whole thing out of court. But I had to keep going in for counseling for a year or so."

"Wait, your *mom* called the cops?" Emma asked, her chest tightening. "You were just trying to protect her."

Ethan turned to look at her sadly. "That's not how she saw it, I guess. No matter how bad things get with my dad, she always takes his side, says she deserves it or whatever."

In the silence that descended between them, they could hear a crooning R&B ballad piping through the sound system up at the house. Emma took Ethan's hand in hers and squeezed it hard. His fingers were limp and heavy in hers, as if he'd turned to wood and could not feel her touch.

"I'm so sorry," she whispered. "I should have let you tell me in your own time. I should have realized it must have been something that was . . . hard for you to talk about." She swallowed. The first tendrils of relief unwound inside her. Ethan wasn't crazy. He wasn't like her mother. He was a victim, just like Emma. "I've been so scared, Ethan. Everything I thought I knew about my childhood, my family, is wrong. It feels like every day I find out some new, huge secret. I guess I just expected the worst when I saw that file. Because the worst keeps on happening."

He nodded, looking down at his lap. "I don't want to have secrets from you, Emma. I want to share everything."

"So do I," she said. She reached for his hand, but he gently disentangled his fingers from hers.

"Are you sure about that? That's not what it looked like tonight."

Emma shook her head. "Ethan, *he* kissed *me*. I drank too much at the party and wasn't thinking clearly enough to stop him in time. It was a stupid mistake. I'm really sorry it happened, and I wish I could take it back. But you have to believe me—I'm not interested in Thayer. I love *you*."

Ethan bit his lip. For a moment he looked so vulnerable, so heartsick, that it was all she could do not to pull him into her arms.

"I'm sorry for what I said," he apologized. "About you, and about Sutton, too. It's just . . . when I saw that piece of—when I saw *him* touching you, I flew off the handle." His fists clenched against his thighs, and he sighed. "Thayer Vega has always gotten everything he ever wanted. He snaps his fingers and the world delivers it to him on a silver platter. And I still have trouble believing that someone like *you* could fall for someone like me, when you could have him." He looked at her seriously. "Emma, no one's ever cared about me before. And now, suddenly, the most beautiful, brilliant, amazing girl I've ever met is my girlfriend? I keep thinking you're going to wake up one day soon and trade me in for someone else."

His words cut painfully into her heart. She knew what it was like to feel unloved. She knew what it was like to live with that kind of doubt. She leaned across the gearshift and rested her head on his shoulder.

"Ethan, I've never felt this way about anyone," she whispered. He wrapped an arm around her, and she snuggled closer to his side. The gearshift pressed into her rib cage, but she didn't care. "From here on out, let's trust each other. Deal?"

"Deal." He looked down into her eyes, his heavy lashes drooping with emotion. "I didn't even get a chance to tell you that you look amazing."

She self-consciously tugged her short dress further down her thighs. "So do you." He'd worn a light gray V-neck sweater, the white collar of the button-down beneath jutting up around his neck. She liked his usual eclectic look, but Ethan definitely cleaned up well, too.

He touched her cheek, placing a tentative, lingering kiss on her lips. A soft sound of pleasure escaped from the back of her throat. She arched her body toward him.

Ethan pulled back and studied her face, tucking a lock of hair behind her ear. "Want to drive farther up the mountain to see if there's a place to stargaze?" he asked.

Emma nodded, surprised at her boldness.

They didn't speak as he turned the ignition and guided the car out through the Chamberlains' high iron gates. Emma watched the curving lines of the mountain road appear and disappear again in the headlights. Ethan's retro Cure CD crooned out dreamy, sad music as the car climbed higher. Ethan kept his eyes on the road and both hands on the wheel, but she could feel the magnetic pull between them, heavy and urgent.

Finally, high on the mountain, Ethan parked in a shallow lookout at the side of the road.

The lights of Tucson twinkled far below them, as

though it were a small toy town. The moon had risen in the sky and paled to a yellow crescent. Emma unbuckled her seat belt, and without a word climbed over the console into the backseat. She kicked a battered paperback copy of *On the Road* to the floor and curled her legs up under her while Ethan climbed back to join her. Without hesitation they reached for each other, one kiss blurring into the next, their hearts seeming to beat in perfect sync.

Emma put a hand on Ethan's chest, pushing him gently away. She sat up and slowly reached behind her head to untie the knot of her halter. The silk tumbled down around her waist, as soft as flower petals on her skin. A flush swept her cheeks, but she looked up shyly to meet his gaze. His eyes were full of a tenderness that took her breath away. He pulled her to him, running his hands slowly over her shoulders and then her back, tracing the lines of her body one by one. Outside the car, the stars burned bright against the dark sky.

29

ARTS AND CRAFTS TIME

When Emma woke the next day, the late-morning sun poured through the sheer curtains of Sutton's room. She blinked in the light, stretching across the bed. She'd been blissfully nightmare free for the first time in weeks.

Her memories of the night before came back to her in a flood, and she flushed with pleasure, wiggling her toes down under the covers. Ethan had been amazing— tender and thoughtful, sweetly awkward at first, and then passionate as their inhibitions faded one by one. It was perfect. She lay across the bed, smiling, for a long while, not ready to break the memory's spell.

I tried to remember my first time. Had I even had one?

SARA SHEPARD

Garrett had seemed to think we were going to lose our virginities together, but I hoped I'd been with Thayer before I died. I hoped we had had a perfect moment together, somewhere in the middle of our tumultuous relationship.

A high peal of laughter from Laurel's room broke through Emma's reverie. It sounded like Madeline. She cocked her head and listened. Then she remembered—the Lying Game girls were there to work on the prank.

Emma rolled out of bed and pulled on a pair of yoga pants, then padded through the bathroom and opened Laurel's door.

All the girls were scattered around Laurel's room in T-shirts and jeans. Lili and Gabby lay sprawled across Laurel's bed, both typing rapidly on their iPhones. Laurel sat at her desk, applying mascara in a magnifying mirror, while Madeline and Charlotte organized art supplies on the floor. Nisha was there, too, setting up a microphone and an old-fashioned audio recorder. Emma was glad to see that the other girls seemed to have accepted Nisha so easily.

"Good morning, Cinderella," Charlotte said. "I brought you your glass slipper. And sustenance." She pointed to the desk, where Emma's gold heels—the ones she'd abandoned on Charlotte's driveway in order to run barefoot after Ethan—sat next to a steaming coffee. Emma picked up the cup gratefully, blowing at the steam. She sat down on the floor and hugged Charlotte tight.

"Char, I'm so sorry about last night," she said. "I hope the fight didn't ruin your party."

"Are you kidding? Everyone's talking about it on Twitter," Lili said without looking up from her phone. "Between that and my totally newsworthy conquest of Danny Catalano, this is the party of the year."

Madeline snorted. "No one is talking about Danny Catalano but you. He's been untouchable since that awful haircut."

"It's growing back," Lili protested. "Plus, he's an awesome kisser."

Char turned to Emma. "It's okay, Sutton. I know that craziness wasn't your fault. But Twitter-Dumb is right—it did liven things up. Before Ethan went all Incredible Hulk on Thayer's ass, the most exciting thing to happen was a spray-cheese fight some of the morons from the wrestling team got into on the back patio."

Before Emma could say anything else, Madeline pointed at her accusingly. "So what's going on with you and my brother, anyway? I thought you said you were through with him."

"I *am* through with him, I promise." Emma lifted her hands defensively. "We were talking, he kissed me, I didn't pull away quickly enough, and Ethan saw. End of story. It was an accident."

Madeline snorted. "You're quite the safety hazard.

Thayer sure seems to have a lot of *accidents* when you're around."

"Is he okay?" Emma asked. She felt a little guilty that she'd run after Ethan last night without checking on Thayer, but it had looked as if they hadn't had enough time to do any serious damage. Plus, Ethan was her boyfriend, not Thayer.

"He's fine," Laurel said without looking up from her makeup. One eye was painted with bright teal glitter shadow, and the other was still natural, giving her a weird *Clockwork Orange* squint. "I drove him home right after the fight and helped him clean up. As usual," she added pointedly.

Emma cringed. "I didn't mean for anyone to get hurt," she said softly. She picked up a stuffed fox from Laurel's bed and hugged it to her chest.

"You can't help it. You're basically catnip to boys," Charlotte said dismissively. "Speaking of boys, did you make up with Ethan all right?"

"Um, yeah." Emma hid her face behind her coffee cup, her cheeks burning. Charlotte's eyes narrowed.

"Sutton, is there anything you'd like to tell us?" she asked, a wicked smile slowly stretching across her face. Madeline looked up curiously from the magazine she'd been leafing through. Even the Twitter Twins put down their phones.

"Is she, like, glowing?" Charlotte asked the others.

"I'd say she definitely made up with Ethan okay." Madeline grinned.

Emma hugged her knees to her chest and beamed through her blushing cheeks. Laurel poked her in the side. "Talk, woman!"

"Okay, okay!" Emma said. "Ethan and I . . . last night, we . . . you know . . ."

The end of her sentence trailed off, but it didn't matter. The room roiled with shrieks and giggles. Only Nisha was looking at Emma with concern. Emma cringed, remembering how she'd spilled the story of Ethan's file to Nisha last night.

Emma ducked, trying to fend off the girls' demands for details. "Use your imagination, ladies," she said.

Madeline smirked. "You don't want us to do that," she deadpanned.

After that, all was forgiven, and the Twitter Twins started typing away on their phones, alerting their followers to "stay tuned" for a big event that night.

"Don't give it all away," grumbled Madeline. "If Celeste catches wind of anything, the whole thing is blown."

"I don't think she gets Twitter feeds on Mars," said Gabby.

Laurel put on the new Rihanna album, and soon they were all sprawled across the floor, making various props and chatting about how the séance would turn out.

Emma went downstairs to grab a bag of pretzels and some Diet Cokes from the kitchen. She stopped in the living room, where Drake was curled up happily atop a sofa he definitely wasn't allowed on. His tail flopped lazily against the cushions as she stroked his neck. For the first time in ages, she felt as if she was where she belonged.

"Hey." Nisha's voice interrupted her thoughts. She came over and rested a hand on Drake's ear. "I love this dog," she said, scratching him. "My dad's allergic, so we've never been allowed to have one. I'd probably get something little that I could put clothes on, though."

"You could wear matching tennis outfits and carry it in your duffel," Emma said. They both laughed at the image.

"So did you and Ethan talk about . . . you know?" Nisha asked.

Emma flushed and craned her neck to look up and down the hall. Mrs. Mercer was in the backyard gardening, and Mr. Mercer was out playing golf. She pulled the key card from her pocket and handed it back to Nisha.

"Yeah, he explained everything to me. It's not a great story—things haven't really been easy for him." She blinked uncomfortably. "I'm sorry I unloaded all of that on you, and I'd really appreciate it if you could, you know, keep it to yourself." She lowered her gaze. "But thank you for checking on me," she added. "You've been a really good friend."

Nisha opened her mouth as if she was about to say something, then closed it again. They stood looking at each other, secrets still hanging in the air. Then another burst of laughter came from Laurel's room.

"I guess we'd better get back to work," Emma said.

Nisha looked down, suddenly shy. "Sutton—thanks for letting me do this with you guys. I'm really excited about it."

Emma hooked her arm through her friend's and straightened her shoulders. "No, thank *you*. For the idea, and for all your help with my mom. Now, let's go put on a show."

"Let's punk this bitch," Nisha agreed. And arm in arm, my twin sister and my former archrival went upstairs.

30

THINGS THAT GO BUMP IN THE NIGHT

A car door slammed in the darkness, and a middle-aged woman wearing a shiny gold turban stepped into the clearing. The sun had just slipped behind the mountains. Sabino Canyon was alive with sounds: Crickets and birds sang in the undergrowth, while farther away a chorus of coyotes started their nocturnal howls. An early owl swooped overhead.

Along with the turban, the woman had on a long purple velvet cloak and dramatic blue eyeshadow that swept up to her thinly plucked brows. Enormous gemstones glittered on each of her fat fingers. She lit a cigarette and took a long drag. "This is the séance?" she asked, blowing twin tusks of smoke out through her nose.

"Great, you made it," Madeline said, walking over to the strange woman and shaking her hand. She'd told the other girls that she had a last-minute surprise for them, but Emma hadn't imagined it would be this good. "Ladies, this is Madame Darkling. She's a, um, *real* medium."

The other girls barely concealed their grins. Madame Darkling looked as if she'd just come from central casting for a phone-a-psychic infomercial. Emma could see a grubby gray tennis shoe poking out from under her robes.

"Perfect," said Charlotte. She rummaged in her shoulder bag and pulled out a manila folder, which was labeled GHOST WHISPERER PRANK in deceptively cheerful pink marker. "Here's the intel on our subject," she explained, handing it to the psychic. "We did a little research. Her grandmother was a pretty well-known writer. She died last year, but Celeste was close with her. Might be a good angle."

Madame Darkling rifled through the pages. A photograph of Celeste's grandmother, a plump old woman with rust-colored hair and too much rouge, fluttered to the ground.

"Jeanette Echols? Sure, I know her stuff. Piece of cake," the medium said, leaning over to retrieve the photograph. She stubbed out her cigarette in the dirt before carefully picking up the butt and whisking it into a pocket hidden somewhere in her cloak. Laurel and Emma exchanged glances, stifling their giggles.

"Where'd you find her?" Charlotte whispered to Madeline as Madame Darkling helped herself to the carrots and dip they'd been munching on while they set up.

"Craigslist, of course," Madeline said. "The venue of all lost souls."

"She just stuck a finger in the hummus, you guys," Laurel said under her breath.

"Maybe it's haunted hummus," Emma joked.

The girls had spent the afternoon running last-minute errands and setting the stage for the prank. They all wore long black robes embroidered with metallic stars that Charlotte had rented from a costume shop. Everyone except Nisha, that is, who wore black jeans and a black T-shirt, like a stage tech. Her job was to hide in the bushes and activate all the "special effects" they had devised for the prank, including a portable surround-sound system preloaded with Halloween noises like groans and rattling chains. But the best part was a group of helium balloons painted with scary, glow-in-the-dark faces that Nisha could drag around on a ribbon. The girls had tested them in Laurel's bedroom earlier. In the dark, they gave a perfectly terrifying impression of floating disembodied heads.

I was proud of my friends for coming up with such a great prank—but I felt a little sad, too. They were about to conduct a fake séance in the same place I'd spent the last few hours of my life. If only there was a way I could really talk to Emma. If only Madame Darkling was a bona fide medium and I could use her to communicate with my friends. I'd tell Madeline and Charlotte how much I missed them. I'd remind Laurel that I was proud of her, and sorry we'd grown apart. I'd tell Emma that I love her, and thanks for everything she's done for me. I'd even say hi to Nisha and the Twitter Twits. You don't know how much your friends mean to you until you're forced to watch them from the far side of the breach.

Emma's skin hummed as if an electrical storm were brewing overhead, though the evening sky was clear and starting to fill with stars. She hadn't been in the canyon since her first day here, when she'd waited for hours for Sutton to meet her. Her mind kept busily reconstructing what she knew about her sister's last night—the date with Thayer and the runaway Volvo that had hit him, the argument with Mr. Mercer, and then . . . Becky. How could Becky have killed Sutton? Had she strangled her, or had she used a weapon? She'd had a knife when the cops took her to the hospital; maybe that had been the murder weapon.

And where had she hidden the body? It could be anywhere, even the underbrush just out of sight of the clearing. Emma took a few steps toward the woods, then stopped. Someone would have discovered it by now, if it were so easy to see. Here in the dark was not the time to hunt for clues.

"Almost showtime, ladies," Madeline announced. Emma turned back to the circle, where the girls were gathering. Anticipation hung thick in the air. Charlotte held up her hands like a camera lens, surveying the area one last time. The Twins were doing some kind of theater warm-up exercise, saying "The lips, the teeth, the tip of the tongue" back and forth to each other. Madeline started handing out small cardboard boxes.

Emma lifted the top of hers. Inside was a papier-mâché mask in the form of a horned satyr, nestled in a bed of tissue paper.

"These are awesome," Lili said. She and Gabby wore comedy and tragedy masks, one smiling and one frowning. Once they'd put them on, Emma couldn't tell which girl was which. There was a whiskered black cat for Laurel and an eerie porcelain-doll face for Charlotte. In true diva form, Madeline had secured the only beautiful mask for herself—a red, feathered domino that covered her eyes and cheeks.

"Be careful with these. They have to make it back to the ballet closet by Monday morning, or I'm screwed," Madeline warned.

A rhythmic chanting from behind the rocks made

Emma jump. Nisha had started the music. Tendrils of "mist" from the smoke machine crept across the clearing. Even being in on the joke, Emma felt the short hairs on the back of her neck prickle. A few years earlier she'd had a job at the ticket counter for a Halloween haunted house. She remembered how silly the whole thing had looked when the lights were on—anyone could see how fake the foam monsters were, and even the professional-quality monster makeup seemed cakey and silly in the harsh light of day. But when the lights went down, when the smoke machine billowed and the music echoed creepily and the actors hid in the shadows waiting to jump out at their victims, the house became greater than the sum of its parts.

"Excuse me?" A girl's voice broke in over the droning music. A figure emerged from the mist, looking around uncertainly. "Is this the Conference of the Dead?"

The girl's face was hidden by a Venetian *Carnevale* mask in gold and white, but her hair was unmistakably Celeste's, her braids jutting in every direction. Her robe was deep velvet and embroidered all over with esoteric symbols in gold thread.

"I bet you she just happened to have that robe hanging around in her closet," Laurel whispered. Emma grinned behind her mask.

The girls nodded slowly. Madeline, now transformed into some kind of glowing mystical creature, gestured to the empty space in the circle. Celeste stepped hesitantly down the path to join them, the whites of her eyes clearly visible behind her mask as her gaze darted around the clearing.

Despite Emma's skepticism about Madame Darkling's authenticity—when the curtain came up she was all pro. A theatrical intensity infused every gesture she made. She walked around behind them counterclockwise, sprinkling salt to mark out a circle. "Within this circle we invite all benevolent spirits who would communicate with us. All those who would do us ill are banished to the outer darkness." Her voice seemed to have mysteriously acquired a strange, choppy accent. Emma locked eyes with Charlotte across the circle and had to bite her lip to keep from laughing out loud.

The medium rejoined the circle, waving her hands over a small cauldron that Emma recognized as a fancy potpourri diffuser. She reached into a little leather pouch around her neck and drew out a pinch of some kind of dried herb. When she sprinkled it into the fire the flame grew brighter. The smell that came off it was something like mint tea mixed with a locker room.

And then, suddenly, her eyes snapped up and locked right onto Emma.

"You," she said, her voice throaty. "Someone is here for you, dear."

Emma was glad that the mask on her face was covering her confusion. Had Madame Darkling forgotten who was who? Maybe this was just an opening act, her way of building up to the final reveal.

The music from the underbrush was low and ominous, a soft rumble of chanting monks. "I sense loneliness. Pain," said the medium. The cauldron's low flame played across her face. In that moment she looked like a witch, eyes alight with unearthly knowledge. "Someone who died too young."

And then, somehow, I detached myself from Emma's senses for the first time since I'd died.

I drifted away from her, around the circle toward Madame Darkling. I could smell the herbs, feel the heat of the fire and the coolness of the breeze, all on my own—not just through Emma. It wasn't like having a body again so much as connecting with this place. The moonlight on the clearing, the wind, the soil, the quiet chorus of crickets, the mesquite branches gnarled against the sky like skeletal fingers—it was as if all of those things were connected and I was one of them.

Had this faux medium managed to inadvertently tap into something real? Or maybe my body was close, and being near it made me feel a little more alive again.

"Can you hear me?" I asked the medium. Her eyes flickered in answer. She didn't seem to see me, but maybe she *felt* me.

"Tell her," I said, speaking as clearly as I could. Madame Darkling's pupils were wide in the darkness. "Tell her I wish I could have met her."

"I wish I could have met you," Madame Darkling said, her voice flat and distant. Emma gasped softly.

Emma closed her eyes. This couldn't be real. She didn't believe in ghosts. But more than ever, she wanted to believe. She tried to quiet her thoughts, to empty her mind and wait for another message to come. *I'm listening*, she thought desperately. *Sutton, are you here? Is that you?*

I could have hugged the woman, gold lamé and all. She could hear me. She could communicate with Emma for me, and we could work together to solve my murder.

"Tell her I'm worried for her," I said. "She's in danger. I only wish we'd had a chance to meet. We would have been an unstoppable team. Tell her I'm grateful for everything she's done. Tell her I love her."

Madame Darkling's sonorous voice came across the circle. "He's a handsome young man—one you have loved in a distant past life, and lost. He stands at the edge of an abyss and reaches to you . . . reaches . . . but the chasm between life and death is too wide, and he turns away again." Madame Darkling touched a hand to her brow. "He says . . . he says he will see you one day. On the other side."

Next to Emma, Madeline snorted softly. "Sutton

Mercer, breaking hearts on both sides of the grave," she whispered.

I groaned with frustration. It had felt so real for a moment, but it was just part of the medium's performance. No matter how strong I felt here, I was still stuck in this limbo, alone and powerless.

Emma's shoulders slumped. It'd been so easy for her to believe her sister was still out there, watching over her. But that was how con artists worked, right? They figured out what you wanted to believe and served it up on a silver platter. She couldn't afford that kind of denial. Sutton was dead and gone.

"Dead," I whispered sadly, "but not gone. I'm here, Emma."

Tendrils of mist blew across the clearing, and the music shifted to a quiet murmur. Madame Darkling turned her turbaned head toward Celeste. The Venetian mask glittered in the ambient light.

"You, dear," said the medium. "Someone's arrived for you. An older lady. She only crossed over very recently. A woman of letters, perhaps?"

Through the holes in her mask, Celeste's eyes became very round. "Grandmama?" she squeaked. "Is that you?"

Emma felt a pang of guilt. It was obvious Celeste had been close with her grandmother. Maybe that was where all her otherworldly nonsense had come from—the desperate desire to believe her grandmother was still there. It felt cruel to aim for such a vulnerable spot, especially since Emma had just found it so easy to believe that her dead sister was still with her.

"She's trying to tell me something," Madame Darkling intoned, touching her hands to her temples. She looked like she was straining to hear. "She says she does not approve of the boy you are seeing. Gareth, I believe?"

"G-g-g-garrett, Grandmama," Celeste said, her voice so soft Emma could barely make it out. Madame Darkling nodded.

"She says . . . that he uses more hair product than you do." Charlotte broke into a fit of coughing next to Emma. "And that he doesn't truly care for you. She says that he's using you to get revenge on his true love, a devastatingly beautiful girl who broke his heart."

Emma couldn't believe Charlotte had told Madame Darkling all this. Celeste's lips pressed together tightly.

"I knew it," she growled. "Don't worry, Grandmama. We're through. I won't waste any more time on him."

Madame Darkling clutched her head. "Silence!" she snapped. The girls went still. From the underbrush the music built, a violin's tense tremolo joining the low drums. A gust of wind blasted through the clearing.

When it passed, the medium opened her eyes. "Something else is here," she said, her tone afraid. A low moan came from somewhere to the left, then seemed to move around them as if they were being circled. Celeste's head snapped up, her lips parted.

"Grandmama?" she whispered.

Multicolored lights began flashing from the underbrush, and the sound of footsteps reverberated all around the clearing. The fake cactus writhed as if it was possessed. For a moment Emma almost forgot that it was one of their props, controlled by Nisha in the darkness.

"No," Madame Darkling said, her voice dropping low, a strange, half-mad grimace on her face. "Grandmama isn't here anymore, Celeste. This is a malevolent being. Everyone, remain strong in your minds and intentions and we can banish it together. Forces of evil, leave us be. Forces of evil, leave us be . . . ," she began to chant.

A scream echoed from somewhere, and then another answered it on the other side of the clearing. Celeste gasped, one hand flying to her lips, the other pointing upward at the leering green faces swooping overhead. She whimpered and scrambled backward, scuffing the circle of salt with her sandals.

"You have broken the sacred circle!" Madame Darkling cried, raising a trembling finger to point at Celeste. Celeste opened and closed her mouth like a fish. She glanced wildly around, her face pale under her mask. Emma watched something move in the shadows behind her. It was Nisha, reaching out from behind a rock with a peacock feather in her outstretched hand. She tickled Celeste on the back of the neck and vanished before the other girl turned.

"Celeste . . . ," a strange voice crooned from the bushes. Nisha had cued up the best of their sound bites, a superdistorted recording of Charlotte calling Celeste's name in a creepy singsong. Nisha had warped it and added reverb until it was scarcely recognizable. The same call came from the other side of the clearing, and then from a third angle. Soon they were surrounded on all sides by the voice.

Goose pimples sprang up along the back of Emma's neck. Even *I* shuddered, and I knew perfectly well that I was the only ghost in the canyon tonight.

"The spirits have come to claim you!" Madame Darkling screamed.

Celeste was huddled over, her hands covering her head, trembling. The chorus of voices overlapped and grew to a fever pitch, an insane babble. But just when Emma didn't think she could take any more, the sounds stopped at once.

"Gotcha!" the other girls screamed on cue, all except Emma.

Light flooded the clearing. The girls whipped off their masks, clutching their sides with laughter. Madeline had tears pouring down her cheeks. Laurel could barely breathe, crouched over her knees in hysterics. Nisha sauntered out of the bushes smirking.

Celeste blinked into the bright lights, a dazed and blank expression on her face. She didn't remove her mask but stayed crouched in the leaves and dirt.

Charlotte tossed her hair to fluff it after having it crushed under the mask. "How's Sutton's aura looking now?" she sneered.

"Did you get it on tape, Nisha?" Madeline asked. Nisha held up her iPhone.

"It's uploading to YouTube as we speak."

"On it!" the twins exclaimed, whipping out their phones to retweet the link.

Celeste stood up slowly. Dirt and leaves stuck to her cloak. One of her braids had flopped over the top of her head and jutted outward.

"We really got you, didn't we?" Madeline asked. "I mean, shouldn't you have seen it coming, in the stars or the tea leaves or whatever?"

"Hilarious," Celeste snapped. Her voice was substantially less dreamy than usual. "You're hilarious."

"We know," said the Twitter Twins in perfect unison. They were dancing around each other in a taunting do-si-do.

Celeste walked slowly to the side of the clearing and picked up her hemp knapsack. It was covered in patches and buttons that said things like FREE TIBET and VEGANS TASTE BETTER. Then she turned on her heel to face them.

"You shouldn't play with forces you don't understand," she spat. She locked eyes with Emma. "It can be dangerous. You can accidentally call all kinds of problems down on yourself."

"I think it's time you stop with the lame aura warnings," Charlotte said. "You're the one who called down all kinds of problems on *yourself* when you messed with us. Remember that the next time you try to get in Sutton's head."

"You've been warned," Celeste insisted, shaking her head slowly. "The spirits will not be mocked." She tossed her bag on her shoulder and started up the path away from them. A moment later they heard a car start and drive away.

"That was brilliant," Madeline told Madame Darkling. The medium had already lit a cigarette and stood to the side, examining their props. Charlotte handed the woman an envelope bulging with cash, and she opened it and began counting the bills.

"I'm going to have to remember some of this stuff," she said. "Glow paint and balloons. Nice touch."

Emma stood back, mask still on, not joining in the celebration of the rest of the group. She watched as the woman shoved the envelope somewhere inside her robes, then took off down the same path Celeste had, toward the parking lot. Laurel wheeled a cooler out of the underbrush while Gabby and Lili built a teetering pyramid of kindling. Nisha cued up a Black Eyed Peas album on the surround sound. Soon they had a fire crackling, marshmallows speared on sticks and browning in the heat. The clearing, which just minutes before had been spookier than a graveyard, became bright and cheerful.

"That could *not* have gone better," Madeline said, reclining in a camp chair. The Twitter Twins were reading aloud tweets hashtagged "séance." They had gotten the prank trending locally within the past few minutes.

Emma pulled Sutton's wool jacket closer around her torso. "You guys, I feel a little bad," she said.

If there had been a DJ playing in the bushes, his record would have scratched and gone silent. The girls turned to gawk at her. Sutton rarely felt bad about anything, and she wasn't big on regret. But Emma couldn't help but think of how desperately she'd wanted to believe that her sister could still speak, and how lonely she'd felt in the split second after she'd realized the medium was a fraud. It had felt almost as awful as those moments after she'd found the murderer's first note—almost as if she'd lost Sutton all over again.

"I just mean, you know . . . her grandma recently died. Maybe we shouldn't have gone there," she said softly.

Surprisingly, it was Nisha who spoke first, her voice tense.

"If she was stupid enough to think her grandma would talk to her through some cheesy lamé-wearing hack, she deserved to be punked," Nisha said. "The dead don't come back. No matter how much you want them to."

Emma bit her lip. Of course solid, sensible Nisha would have no patience for the desperate, delusional hopes of the grieving. Her voice was harsh with bitterness. She sounded as if she was mocking her own grief as much as anyone else's.

The song ended on the stereo system. In the silence before the next started, they heard the distant bark of a dog down in Nisha's subdivision. Then they heard a low, mournful cry.

"Did you leave the sound effects on?" Laurel asked Nisha. Nisha shook her head. Something crashed in the bushes nearby. Emma strained her ears.

"Seriously, guys?" Madeline said. "Who counter-pranked? I thought we agreed not to pull those anymore. That stopped being clever in middle school. I think whoever did it should have to sit out the next prank as punishment."

"I didn't do it!" Laurel quickly protested. "Cross my heart and hope to die!"

Everyone quickly repeated the safe word. They looked uncertainly at one another.

"Okay," said Charlotte, rolling her eyes. Her robe hung open, revealing a pink sequined camisole. "It's obviously just Celeste."

Madeline slapped her forehead. "Oh my God, you're right."

"But we heard her leave." Emma frowned.

Charlotte raised an eyebrow. "Excuse me, are you new to this? She circled around somehow. There are trails all through here—it wouldn't be hard. She's just trying to make us think there's some evil spirit on the loose."

"I can't believe she's asking for seconds," Laurel said.

"Just ignore her," Charlotte said. "I'm so over that weirdo."

The explanation seemed to be enough for the other girls. Nisha turned the music back up. The Twitter Twins replayed the whole séance on their new iPad, reading the comments that had already popped up on YouTube. "Spaceman77 says, 'Who's the babe in the satyr horns, she's hawt!!'" Gabby turned to Emma, but Emma hardly noticed.

They were probably right—it must be Celeste, hoping to get back at them. But what if someone was hurt? The voice had sounded like it was crying. What if someone had gotten injured out in the woods?

Or . . . what if Becky had come back to the scene of the crime and taken another victim?

Emma imagined Sutton bleeding and running through the woods, trying to get away from Becky. What if someone had been in the clearing that night? What if someone could have helped her but had ignored her instead? Sutton could be alive now, at the fire with the rest of them. She couldn't let Becky get away with it again.

She stood up and dusted off her butt. Out beyond the cheerful firelight the canyon was pitch-black. She peered up the trail in the direction she'd heard the crying.

"What are you doing?" Madeline asked, staring at her.

Emma glanced around at her friends. There was safety in numbers, in the clearing. But then she set her jaw in determination.

"I'm going to go prank Celeste back," she said. "You guys stay here."

"Wait, we want to come," Gabby and Lili said, starting to stand up, but Emma held out a hand.

"I'm invoking Executive Diva privilege," she announced, citing Sutton's official Lying Game title. "You can hear about it later. I'll give you an exclusive." She tried to be lighthearted, but her heart was hammering. No matter how much she didn't want to go out there alone, she would never be able to live with herself if she got one of her friends hurt.

"Okay, raise your hand if you don't think it's a brilliant idea for Sutton to go wandering in the woods by herself,"

278

Laurel said, throwing her own hand in the air. Emma snorted.

"Whatever, guys," she said, starting up the path with a flashlight.

"All right, but if you get murdered in the woods, I'm going to say I told you so," Charlotte's voice rang out behind her.

Touché, I thought.

The pale beam of the flashlight swept over the brush on either side, small bushes and cacti casting deep shadows. Emma stopped and listened for the sounds again. From farther away than before came another whimper, a rustle of leaves. She started jogging along the trail, trying to land softly on her feet so she could hear where the sound was coming from. A human groan echoed off the desert rocks. The trail led her higher up the mountain. She moved in silence for several minutes, until the bonfire glittered far below her, a tiny pinprick of light shining through the sparse trees.

Emma arrived at an overlook, with a park bench facing the neighborhood where Ethan and Nisha lived. She thought she could just make out Ethan's porch light. Was he looking at the stars? She wished she could run all the way down the mountain and into his arms.

While Emma stared out over the city, I saw a figure step quietly out from the shadows. It was a gaunt woman, mascara and tears trickling down her cheeks. She watched Emma for a moment, chewing her lip. An old hospital bracelet still stuck to her wrist, as if she'd forgotten to cut it off.

Becky.

Emma's back was to her. I couldn't believe how silently our mother could move when she wanted to—just a moment ago she'd been crashing around through the underbrush, but there was nothing here to trip her up. She stepped toward Emma, eyes glued to her back.

A few pebbles dribbled down the side of the mountain from where Emma's feet displaced them. It was a sheer drop to the next overhang, forty feet or more. Becky kept advancing, her eyes glowing strangely in the darkness, like a mountain lion's.

"Emma!" I screamed, as loudly as I could.

Emma cocked her head. "Hello?" she whispered. The voice that had called her was so tiny, so faint it was almost like a breeze.

My knuckles clenched. She'd heard me. I was right—I was stronger here, for some reason.

"It's Becky!" I shrieked, focusing every fiber of my ghostly being on the words. "She's right behind you!"

"Sutton?" Emma breathed. But before I could answer, before Emma could make another move, a hand clamped on her arm. Emma's body spun forcefully around so she was looking into Becky's face.

And just like that, something snapped into place at the back of my mind. That familiar feeling came over me, of something unknown finally making sense, and a memory tugged me backward in time . . .

31

ORIGIN STORY

My lungs burn in my chest as my mother's arms tighten around me. Bright colors kaleidoscope behind my closed eyes, reds and greens exploding across my vision. Some ancient part of my brain, a primitive survival instinct, kicks in. My body wrenches around in her grasp. She's stronger than she looks—but so am I. I thrash back and forth, gasping for breath, my arms and legs writhing in all directions. And then all at once I break free and stagger away from her.

I fall to the ground, too dizzy and breathless to move.

She steps toward me. I open my mouth to scream for help, to scream at her to stay away from me, but my lungs are flat inside of me. Her face is hidden in the shadows of her hair. She walks over like some kind of monster, in a halting shuffle, and kneels down next to me.

The moon blazes out from behind a cloud, and suddenly I can see her face as clearly as if it were day. She's crying.

"Sutton, I know you're upset, but you have to breathe, sweet-heart. Take a deep breath. You're hyperventilating." She reaches for my hand. I search her face for the grotesque sneer, the anger that I thought I had seen just a few seconds earlier, but I can't. With a jolt, I wonder: Was that just the face of a woman trying not to cry?

I take a deep, shuddering breath, and when I exhale, the world seems clearer.

"What do . . . you want from me?" I pant.

Becky shakes her head back and forth, her lip quivering. "I just wanted to meet you, Sutton. That's all. I'm sorry. I shouldn't have just grabbed you like that. But . . . I've wanted to hold you for almost eighteen years now."

Wanted to . . . hold me? That was a hug? My mind reels. A humiliating realization dawns on me—she didn't crush me at all. I had just panicked when she put her arms around me.

Some prankster queen I am. I almost just asphyxiated myself in fear.

I take three or four more gigantic breaths. She doesn't touch me again, but she sits down beside me, watching me with concern. Her eyes are still wet, but her tears have stopped running.

"Here we are, sitting in the dirt again," she says. I don't say *anything.* She bites her lip. *"I'm sorry, Sutton. I always do this. I always find a way to mess things up."*

She looks so forlorn sitting there that I almost feel sorry for her. But I'm not ready to feel sorry for her yet, to forgive her. She did mess things up, starting when she left me behind with my grandparents, and ending with us screaming at each other in the mountains.

Becky's eyes fall to the locket I always wear. I grip it in my hand self-consciously, half to hide it from her, half to reassure myself that it's still there.

"You're still wearing my locket," she says softly.

My hackles go up again. Her locket? This is my trademark, the centerpiece of my style. My parents gave it to me when I was little, and now everyone knows that I'm never seen without it. The little silver sphere is cold in my fingers. I don't want to believe that something of hers has been hanging around my neck all this time.

"Mom and Dad gave this to me," I say, as snidely as I can. "If it was yours, it's not anymore."

"No, of course not. I didn't mean—I mean, I left it for you, Sutton. I left it so you would have a piece of me. Something to remember me by."

We're silent for a long moment. An owl calls out overhead, on the hunt. I pick at a sticker embedded in my jean shorts from my long tumble through the woods. Finally, I speak.

"I wear it every day," I whisper. The silver starts to get warmer in my grip.

Becky plucks a rubber band from her wrist and pulls her hair back in a low ponytail. With her hair tamed she looks calmer. She takes a deep breath.

"Maybe now you can see, a little, why I had to leave you. I'm no good with people, Sutton. I get . . . agitated. Easily confused. Short-tempered."

"What made you like that?" I blurt. Her forehead crumples into a sad frown. She shrugs.

"It's just how I am. Mom and Dad . . . your grandparents, I mean . . . they did their best for me. But some people are just damaged on the inside, no matter what their lives look like. Sometimes I get better for a little while. I think I can take care of myself, maybe even of you . . . but it never lasts." She exhales loudly. "Leaving you with my parents was one of the hardest things I've ever done. You have to understand that. I didn't want to do it—I kept trying to convince myself that I could look after you. After you and your sister both."

I frown. "Laurel's yours, too?" That doesn't make any sense. Laurel is only six months younger than me. It'd be impossible.

"No, no." She stands up and slaps the dead leaves and branches off her bottom. She stretches, then looks out over the city lights, her back to me. "Have you ever wondered what the 'E' in your locket stands for?"

I shrug, even though she's not looking at me. I push myself up with my raw, tender palms. My legs are one big scrape, and there's an ache in my lower rib cage that I know is going to be a serious bruise. My shirt is pretty much ruined, torn and covered in dirt. I sigh, moving next to her on the ledge to look down over the subdivision.

When I was little, I used to have this recurring dream that my reflection would step out of the mirror and we would play together. When I explained the dreams to Laurel, she said they sounded scary, but they never were. My reflection and I would run across a playground hand in hand while the sun rolled up into the sky. I knew, the way you know in dreams, that we were two parts of a whole, that we were each incomplete without the other. I would wake up from those dreams feeling complete in a way I never did during my waking life. I never told anyone, but I used to pretend that the E in my locket stood for my reflection.

"Mom always said the locket was vintage, and it stood for whoever owned it before me." I take a deep breath. "But when I was little I pretended it belonged to a friend of mine."

Becky nods slowly. She reaches into her back pocket and takes out a hard pack of cigarettes. She slides one between her lips, then fumbles with a match. Her hands are shaking, and the flame wavers for a moment before she gets the cigarette lit. She takes a long drag and exhales.

"When I got pregnant with you," she says very quietly, "I was really excited. I mean, it wasn't a planned pregnancy, obviously. I was young, I was constantly in trouble. I didn't know how I was going to take care of you. But when I felt you kick for the first time, I knew I couldn't give you up."

I open my mouth to interrupt her, but she holds up a finger. "Please, Sutton, this is hard for me to talk about. Just wait and let me tell you the whole story. Then you can yell at me some more."

I bite my lip, but nod. She takes another drag from her cigarette, the smoke wreathing her face. "I started getting ready for you. I scraped together enough money for a stroller and a crib. I read a bunch of books from the library about babies. I didn't have any money for an ultrasound or any of that, but I took vitamins and ate green vegetables every day and played music for you. You loved salsa music. You'd go crazy in there." She laughs, and for a moment she almost sounds like a normal mom.

"Then I went into labor. I'll spare you the details—hell, I don't remember most of the details. You weren't positioned right, and they had to operate. They gave me so much pain medication that I didn't really know what was going on until it was over. Then they brought you to me. You—and your sister. Your twin. Emma."

For a long moment I can't move. I can't speak. I look up and she's watching me, a tentative, hopeful expression on her face. I shake my head slowly.

"You're imagining things," I say. "You must have been high as a kite. I don't have a twin. That's impossible."

"You do have a twin," she says. "I never told my father. I've never told anyone. But I want you to find her, Sutton." A single tear fights its way loose and rolls down her bony cheek.

I think about my recurring dream, me and my reflection ruling the playground. I think about the feeling I've always had of missing somebody, missing somebody who should be right next to me and isn't. I'd always assumed the feeling was about my birth mom, but now I wonder—have I always known she was out there, deep in my blood? My twin?

And suddenly, I know Becky's telling the truth.

My mind is swimming, but a barrage of questions comes pouring out of me. "Where is she?" I ask. "Does she know about me? Does she know about our—our grandparents?"

"No. She doesn't know any of it." Becky stubs her cigarette out in the dirt, pocketing the filter. "I don't know where she is anymore. I've lost track of her. The last time I knew where she was, it was a foster home in Las Vegas, but Family Services moves her around so often I don't know where she is now. Her last name's Paxton, unless she's changed it."

"Well, how am I supposed to find her, then?" I ask. Becky just shakes her head.

"You'll figure it out. You two are meant to find each other, Sutton. You need each other. I should never have separated you in the first place." She crosses her arms over her chest and heaves a loud sigh. "I have to go now, or everything will get too complicated."

"What do you mean, go? You just got here. I just met you. And you have to help me find my sister," I protest. A heavy feeling starts to knot up in my stomach. I'm not sad that she's leaving, exactly. But I don't want her to go either.

A strange look comes over Becky's face. A few minutes earlier it might have looked sinister to me, but now that I'm really looking I can see that my mother just looks shattered. Heartbroken. It's the look of someone who has already lost everything.

"I'm sick," she says slowly. "I'm okay right now, but I can feel it coming on. Another episode." Her body shudders again, as if the very thought is repellent. "I can't be there for you. I'm so sorry. You'll never know how sorry. But that's why I gave you up. I thought you'd be safe with your grandparents, have a shot at a normal life." She wraps her thin arms around her body. "You know, I tried to come back for you once, when you were a few years old, but Dad wouldn't give you up. You were his daughter by then. He could finally have a daughter he was proud of. I never gave him that. But you? Sutton, you're my second chance."

She smiles, and for just a moment she looks almost pretty again, almost young. The lines in her face relax and in the moonlight she seems smooth and innocent. Pure.

Then she turns, and without another word, she disappears into the night.

32

HELLO, AND GOOD-BYE

Becky's hand lingered on Emma's arm, as if it were hard for her to let go. Then she released her and took a step back. "Sutton," she said softly.

Emma's muscles were tense, ready to bolt. Even to fight, if it came to that. But something held her back. This was her chance to get answers. This was her chance to find out what had really happened that night between Sutton and Becky. She whirled around to face her mother, planting her legs firmly on the ground and crossing her arms over her chest.

Becky had changed out of her hospital clothes and into a pair of jeans and a secondhand T-shirt that said

SOMEBODY IN VIRGINIA LOVES ME. Her face was still too thin, shadows collecting in its pits and hollows, but something about it had softened. Her eyes were clear, and the rictus had left her lips. She looked almost like the young, beautiful mother Emma remembered from thirteen years before, a little older, a little more weathered, but recognizable. Tears and makeup had dried on her face. She looked Emma up and down.

"You've got a lot of nerve, coming back here. To the canyon," Emma said. Her pulse throbbed in her neck. A charge of fear swept over her skin like a light fingertip, sending the hair on her arms straight up. She couldn't see the girls' bonfire at all anymore. Down in the subdivision she heard a motorcycle accelerate and then disappear. It echoed strangely off the canyon rock.

"I know," Becky said. She hung her head, wringing her hands in front of her body. "But I wanted to see you before I left."

"Before you leave?" Emma's voice was sharp. She narrowed her eyes. She wasn't letting Becky leave until she'd paid for what she'd done.

"Emma," I protested. I tried to clutch at her, knowing even as I did that it was hopeless.

But this time, something was different. My touch didn't move through her. It rested lightly on the surface of her skin, as soft as a kiss. I could *feel* her heartbeat, so warm, so alive.

Emma was still staring at our mother, a determined look on her face. She didn't seem to have felt anything. But I had. Even if it only happened once, I had touched my sister.

"She didn't do it," I said, summoning up all my strength. Emma needed to know this, to stop following Becky's trail so that she could find my real murderer. I concentrated everything I could on making her believe me. "Emma, she didn't do it!"

Then Emma realized something: Becky had called her Sutton. Not Emma. Either she was a very good actress, or she truly didn't know Sutton was gone.

Relief and suspicion mingled inside of her. Maybe Becky was innocent, or maybe Emma was just lying to herself again, wanting to believe in her mother despite the evidence to the contrary. She bit her lip.

"Where are you going this time?" she asked.

Becky shrugged. "I don't know. I just need to get out of Tucson. This place has a lot of bad memories for me. There are too many people here that I can hurt. That I do hurt," she said, swallowing hard.

Emma tensed again. "People you *hurt*?"

Becky looked up at her, her long lashes still damp with tears. She took a deep breath.

"I know you probably won't believe me, but I don't remember much from the hospital. They had me pumped full of so many drugs I didn't know what was going on.

But I remember enough to know that I must have really scared you. I'm so sorry." She rolled a pebble back and forth under the toe of her shoe. "I'm so sorry I couldn't explain sooner, Sutton. I was too scared to tell you the truth, about my history, about my illness. That night we met here, it was so hard to leave you with all your questions. I almost came back to explain, but I was afraid."

Emma turned away from Becky, pacing in a little circle, trying to clear her head. *Leave you? Come back?* It sounded like when Becky left, Sutton was still safe. But could she take Becky at her word? She *was* crazy.

But Becky looked so much more lucid now, her eyes focused, her breathing even and calm. All of the memories Emma had clung to over the years seemed to crowd in around her. Becky singing off-key along with the radio, teaching her the words to all the Beatles songs. Becky taking her to the free shows along the Vegas strip, her face reflecting the light from the Bellagio fountain. Becky stroking her hair out of her face, carrying her into the apartment after an afternoon playing outside, and tucking her into bed, Emma pretending to be asleep so she could lay against her mother's shoulder. And here she was, right now, telling Emma she had walked away from a still-living Sutton in the canyon the night they'd met.

"Becky didn't kill me," I whispered urgently. "Believe her, Emma."

And suddenly, as though she had heard me, Emma did.

But just to be certain, she asked Becky another question. "Where did you go, after that night?"

Becky sighed. "Vegas, actually. I had a feeling your sister might be there. I even got a job at the diner in the Hard Rock, so that I could stay longer and look for her. But I never found her." She stopped, suddenly looking hopeful. "Have *you* made any headway in tracking her down?"

Vegas, Emma thought. If things had been different, Becky might have come for her and reunited the twins herself. Then she realized what Becky's words meant: Becky had told Sutton about Emma. The knowledge brought a fresh crush of sadness over her. In her last few hours of life, Sutton had known she had a sister.

"Yes and no," Emma said softly.

Becky's hand squeezed hers in the darkness. "I loved her so much. Giving both of you up was the biggest mistake of my life. Find her, Sutton. Her life hasn't been as easy as yours. Give her the chances you've gotten."

Emma took a deep breath. "You have another daughter, too, don't you?"

Becky's eyes widened, her mouth dropping open for a moment. She blinked several times, then nodded. "Yes," she said softly. "How'd you . . ."

"Where is she?" Emma pressed.

"California. With her father. I was declared unfit to

care for her five years ago. I haven't seen her since."

"How old is she now?"

"Twelve," Becky said. "I was pregnant with her when I gave up your sister." She shook her head sadly. "I know it doesn't make any sense. All I can tell you is I wasn't in my right mind. I was off my meds, and it seemed like a good decision at the time." She was quiet for a moment. "I haven't stopped feeling guilty about it ever since."

Emma's heart twisted in her chest. She knew she'd been abandoned for another child, but it was even harder hearing Becky say it aloud.

Then she imagined Becky's life: traveling from town to town, unable to go home, to see the people she loved. Yes, she'd been destructive. She was alone because she'd hurt the people in her life too much. But Becky hadn't chosen to be mentally ill. And in her own twisted way, she'd tried to do what was right.

Emma stepped toward Becky. She looked her mother up and down again. She'd call the Hard Rock Hotel later and confirm that Becky had been working there after Sutton died—if she was in Vegas, she couldn't exactly be leaving Emma threatening notes and rigging light fixtures to crash on her head. But she already knew what they would say. Becky was telling the truth.

Under the smell of tobacco, she caught a whiff of the same cheap herbal shampoo Becky had always used when

Emma was a child, chamomile and mint. She remembered that fragrance washing over her when her mom leaned down to kiss her good night. Her lip quivered, her eyes brimming with tears.

"Mom," she said hesitantly. "Did you see anyone else in the canyon that night? Someone stole my Volvo and hit my—and hit Thayer with it. I need to know who has it out for me."

Becky frowned, shaking her head. "I don't think so. Dad and I got out there early in the evening and it was pretty crowded, but by the time you and I talked it was empty."

Emma stepped forward and wrapped her arms around Becky in a tight hug. For a moment Becky seemed frozen in shock. Then she put her arms around Emma, too. Emma held her mother for the first time in thirteen years. So the investigation was at a dead end again. No new leads, no new suspects. But at least her mother had been crossed off the list. And she'd finally gotten some answers about her family, about her own history.

Minutes ticked by as they stood there, embracing. Emma's tears came hot and silent and soaked into Becky's T-shirt. Over the years she'd kept a list of *Things She'd Say to Mom* if her mother appeared again. But now that Becky was here, she didn't want to say any of them. Hateful, angry words wouldn't solve anything right now.

I moved nearer to my mother and my sister, hovering

close to pretend that I was part of their hug, too. I knew neither one of them felt it, but for a moment I was there with them, mother and twins reunited after eighteen years.

Then all three of us let go.

Becky scratched at her earlobe awkwardly. "I should leave, Sutton. I need to get out of here."

For a second Emma thought about asking her to stay. They could go to the Mercers' house together. They could talk to Mrs. Mercer and make her understand. Emma could help Becky get better—she could look after her, just like she had when she was a little girl. She'd make sure she took her meds every day, and they could move in together. They could be a family.

But even as she pictured it, she knew it could never happen.

Emma nodded, her throat dry. "Take care of yourself, Mom. For me."

Becky just smiled and turned away. And then she was gone, slipping into the shadows, her footsteps crunching on the ground and fading out of earshot.

My mother—strange, sad, damaged beyond repair— but not my murderer.

❧ 33 ❧

THE MOST IMPORTANT MEAL OF THE DAY

Emma woke up the next morning with her stomach growling. Early-morning light poured through the half-closed drapes. The clock read 5:57. She buried her head under the pillow, smelling the lingering wood smoke on her hair and skin from the bonfire the night before. She didn't have school for another two hours. She squeezed her eyes shut, trying to will herself back to sleep.

But her stomach growled traitorously, and Emma realized she'd been picking at her food for over a week, ever since that first night she and Mr. Mercer went to the hospital. She rolled out of bed and went to the closet, pulled on a sweater dress, and raked a brush through her hair.

The house was dark and quiet as she crept down the stairs to the kitchen. Outside, the sky was the dusky violet of just before sunrise. In spite of the early hour, in spite of the fact that she was back at square one yet again, Emma felt almost buoyant. Becky hadn't killed Sutton. And for the first time since she was a little girl, Emma had gotten to sit next to Becky, to talk to her. She was starting to understand her own family history. It wasn't simple, and it wasn't pretty. But it was hers.

Mr. Mercer was already sitting in the breakfast nook, dressed in chinos, a button-down shirt, and a blue silk Burberry necktie Laurel and Emma had given him for his birthday a month earlier. The *New York Times* was spread across the table in front of him. He was always an early riser, from all the years of keeping odd hospital hours. When Emma came into the room he pushed his reading glasses up on his forehead and blinked at her. "You're up early."

"I'm starving," she admitted.

He folded his newspaper and set it aside. "Well, what kind of father would let his little girl go hungry? Let's go out for some breakfast."

Once inside, Emma rolled down the window of Mr. Mercer's SUV. She let her hand catch the air as they drove, and nodded her head absently to the music he had on the radio. The sun poked its head above the mountains, casting orange light over everything. She didn't know the last time she'd seen a sunrise. She'd forgotten how beautiful they could be.

Mr. Mercer looked at her out of the corner of his eye, a smile playing around his lips. "I haven't seen you this happy in a while," he said.

"Yeah," she admitted. "It's been a confusing . . . month, I guess. Year."

They pulled into the parking lot of an adobe bistro. Inside there were fresh pink flowers on every table and the smell of bacon and hash browns in the air. The restaurant was already bustling with the early-bird crowd. A half dozen senior citizens in tracksuits laughed loudly from a booth at the back. At a table by herself, a bleary-eyed college girl wearing a sweatshirt and glasses nursed a steaming cup of coffee while typing furiously at a laptop, probably trying to finish a paper at the very last minute. Emma's mouth watered as she watched plates laden with pancakes, eggs, French toast, and home fries swirl around the room in the waitstaff's hands. She and Mr. Mercer took a seat next to the window, where the early-morning sun filtered in around the clean white curtains.

Mr. Mercer looked at her over the top of the menu, then sighed and set it down. He leaned forward, resting his arms on the table.

"Sutton," he said carefully, "Becky came to see me yesterday."

Emma nodded slowly. She folded and refolded the napkin across her lap. "I saw her, too."

He nodded. "I thought you might have. She wanted to know where you were. I told her I didn't know, that I could call you and set up a meeting—but Becky doesn't like things to get too set in stone. She doesn't do well when people expect anything of her."

"Maybe it's because she's let people down so much she's afraid she'll fail," said Emma.

Mr. Mercer cocked his head at her. "That probably has something to do with it." The waitress came over and poured him a cup of coffee, and he added milk and sugar before taking a sip. "Is it my imagination, or have you grown up a lot in the past few months?"

Emma wished yet again that she could tell her grandfather the truth. He deserved to know. Maybe he would be able to help her figure out what to do next, to find Sutton's killer and lay her spirit to rest.

But every time she had almost convinced herself to tell him, she thought about the threatening messages she'd received. The killer was obviously still watching her. The killer could be here right now, in this very restaurant. Her eyes flicked around, studying the waiters, the people walking outside in the parking lot or waiting in line at the smoothie counter next door. She shivered. Who knew what Sutton's murderer would do if she told

Mr. Mercer? She couldn't risk her grandfather's safety.

Mr. Mercer looked sideways out the window, too. "I'm glad Becky found you," he said. "I know she didn't want to leave things like they were the other night at the hospital." He sighed. "Part of me thinks I should have sent her back there, but she seemed so much healthier last night. She said she needed to get out of here, so I gave her some money and made her promise to call me soon. I know from experience it's no good trying to force her into treatment. She has to *want* to take care of herself."

Emma nodded. "She told me she was sorry. I guess I just don't understand why she feels like she has to leave. Can't she stay here and try again? We could help her, Dad. Our family is worth fighting for."

He turned his serious eyes back to meet hers. "Oh, Sutton, of course we are. Of course *you* are. And in her own way, Becky has tried harder than the rest of us can ever fully appreciate. Even if you don't believe anything else about her, believe that."

"I know. I do," Emma promised.

Mr. Mercer opened his mouth, but before he could speak, the waitress appeared at their table to take their order. Emma fumbled at the menu, trying to decide what she wanted. She felt hungry enough to eat a half dozen pancakes, but she finally settled on a vegetable omelet with a side of bacon. Mr. Mercer ordered the eggs Benedict, his favorite, then turned back to Emma and dropped his voice.

"Sutton, honey, did your mother say anything else to you last night?"

Emma's heart picked up speed. "Like what?"

He frowned down at his hands, then shook his head. "I don't know. She insinuated some very strange things to me, and I don't know what to believe. Time will tell, I guess." He stirred his coffee, his eyes looking somewhere far away.

Emma wondered what, exactly, Becky had hinted at. That there was a lost twin in Las Vegas? Another daughter in California? Something else entirely? She waited for him to say more, but he'd gone quiet and pensive, sipping from his mug.

My sister was still in so much danger—and along with her, all the other people I loved. I was glad that Becky had been cleared. But Emma needed to keep investigating the night that I died. The case was getting colder by the minute. We didn't even know where my body was, and we had no new evidence, no leads. All we had was my murderer, watching Emma's every move.

"Where do you think she'll go this time?" Emma asked softly.

A sad smile turned the corners of Mr. Mercer's mouth up. "I don't know if she even knows. She told me she'd let me know when she landed somewhere. I hope she does. As difficult as things can be with her, I miss her when she disappears."

Emma nodded. She understood the feeling more than she could tell him.

"I'm glad that you've had Ethan through all of this," Mr. Mercer said, and Emma looked up in surprise. "He seems like a nice young man. Maybe you should invite him to dinner tonight? Your mom is cooking her special enchiladas."

Emma smiled. "That sounds like a great idea."

The waiter arrived with plates of steaming food. Emma dug into the melted goat cheese center of her omelet. She glanced out the window once more. A cluster of pigeons pecked at invisible crumbs on the sidewalk. Beyond the parking lot the university campus sprawled, the red tile of the roofs bright in the morning sunshine.

By now Becky could be anywhere—on her way to California, Las Vegas, or somewhere new, somewhere she could make a fresh start. Emma pictured Becky driving through the desert, greeting the sunrise with tired eyes. Drinking a cup of truck-stop coffee and tuning the radio until she found a station that played loud, happy music. Becky's life had been full of mistakes and bad decisions; it seemed naïve to hope she'd suddenly change, so Emma settled for hoping that Becky would survive. As long as she did, as long as she was alive, there was always a chance to keep growing up. There was always a chance for them to be a family again someday.

34

KISS THE GIRL

By the time Mr. Mercer dropped Emma off at school, news of the séance prank had already made the rounds. Word traveled fast at Hollier, especially when the topic was the Lying Game girls. Some boys from the football team tried to high-five Emma in the hallway. Kids she recognized from Charlotte's party hooted about her "insane weekend."

She didn't catch sight of Celeste until third period German. Frau Fenstermacher's classroom was decorated with declension charts and pictures of German and Austrian landmarks. A panorama shot of Neuschwanstein hung next to the chalkboard, a black-and-white shot of the Brandenburg Gate over the radiator. The Frau sat at her desk, grading a stack of papers while the students settled into their seats.

Two girls sat on either side of Celeste. Emma couldn't think of their real names—the German aliases they'd given themselves were Klara and Gretl. Klara had a tiger-striped Mulberry purse on her desk, and Gretl wore a black motorcycle jacket and skintight leggings. The first girl moaned like a ghost, waggling her fingers at Celeste, while the other giggled shrilly. For her part, Celeste sat silently, staring forward, determined to ignore them. She wore a tie-dyed baby-doll dress and her usual armory of silver jewelry, but her hair had come out of its customary braids. It fell long and somewhat flat around her shoulders, as if she'd been deflated.

Emma slammed her books down on the desk next to Gretl. They all jumped, and Celeste turned quickly away.

"Hey, Sutton. Nice one this weekend," Gretl congratulated her.

"Yeah, well, I'm pretty sure Celeste learned her lesson," Emma snapped. "So why don't you leave her alone?"

The grin quickly faded. Gretl made a face. "Oh, come off it, Sutton. What's with the high horse? You're the one who pranked her."

"Sure. And now the prank's over, so let it go. It's bad enough you're wearing those knockoff Jimmy Choos.

Don't think you can get away with knocking off my genius pranks, too." Emma tossed her hair over her shoulder and looked at both girls with maximum Sutton attitude. After a moment, they shrank back into their chairs.

The bell rang. Frau Fenstermacher paced the front of the classroom, occasionally slapping a wooden pointer against her palm for emphasis as she led them through their conjugation exercises. Emma felt Celeste's eyes dart toward her during class, but she kept her eyes on her own textbook. "*Kennen,*" she said, when the teacher asked her the verb "to know." "*Ich kenne, du kennst, er kennt, wir kennen, sie kennen.*" *I know, you know, he knows, we know, they know.*

WHERE ARE YOU? Emma texted Ethan under the desk. He was supposed to be in German, and wasn't one to skip class.

HOME SICK, he answered.

OH NO! MY PARENTS WANTED TO HAVE YOU OVER FOR DINNER ☹ WE'LL DO IT ANOTHER TIME!

ARE YOU KIDDING? FOR YOU, I'LL DEFINITELY BE BETTER, he answered.

"*Sehr gut!*" exclaimed Frau Fenstermacher, and Emma quickly slid her phone back into her bag. The frau still watched Emma with suspicion after she answered a question correctly—as if waiting for the *teufelkind* to reemerge, the demon child everyone knew Sutton Mercer to be. But when she handed back their graded quizzes, Emma's had a silver star stuck to the top of the page, and an exclamation point scrawled after the "100%!"

When class was finally over, Emma shoved her textbook and her pencil bag into her messenger bag. Celeste was waiting for her near the door.

The girl's face seemed less luminous than usual, her eyes tired and red. "You didn't have to do that," she said, gesturing back toward the seat Gretl had occupied. "But thanks."

Emma opened her mouth to speak, but Celeste held up her hand. "Listen, I'm sorry if I was being weird about the aura stuff. I promise you I won't ever say this again. But I just want you to know that I wasn't pretending." Her voice wasn't its usual breathy tenor, but low and intense. "I really do get feelings about these things, and I can't shake the sense that you're in real danger. I only hope I'm wrong."

A chill raced across Emma's scalp. Of course Celeste was right—but it wasn't like her weird prescience was telling Emma anything she didn't already know. She'd been in danger since stepping off the bus in Tucson. Maybe Celeste *did* have some kind of supernatural instinct, but unless it could lead her to her sister's killer, it was no good to her.

Just then Garrett appeared in the doorway and threw an arm protectively over Celeste's shoulder. "I can't believe what you did, *Sutton*," he said. The way he emphasized her twin's name sent a shiver down Emma's spine, almost like he knew it didn't really belong to her. "Watch your back."

Emma's phone vibrated in her purse. She glanced at the screen; it was Nisha. She hit IGNORE—but not before Garrett saw the screen, too.

"So you and Nisha are best friends now, huh?" Garrett laughed once, a harsh, angry sort of laugh. "Well, I guess you do have one thing in common—me."

"Come on, Garrett," Celeste interrupted, pulling his sleeve and shooting Emma an apologetic glance over her shoulder.

Emma stood there in confusion. Then she shook her head and turned out of the classroom. And walked smack into Thayer Vega.

She grabbed his arm to steady herself. She hadn't seen him since the party, since the kiss that had lasted too long. Her lips burned at the memory.

Thayer was looking a bit worse for wear. His eye was bruised and shiny, and his lip was split down the middle where Ethan had punched him. "Oh my God," Emma whispered. She reached up toward his cheek to touch it, but he recoiled from her hand. She winced. She deserved that. "Thayer, I'm so sorry."

He shrugged. "You've got Calc next, right? I'll walk you."

They moved through the hallways together in silence, a trail of whispers in their wake. "Are those two back together?" one girl asked another, loud enough for Emma to hear. Emma just kept her eyes straight ahead. Let them think she was some kind of man-eating bitch if they wanted. She had bigger things to worry about, a murder to solve. The people who really mattered knew the truth about her.

Her phone vibrated in her purse. She glanced at the screen, then hit IGNORE. Nisha could wait a few minutes.

"Come on," Thayer said, leading her into a narrow hallway that connected the math wing and the arts wing. There weren't any classrooms in the corridor—just a janitor's closet, a pair of bathrooms, and the photography darkrooms. They were alone except for a pimpled marching band couple making out against the wall under an army recruitment poster.

"I need to talk to you," he said, stopping next to a fire alarm. His lips were pulled into a serious line. The bruise on his eye looked almost green under the fluorescent lights.

Emma laughed nervously. "Okay. What's up?" Her phone vibrated again and she glanced at it. Nisha. *Take a hint*, she thought, hitting IGNORE again.

He grabbed her arm. Her gaze shot up to meet his, his touch seeming to scald her.

"There's something different about you," he whispered angrily.

Emma's heart skipped in her chest. She pulled away from him and crossed her arms over her chest.

"Of course there's something different, Thayer. Look, we're not together anymore. You shouldn't have kissed me. I'm not the girl you used to date, not anymore."

Her phone rang again, and Thayer gritted his teeth. "Do you need to get that, or what?"

"No," she said shortly, hitting IGNORE. She looked back up at him. He was searching her features, like he was trying to solve a puzzle and couldn't figure out which way to turn the piece.

He shook his head. "Something's going on with you. It's not just Landry. There's something . . . off. I don't care what you say, Sutton. I'm going to find out what it is."

Emma tossed her hair flippantly, even though her entire body had gone cold. "Are you off the wagon? Because you're acting totally high."

Thayer gave her a long, piercing look. She had to get away from him, had to hide from his gaze before he saw something in her that he shouldn't. She pushed his shoulder playfully. "Now I'm going to class, Mr.

Conspiracy Theory. Hurry up or you'll be late to English. Mr. Abernathy isn't going to let you off the hook a third time."

With that she spun on her heel and walked away, feeling his eyes boring into her back as she strutted down the hallway.

I'm right here, I whispered to Thayer, before my attachment to Emma tugged me forcefully along after her. Even though I didn't want Emma's cover blown, my heart swelled. At least Thayer had finally noticed that Emma wasn't a perfect Sutton replacement. Had finally sensed that I was gone.

Emma looked at her phone again. CALL ME ASAP, I HAVE SOMETHING TO TELL YOU, Nisha had texted her. But before she could dial, the bell rang. Kids disappeared into the classrooms up and down the hall. She turned off the ringer and put the phone back into her purse. Nisha would have to wait until tennis practice.

35

CALL ME MAYBE

Later that night, the Mercers sat at the patio table in their backyard, waiting for Ethan to arrive. Despite Emma's insistence that he really didn't have to come, Ethan had been determined to make the effort, saying he felt much better. Citronella candles flickered around them to keep the bugs off. Mr. Mercer had put a jazz record on the outdoor sound system, and even though Emma muttered that it was "so lame," she secretly liked the effort they'd put in for her boyfriend.

Ethan had texted her to tell her he was running late: SORRY, MOM STUFF, BE THERE SOON. Ever since Ethan had told her that Mrs. Landry had defended her abusive husband and called the cops on her own son, Emma had found it difficult to feel charitable toward Ethan's mother. Of course it was terrible that she was sick. But Ethan was trying so hard to take care of her, and she treated him like dirt.

Emma picked at the chips and salsa, fiddling with her phone. Nisha hadn't been at tennis, and she was a little worried. She'd called and texted her friend a dozen times since school got out, but there was no answer.

Laurel eyed her over the table while Mr. and Mrs. Mercer wrestled with a stubbornly corked wine bottle.

"Everything okay?" she asked softly.

"Um, yeah," said Emma. She couldn't very well tell Laurel that she felt perched on the verge of exposure. Thayer suspected she wasn't who she claimed to be. She kept thinking about the look on his face when he'd said he would find out what she was hiding. He'd meant it. The question now was, what would he do next?

The doorbell rang, and Emma jumped up to answer the front door. Ethan stood on the step, holding a bouquet of lilies and roses. He wore a sports jacket that she'd bought with him at Nordstrom a few weeks earlier, and his usually disheveled hair had been neatly styled. She leaned up and kissed him softly on the cheek.

"You look great," she said. He looked her up and down.

"So do you," he said. She'd changed into a short

coral-colored shirt dress, casual enough for a patio dinner but still splashy enough to get his attention. He picked up a lock of her hair and smoothed it back.

"How are you feeling?" she asked.

"Much better, now that I've seen you." He kissed her lightly on the cheek. "I'm so sorry to be late for your parents. I had to get a refill on one of my mom's medicines at the last minute. I just wish she'd told me earlier."

For a moment she thought about telling him what Thayer had said to her, asking what he thought they should do. But she didn't think bringing up Thayer right now was a great idea. She didn't want a fight right before dinner with her family. They could discuss it later, when they were alone.

"Hi, Ethan," Mrs. Mercer said brightly as Emma led him out to the patio. She wore a lemon-yellow apron over her silk button-down shirt. She'd been to the salon just that afternoon, and her dark hair hung in perfect waves around her shoulders. "You're just in time. The enchiladas are ready."

"They smell terrific," he said, handing Emma's grandmother the bouquet.

"You shouldn't have!" Mrs. Mercer exclaimed, breathing in the smell of the flowers. "I'll run in and get a vase."

"Suck-up," Emma muttered at Ethan. He grinned.

Mr. Mercer took a sip of his wine, watching Ethan

warily over the top of his glass. "Well, Ethan," he said, clearing his throat. "How's school going?"

Emma stifled a giggle—whenever Mr. Mercer talked to Ethan he unconsciously adopted a stern, paternal air, a don't-you-dare-hurt-my-little-girl tone of voice.

Ethan fidgeted nervously under his stare. "It's going great." He smiled shyly at Emma. "I was going to tell Sutton in private, but now's as good a time as any. I actually got my early admission letter from UC Davis today. A full ride and everything."

Emma squealed loudly, her hands flying to her lips. "Ethan! That's awesome!"

"Well, congratulations, son," Mr. Mercer said, setting his glass down. "Did Sutton tell you that's my alma mater?"

Emma looked at her grandfather, surprised. She hadn't known that. He was smiling warmly at Ethan now, his lecturing tone melted away.

"No, she didn't," Ethan said, glancing at Emma.

"It's a great school," he continued. "You'll fit right in there, Ethan. And you won't find a better education anywhere." He lifted his glass again. "This calls for a toast, I think."

Emma picked up her iced tea, raising it high. She was so proud of Ethan.

"To the future," said Mr. Mercer. "To past and future Aggies."

"Hear! Hear!" cried Emma, laughing. They all clinked their glasses together over the table. Emma rested her foot against Ethan's under the table.

"So I guess the science fair stunt didn't hurt you too much after all," Laurel said, winking at Ethan. Emma flinched. She didn't know the whole story, but she knew that Sutton and the Lying Game girls had ruined Ethan's chances for a scholarship a few years earlier through some kind of prank.

Ethan just laughed. "No, but I'll hang on to it, anyway. I need something to hold over her head." He squeezed Emma's hand, and they shared a private smile.

Soon their plates were heaped with blue corn enchiladas, Spanish rice, and avocado salad. Emma sipped at her tea, listening to Mr. Mercer reminisce about his years in college. Ethan listened eagerly, asking questions about the town and the school. Their laughter rang out in the cool fall evening, the stars bright overhead. Right now, in this moment, everything was perfect.

Then Mr. Mercer's ringtone, the shrill old-fashioned jangle of a rotary phone, broke through their conversation. He pulled it out and looked down at the screen. Mrs. Mercer cleared her throat. "We're eating, dear."

"I know, I'm sorry. I have to take this—I'll be right back." He rose and stepped into the house. "Sanjay, calm down," Emma heard him say before he slid the door shut behind him. She stopped eating and looked toward her father, watching him through the sliding glass door. Sanjay? That was Dr. Banerjee's first name. Had something happened to Becky?

Emma strained her ears to try to catch what Mr. Mercer was saying on the phone, but she couldn't hear anything. His face had gone very white. She made out the words "You found her where? Are you sure?" Emma's stomach clenched and she pushed the rest of her enchiladas away across the table. It had to be Becky. After all that, Becky hadn't even made it out of town. Ethan's eyes flashed questioningly at her.

The door slid back open. Mr. Mercer stood helplessly in the doorway. His face was twisted with grief. When Mrs. Mercer looked up and saw him there, she rose to her feet automatically. "Ted . . . what is it?"

Mr. Mercer licked his lips. In the porch light his face was heavily shadowed.

"That was Sanjay Banerjee," he said in a low, broken voice. "He just found Nisha facedown in their swimming pool. She's dead."

∽ EPILOGUE ∽

My family stares at one another over the round table filled with steaming dishes and wine glasses smudged with lipstick and fresh flowers springing out of their vase. Laurel's hands have flown to her mouth and frozen there, while Mrs. Mercer sits in mute shock. Ethan's eyes are wide with horror. And Emma—who is no stranger to violence by now—clenches her phone in one hand. The screen shows all the phone calls from Nisha she'd ignored. They'd stopped abruptly that afternoon, right after school.

Could she have saved Nisha's life if she'd just picked up the phone?

As I watch my family grieve, I wonder where Nisha's

soul has gone. If she has attached herself to someone else, hoping to wrap up *her* unfinished business. Will I be able to see her if she's there, or will she be as invisible as I am to the people at this table right now? I look around, half hoping to see my old nemesis. It would be a relief to have someone to talk to, even if I'm not sure what I'd say. *So, death sucks, right? I'm glad you and my sister became friends.* But there's no sign of Nisha in the yard. Emma sobs suddenly, a sound like an awkward hiccup, and Ethan pulls her into his arms.

Was Nisha's death a suicide? An accident?

Or did she find out something my murderer didn't want her to know?

A vague memory of Nisha at a junior high day camp comes back to me. The rest of us spent our afternoons splayed out in deck chairs working on our tans, but Nisha couldn't seem to stay out of the water. She swam like a fish. She beat everyone at the end-of-summer races that year and got a fake gold medal during the camp's closing ceremony.

No, it hadn't been an accident. Deep down, Emma and I both knew it. Nisha had something she wanted to tell Emma. Whatever it was, my murderer somehow found out that she knew it—and made sure she was silenced, permanently.

Emma's investigation unearths as many questions as

it does answers. Emma and I have another sister some-where, who may or may not know anything about us. Becky's illness has brought Emma and my dad together, but Mrs. Mercer still doesn't know they've been in contact with my birth mother. And no one seems to know about Emma's existence, much less that she's taken my place.

Now there are even more questions to add to the list. What happened between Nisha's last call to Emma and Dr. Banerjee's grisly discovery in the pool? What had she so desperately wanted to tell Emma?

My killer is still out there, clearly willing to kill again. Emma needs to find my killer, fast, before the cracks in her performance start to show. Thayer's already onto her. And if she's exposed, she'll either be blamed for my death—or she'll be next.

Celeste's warning drifts back to me. *You're in real danger.*

Time is running out. Emma needs to make the next move soon, or my killer will make one for her.

⮜🙟 ACKNOWLEDGMENTS 🙝⮞

Huge thanks as usual to Lanie Davis, Sara Shandler, Josh Bank, Les Morgenstein, Katie McGee, and Kristin Marang from Alloy Entertainment—such a great Lying Game team! Also to Jennifer Graham—I don't know what I would have done without you. Much appreciation to Kari Sutherland and Farrin Jacobs at HarperCollins. Thanks, too, to all of the readers of this series and viewers of the show, and a huge good-luck to all of the great people I met at the Society of Children's Book Writers and Illustrators conference in Los Angeles this August. Love to MS, MG, CM, SC, AS, and CC. You all rock!

Read on for a preview of

THE LYING GAME
book six

SEVEN
MINUTES
IN
HEAVEN

⌒⊃ PROLOGUE ⊂⌒

The walk-in closet would be any girl's dream. A thick pink rug lay on the hardwood floor, perfect for bare toes first thing in the morning. Shelves and cubbies lined the walls, filled with designer purses and jewelry and dozens of shoes. Luxurious clothes in every color of the rainbow hung in careful rows: blouses and skirts in silk, cashmere, cotton.

For most girls, this closet would be heaven. For me, it was just another reminder that heaven was exactly where I wasn't.

Next to me in the narrow space, my twin sister, Emma Paxton, ran her fingers through the rich fabrics of my clothes, her heart clenched in a knot of grief. She has my exact chestnut hair and long legs, the same marine-blue eyes lined by dark lashes. She is my identical twin, after all. But even though I stood right next to her, hers was the only reflection in the three-way mirror at the end of the closet.

Ever since I died, I'd been invisible. But somehow I still lingered among the living, attached through forces I don't understand to the long-lost sister I never had a chance to meet. The sister who'd been forced by my killer to take over my life. Since my death, Emma had fooled all my friends and family into thinking she was me, Sutton Mercer. She'd been fighting tooth and nail to find out what happened the night I died, and she'd managed to eliminate my family and my best friends as suspects. But the leads were quickly dwindling, the clues drying up. And the killer was still watching, somewhere in the shadows, making sure she didn't step out of line.

Suddenly, Emma began to tremble. She sank to the plush rug, hugging her arms around her knees as tears rolled down her cheeks.

"What happened to you, Nisha?" she whispered. "What were you trying to tell me?"

It'd been nearly two weeks since Nisha Banerjee, my old rival, was discovered floating facedown in her pool. The announcement sent shock waves through the school.

While she wasn't quite the queen bee I'd been, everyone knew her. The rumor mill started up almost immediately. Nisha was athletic and a strong swimmer—half the school had been to a pool party at her house at one time or another. How could she have drowned? Was it just a freak accident? Or could it have been something darker— a drug overdose? *Suicide?*

But Emma and I knew better. The day of her death, Nisha had been desperately trying to reach Emma, calling her over and over. Emma hadn't called back at first because she'd been so distracted by my secret boyfriend, Thayer Vega, insisting that there was something different about her and that he was going to find out what it was. By the time Emma did call her, Nisha was already dead, and Emma had a feeling that it wasn't a coincidence.

If Emma was right, if Nisha stumbled on some kind of information about my death, then she was the latest victim in my murderer's deadly game. Whoever killed me was still out there—and was willing to kill again to keep his or her secret buried.

Emma finally got to her feet, rubbing the tears away impatiently. Grieving for Nisha was a luxury she couldn't afford. She needed to figure out what happened the night I died, before someone else she cared about paid the price— and before the killer eliminated her, too.

1

WHAT A TANGLED WEB WE WEAVE

"It was almost two weeks ago that this local girl was found dead in her family's pool," the newscaster's voice intoned as an image of Nisha filled the screen on a Saturday in late November. Emma stood in front of Sutton's desk, streaming the local news coverage about Nisha while she got dressed for Nisha's funeral. She wasn't sure why she was watching; she knew the details already. Maybe hearing them repeated often enough would make her finally believe it was true: Nisha was really gone.

The newscaster, a slender Latina in a mauve blazer, stood in front of a contemporary ranch house that Emma knew well. Nisha's home was the first place she went as

Sutton, the night Madeline Vega and the Twitter Twins, Lilianna and Gabriella Fiorello, "kidnapped" her from the park bench where she'd been waiting to meet her twin for the very first time. Emma remembered how irritated Nisha had seemed when Emma walked into the party—Nisha and Sutton had been rivals for years. But over the past month, Emma had started to form a tentative friendship with the tennis team cocaptain.

"The girl was discovered by her father just after eight P.M. last Monday. In an official statement, the Tucson Police have determined that there is no evidence of foul play and are treating the death as an accident. But many questions remain."

The camera cut to Clara, a girl Emma knew from the varsity tennis team. Her eyes were wide and shocked, her face pale. NISHA'S CLASSMATE appeared at the bottom third of the screen below her. "A lot of people are saying it might have been . . . it might have been intentional. Because Nisha was so driven, you know? How much can one person do before they . . . they crack?" Tears filled Clara's eyes.

The camera cut away again, replacing Clara with a teenage boy. Emma did a double take. It was her boyfriend, Ethan Landry. NISHA'S NEIGHBOR, said the caption below his face. He wore a black button-down shirt and a black tie and was obviously leaving his house for the funeral. Emma's knees weakened at the sight of him.

"I didn't know her that well," Ethan said. "She always seemed really together to me. But I guess you never know what secrets people are hiding."

The camera returned to the newscaster. "Services will be held this afternoon at All Faiths Memorial Park. The family has requested that donations be made to the University of Arizona Hospital in lieu of flowers. This is Tricia Melendez, signing off." Emma snapped the laptop closed and walked back into the closet.

She'd never been to a funeral before. Unlike most kids her age, who had lost grandparents or family friends, Emma had never had anyone to lose. She took a deep breath and started to flip through Sutton's black dresses, trying to decide which one would be appropriate.

Emma finally decided on a cashmere sweater-dress, taking it gently from its hanger and pulling it over her head. The fit was a little clingy, but the cut was simple. As she smoothed the delicate knit down over her hips, Clara's words echoed in her ears. *It might have been . . . intentional.*

Emma picked up Sutton's iPhone, scrolling through the messages. The day Nisha died, she'd called Emma about a dozen times over the course of the morning, then finally sent her a single text: CALL ME ASAP. I HAVE SOMETHING TO TELL YOU. She hadn't left a voicemail, and there was no other explanation. Hours later, she'd drowned.

It could be a coincidence, Emma thought, tucking the

phone into a black-and-white clutch with her wallet. *There's no proof that anyone killed Nisha, or that her death had anything to do with me.*

But even as she thought the words, a grim conviction settled over the doubt and grief that occupied her heart. She couldn't afford to believe in coincidences anymore.

A soft knock sounded at the door. Emma looked up. "Come in."

Mr. Mercer pushed the door open, wearing a tailored black suit and a blue-and-burgundy tie.

"Hey, kiddo," he said, giving her a tentative smile. "How are you doing up here?"

Emma opened her mouth to say *fine*, but after a moment she closed it and shrugged. She didn't know how to answer that question, but she certainly wasn't fine.

Mr. Mercer nodded, then let out a heavy breath. "You've been through so much." He was talking about more than Nisha. As if her friend's death weren't enough, Emma had recently seen Becky, her own mother, for the first time in thirteen years.

She picked up the small black-and-white clutch she'd packed with tissues. "I'm ready to go."

Her grandfather nodded. "Why don't you come down to the living room first, Sutton? I think it's time to have a family meeting."

"Family meeting?"

Mr. Mercer nodded. "Laurel and Mom are already waiting."

Emma bit her lip. She'd never been to anything like a family meeting before and didn't know what to expect. She followed Mr. Mercer down the staircase.

Emma sat down carefully on the suede wing chair across from Laurel and Mrs. Mercer. From the entryway, the clock gave a single resonant *bong*.

"The funeral starts in an hour," Laurel said. "Shouldn't we get going?"

"We will, in just a minute," said Mr. Mercer. "Your mother and I wanted to talk to you first." He cleared his throat. "Nisha's death is a reminder about what's really important in this life. You girls are more important to us than anything." His voice caught as he spoke, and he paused for a moment to regain his composure.

Laurel looked up at Mr. Mercer, her forehead creased in a frown. "Dad, we know. You don't have to tell us that."

He shook his head. "Your mother and I haven't always been honest with you girls, Laurel. We want to tell you the truth. Secrets only drive us apart."

Emma suddenly realized what he was talking about. Neither Mrs. Mercer nor Laurel knew that she and Mr. Mercer had been in contact with Becky. Laurel didn't even know Becky existed. As far as she knew, Sutton had been adopted from an anonymous stranger. As for Mrs. Mercer, she'd banished Emma's mother from the household years before. Emma shot a panicked look at Mr. Mercer. He clung to the back of the chair as if bracing himself.

Mrs. Mercer seemed to notice Emma's anxiety and said, "Honey, it's okay. Your father and I have talked about this. I know everything. You're not in trouble."

Laurel looked sharply at her mother. "What are you talking about?" Her gaze shifted to Mr. Mercer. "Am I the only one who doesn't know what's going on?"

An awkward silence descended on the room.

Emma swallowed hard, meeting Laurel's eyes. "I finally met my birth mother."

Laurel's jaw fell open, her neck jutting forward in surprise. "What? That's huge news!"

"That's not all, though," Mr. Mercer broke in. His mouth twisted downward unhappily. "Laurel, honey, the truth is, Sutton is our biological granddaughter."

Laurel froze for a moment. Then she slowly shook her head, staring at her father. "I don't understand. That's impossible. How could she be your . . ."

"Her mom—Becky—is our daughter," continued Mr. Mercer. "We had her when we were very young. Becky left home before you were even born, Laurel."

"But . . . why wouldn't you tell me something like that?" Angry pink spots appeared in Laurel's cheeks. "This is insane."

"Honey, I'm so sorry we never told you before." Mr. Mercer's voice had a pleading note to it. "We thought we were making the right decision. We wanted to protect you girls from our own mistakes."

"She's my sister!" Laurel snapped, her voice shrill. For a moment, Emma thought she was talking about Sutton—but then she realized Laurel was referring to Becky. "You kept my sister from me!"

Emma had spent so much time thinking of Becky as her missing mother that she'd almost forgotten Becky and Laurel were sisters. Laurel was right; it wasn't fair that she'd never been given the chance to know her.

"Where is she? What's she like?" Laurel demanded. Emma opened her mouth to answer, but before she could, Mrs. Mercer spoke.

"Troubled." Her voice was low and shaky, barely louder than a whisper. "Becky hurt your father and me so much, Laurel. She's a difficult person to care for. We decided that it would be better for all of us if we didn't have contact with her. She's done so much damage to this family over the years."

"It's not all Becky's fault," Mr. Mercer broke in. "She's mentally ill, Laurel, and your mother and I didn't really know how to handle that when she was growing up."

Laurel turned her gaze to Emma again, her face more wounded than angry. "How long have *you* known all this?"

Emma took a deep breath, thinking of what *Sutton's* answer to this question would be. "I met her that night in Sabino Canyon. The night of Nisha's tennis sleepover.

"I'm sorry I kept it from you," Emma said, flinching as she thought of all the other huge secrets she was hiding from the Mercers. "It was really intense, and I just wasn't ready to talk about it yet."

Laurel nodded slowly, conflicting emotions flitting across her face. After a long moment, she laughed quietly.

"What?" Emma asked, cocking her head.

"I just realized," Laurel said, a half-smile twisting her lips to the side, "this makes you my niece, doesn't it?"

Emma laughed softly, too. "I guess so."

"Technically, it does," Mr. Mercer added. He unbuttoned and rebuttoned his suit coat, looking visibly relieved to hear them laugh. "But since we formally adopted Sutton, she's also legally your sister."

Laurel turned to face Emma again, and even though her smile looked a little strained, her eyes were warm. "This is all really crazy . . . but it's kind of cool that we're related. Biologically, I mean. You know you've always been my sister. But I'm glad we're related by blood, too."

Quick flashes of memory crowded my mind of us as little girls. Laurel was right. We *had* been sisters. We'd fought like sisters, but we'd also taken care of each other the way sisters were supposed to.

Mr. Mercer cleared his throat, running his hand over his jaw. "There's one more thing," he said. Emma's eyes shot up at him. More? "Becky said some strange things to me before she left. It's hard to know what to believe. Becky isn't always . . . reliable. But for some reason my gut says she might be telling the truth this time. She says that she had another daughter. That Sutton had a twin."

Emma's heart wrenched to a halt in her chest. For one long moment her vision went blurry, the Mercers' living room turning into a smeared Dali-like landscape around her. They still didn't know the whole truth. When she'd looked at Becky's files two weeks before, Emma discovered that Becky had yet another daughter, a twelve-year-old girl who Becky said lived with her father in California.

"A twin?" Laurel squeaked.

"I don't know if it's true." Mr. Mercer looked down at Emma, his face unreadable. "Becky didn't seem to know where your sister—your twin—was now, Sutton. But her name is Emma."

"Emma?" Laurel turned an incredulous glance at Emma. "Isn't that what you called yourself at breakfast the first day of school?"

Emma was spared answering when Mr. Mercer spoke again.

"Becky told you about her, didn't she?" he asked softly. "That night at Sabino?"

Her mind churning, Emma managed to nod, grateful that Mr. Mercer had provided an explanation. It was most likely true. When Emma had spoken with Becky last week, Becky had talked about Emma like she'd already told Sutton about her once. Either way, Emma knew she had to be very careful here.

"All she told me was her name," Emma said softly. "I should have told you. But I was so mad. I was trying to find out if you knew about her, too. I thought maybe I could pick a fight and you'd have to tell me."

"I'm so sorry we lied to you, Sutton. To both of you," Mrs. Mercer said. "You both have every right to be angry. I hope someday you can understand, and maybe even forgive us."

My own heart ached at the look on my mother's face, full of anguish. Of course I forgave her, even though I could never tell her that. I only hoped she'd be able to forgive herself when the entire truth came out, when she realized how dearly all those secrets had cost our family. That someone had used them against us—against me—by forcing Emma to take my place after my death.

"So what now?" Laurel asked. Her jaw was set determinedly. "We have to find this Emma girl, right? I mean, she's our sister. Our niece. Our . . . uh, whatever."

Mrs. Mercer nodded firmly. "We're going to try to track her down. We would at least like to meet her, make sure she's safe and happy where she is. Maybe make her a part of our family, if she wants to be." She tilted her head at Emma questioningly. "Did she tell you anything else, Sutton? Where Emma might be, or what her last name was?"

Emma bit hard on the inside of her cheek to keep the tears from escaping. It was so unfair—they wanted to look for her, wanted to make her safe, and she was right in front of them, in as much danger as she'd ever been in. "No," she whispered. "Becky didn't tell me anything else."

Mr. Mercer sighed, then leaned over to kiss the top of Emma's head. "Don't worry," he said. "One way or another, we'll find her. And in the meantime—I promise that we'll be honest with each other from now on."

For one brief moment, Emma thought about coming clean. The idea terrified her—they'd be devastated. She would have to tell them that the girl they'd raised as their own daughter was dead—and that she'd helped to cover it up. But it would be a relief, too. She would have help in her investigation, maybe even protection.

But then she thought about the murderer, always watching her—leaving notes on her car, strangling her at Charlotte's house, dropping lights from the catwalk in the theater at school. She thought about Nisha, calling her over and over, and then, just like that . . . dying. She couldn't expose her family to that kind of danger. She couldn't risk it.

Mrs. Mercer cleared her throat. "I know you girls will

want to tell your friends, but for the time being, I'd appreciate it if we could keep this information private. Your father and I are still debating the best way to go about searching for Emma, and . . . there's still a lot for us to talk about."

Laurel's jaw stiffened belligerently for a moment, and Emma was sure she was going to argue. But then she took Mrs. Mercer's hand and squeezed it. "Sure, Mom," she said, her voice gentle. "We can keep a secret."

In the hallway, the clock struck the quarter hour.

"We need to go," Mr. Mercer said softly.

"I have to run to the bathroom," Emma said, needing a second to compose herself. She grabbed her clutch and hurried down the hall. As soon as she was alone, Emma leaned over the sink. In the mirror, her skin looked milky pale. *I'm doing the right thing*, she told herself. No matter what, she needed to keep her family safe.

I was glad Emma was looking out for my family. But as I stared into her face, so achingly like my own, I couldn't help but wonder: Who would keep *Emma* safe?

Photo by Austin Hodges

SARA SHEPARD is the author of the #1 *New York Times* bestselling series Pretty Little Liars. She graduated from New York University and has an MFA in Creative Writing from Brooklyn College. Sara has lived in New York, Philadelphia, Pittsburgh, and Arizona, where the Lying Game series is set.

For exclusive information
on your favorite authors and artists,
visit www.authortracker.com.

PRETTY GIRLS DON'T PLAY BY THE RULES...
THEY MAKE THEM.

 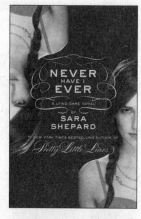 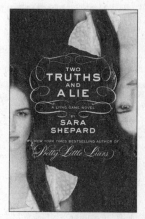

DON'T MISS SARA SHEPARD'S
KILLER SERIES THE LYING GAME—AND CHECK
OUT THE ORIGINAL DIGITAL NOVELLAS
THE FIRST LIE AND *TRUE LIES* ONLINE.

Don't miss a single scandal!

EVERYONE IN ULTRA-EXCLUSIVE ROSEWOOD,
PENNSYLVANIA, HAS SOMETHING TO HIDE ...

DISCUSS THE BOOKS AND THE HIT TV SHOW AT
WWW.PRETTYLITTLELIARS.COM.